MOUNTAIN FREEDOM

NICOLE GARDNER

This book is dedicated to my sons. May you always remember that it's your life. Your story. You get to decide who you want to be.

Thank you for letting me be your mom.

PROLOGUE

Jackson
Past

"Mama's going to kill me," Allison groaned as she kicked a rock, sending up a cloud of dust on the gravel road.

"It's one B. Besides, it's gym class. You got straight A's in everything that matters," I said, unable to comprehend why Allison was so upset. My report card was almost all B's, and I was so proud of it I couldn't wait to show my mom. Not that she'd really care. We both knew it didn't matter what grades I got. My father had already decided my future, and I wouldn't need a diploma for what he had in mind.

"Oh, she'll care," Allison said, rolling her eyes. She changed her voice, mimicking her mom's frequent lectures. "Allison, the only hope you have is to work so hard you get a scholarship. I'm counting on you to be the first person in our family to ever go to college."

"You will be," I said, shrugging it off. I had no doubt Allison would grow up and do amazing things, but I secretly thought her mom took everything a little too seriously. Allison had only just turned thirteen. I couldn't pretend to know anything about college, but I had a hard time believing a B in gym class was going to keep her out of it.

"We'll see," Allison said, sighing dramatically. "If Mama doesn't kill me first." She glanced over at me with a mischievous glint in her eyes. "Race you home!" she said before taking off in a sprint.

I just laughed. I was a year younger than she was, but my legs were way longer than hers thanks to a recent growth spurt. I could give her a ten-second head start and still beat her.

But Allison stopped, her laughter fading as she turned the final corner in the road where our trailers came into sight. My heart sank as I caught up to her. Russell, my dad, was standing in my doorframe, smoking a cigarette as he stared us down, waiting.

I swallowed hard, knowing I was in for it.

"Don't go," Allison whispered, keeping her voice low enough that he didn't have a chance of hearing. "We can turn around and run back to town. I'll go with you. We'll find somewhere you can hide, someone who will let you stay with them."

"I can't," I said, even though the thought had crossed my mind before she'd said it. "You know what happened last time I tried to run away."

She knew enough, anyway. She knew he'd beaten me even worse than normal for not taking it like a man the first time. What she didn't know was that he'd warned me if I ever ran again, he'd punish her, too. He said he'd kill her—slow and painful—then make it look like an accident. And he'd get away with it.

Just like he'd gotten away with it before.

"Jackson—"

"I'll be fine," I said, forcing false confidence into my voice. "Go home. I'll see you later, okay?"

She gave me a worried look. "Meet me at the creek tonight?"

"I'll be there," I promised, hoping it was a promise I could keep.

"Stop dawdling, boy," Russell called out. "I've got work for you to do."

"See?" I said under my breath. "He has a job for me. That's all."

"Be careful," Allison warned, reaching over to give my hand a tight squeeze before running off and disappearing through the doorway of her own trailer.

I walked briskly, knowing Russell expected it—and that I might already be in trouble.

"You're late." He flicked his cigarette at me.

"Sorry, sir. You said you had some work for me to do?" I kept my voice respectful, even though I wanted to tell him exactly where he could put that work of his.

"I do, and time's wasting. You're spending too much time with that pretty little girl. I don't like it." He leveled his gaze at me, as if daring me to say something.

I bit my tongue and stayed silent.

His eyes glinted with something evil and dark. "She's spoken for. She don't belong to you, and she never will. You got that? You're not to touch her. There'll be hell to pay if you do."

"Yes, sir," I answered, knowing it was the only response I could give. I knew what he meant, even if I couldn't explain that it wasn't like that with me and Allison. She was my best friend. But friendship was something Russell would never understand.

"Although," he said, scratching his chin as he mulled things over. "It's high time we found you a girlfriend. That's exactly what you need to toughen you up and finally make you mean." He glanced at my mother, who was peeling potatoes in the kitchen. "Isn't that right?" he asked her, raising his voice. "Worked for me, didn't it?

She nodded slowly, keeping her head down.

Russell chuckled. "That's right. I didn't know I had it in me until I married her." He put a hand on my shoulder, like he was sharing a moment of wisdom with his son.

I wanted to pull away and run from it, but I didn't.

"I still believe there's hope for you, young Jackson. We've just got to find a girl who'll teach you how to get angry. Someone who'll bring out that Sharp blood, finally make a man of you. All women are the same. Don't matter how charming they are at first. Get you a woman and it won't be long before you realize what real anger is." He threw a disgusted look toward Mom, who never looked up, even as her cheeks turned red and her hands trembled.

I nodded, hoping he'd end his speech soon. I'd heard it before, but I was wise enough not to say so—or to mention what a contradiction he was, taking pride in his violence but also blaming it on my mother.

He studied me, then changed tack. "Enough of that. You're on a deadline. Got to deliver these supplies in a hurry." He grabbed the brown paper package he had sitting behind the door and shoved it into my hands.

"The usual place?"

"That's right. And hurry now, or I'm liable to get impatient."

"Yes, sir."

He tugged my ear hard, for good measure. It hurt, but from him? It was practically a sign of affection. "Get going now."

LATER THAT NIGHT, WHEN THE SUN HAD ALREADY SET behind the trees, I snuck out of the trailer and made my way down the wooded pathway to the creek. I saw Allison long before she ever heard me. The moonlight caught on her blonde hair as she sat by the water's edge, hugging her knees, a solitary bright spot in the dark landscape.

I came up behind her and tugged on her pigtail before plopping down next to her.

"Oh, Jackson." She breathed a sigh of relief. "I didn't hear you walking up."

"I've learned to be quiet," I said, forcing a chuckle.

"Are you okay?" She turned to me, those serious eyes studying mine, looking for signs of injury—physical or otherwise.

"I'm fine," I said. "Just had to deliver a package for him."

Her face turned to disgust. She knew how much I despised being forced to help Russell with his drug business. "I'm sorry. But I'm glad that's all it was."

"Me too." I searched her face, realizing I might be okay, but she wasn't. "What's going on?"

She groaned. "Daddy has a poker game tonight. You know how Mama gets about that."

"Big fight?"

Tears pricked her eyes, but she blinked them away. "Yep. But it won't matter. It never changes anything."

"I'm sorry," I said, wishing I could make it all better somehow.

She sighed, turning back to stare at the water. "Someday we'll get out of here. Someday we'll be free."

"Free," I echoed. It was a nice dream. But it didn't feel real. Freedom wasn't my future. Russell would make sure of it.

Allison's voice changed, taking on the dreamy tone it always did when she was imagining something better. "We'll start a new life far, far away from this place. Somewhere amazing, like New York City or Chicago. We'll get a cool apartment, and I'll go to med school. You'll do something awesome. We'll start fresh."

"I hear San Diego's nice," I said, playing along.

It was Allison's favorite game, to dream of a big city life far away from here. I couldn't imagine leaving Rosemary Mountain, even though I wanted to get a million miles away from Russell. I'd go anywhere if it meant being free from him. But secretly, I doubted that even New York City could be as perfect as this creek bank in the summertime. I didn't want crowds of people and big shopping malls.

I just wanted her.

She didn't think of me like that though. Russell was right about that one. Allison was my best friend in the whole world, but she treated me like a brother. We'd grown up side by side, so it was no wonder. She had a boyfriend. She'd even told me about their first kiss, with it never crossing her mind that she might be breaking my heart.

But she was always there when I needed her. She'd drop everything in a heartbeat to be here if she thought I might have a bad night with Russell. And whenever she dreamed of leaving this place, she'd always tell me to come with her. She'd paint a picture of all the fun we'd have wherever we went, and how we'd never have any troubles once we got out of here.

I knew enough about life to know she was wrong about that one. But I liked to hear her dream anyway.

She nudged my shoulder. "You're awfully quiet tonight. What are you thinking about over there?"

I swallowed hard. Talking about feelings was...weird. But tonight felt different. And I had some things I needed to say.

"You're my best friend," I said, knowing it was the understatement of the year. She wasn't just my best friend. She was my *only* friend. The only good thing in my life. The one who had given me strength to survive these last few years.

Without her? I'd have given up a long time ago.

"You're my best friend too," she said, smiling. She picked up a flat rock, kissed it, and skipped it across the dark surface of the creek. Seven skips, each one quietly echoing the sound of the stone when it first hit the water. Seven. Her lucky number.

"I was thinking we should make a pact," I said.

"A pact?" She turned to look at me again. "What kind of pact?"

"To be best friends forever."

She gave me a playful shove, laughing that pretty laugh of hers. "Of course we will be, silly. We'll always be best friends."

I swallowed hard. "Even if I go to jail?"

"You're not going to go to jail, Jackson. You're just a kid, and it's not your fault Russell makes you break the law. If they ever arrest you, I'll tell them how he forced you to do it." She seemed so confident, just like she was about how someday we'd be free of it all.

"Just promise, Allison." For some reason, it felt crucially important. I couldn't say why. Maybe it was the conversation Russell had with me earlier, maybe it was my growing fear about getting caught, or maybe it was the knowledge that Allison's life was moving her a little bit further from mine every day. But something in my gut told me that things were going to change.

And I didn't want them to.

"I promise," she said softly, holding up her finger to pinky swear. "We'll be best friends forever."

"Forever," I echoed.

I meant it with all my heart.

THE NEXT MORNING, I ROLLED OUT OF BED, STUFFED MY FEET into my worn-out sneakers, and grabbed my homework. Then I walked silently through the trailer, taking care to avoid every creaky spot in the floor, and eased the door open so I wouldn't wake Russell. If I didn't slip off to school before he woke, he'd make me run errands for him all day. He saw no value in school. After all, my future belonged to him.

I held the screen door so it wouldn't bang shut. Then I jumped down the stairs and ran over to Allison's trailer. But when I knocked, she didn't answer.

I knocked again, feeling a knot of tension form in my belly.

Silence.

I walked over to her window and threw a rock at it, hoping to get her attention. Then another. And another.

Still nothing.

Allison had never left for school without me.

I glanced around and realized her mama's car was gone. Had something happened? Had her dad finally kicked the bucket?

I went back to the front door and pounded on it until I heard a groan inside. That was it. I grabbed the spare key from underneath the mat and unlocked the door, rushing in to see Brent, Allison's dad, in his usual spot: sprawled out in his recliner, surrounded by empty gin bottles.

"Where's Allison?" I asked, grabbing his shirt and shaking him before I realized what I was doing.

"Gone," he mumbled before letting out another groan.

Gone.

My entire world stopped.

"What do you mean she's gone?" I asked, grabbing his shirt tighter in my panic.

"Gone, like I said," he repeated, his words slurred in a gin-soaked haze. He forced his eyes open before trying to slap at my hands. "Her mama took her and left. Ain't coming back. Now, go on and get out of here."

I didn't leave though. I backed up, shaking. It couldn't be true.

I ran down the hallway to Allison's room and threw the door open. Her dresser drawers were open and empty. Her closet only held hangers. And the stuffed bear she slept with every night was missing from her bed.

I sank to the floor, feeling like the world was spinning too fast for me to stand.

Allison was gone.

CHAPTER ONE

Allison
Present

NERVES MADE MY FINGERS SHAKE AS I PRESSED THE elevator button for the fourteenth floor. Fourteen floors didn't feel like enough time for me to pull myself together. I needed to present myself as the confident, competent professional I was: a full-fledged doctor, finally finished with residency and ready to sign the contract for my dream job.

I did *not* want to present as what I really felt like inside: a nervous newbie who still felt like a child playing dress-up in a lab coat. My mentors had assured me that feeling would soon go away.

I doubted it.

"You've got this," I whispered to myself, taking a moment to smooth my hair in the reflective elevator door. I had chosen my outfit to look professional. Smart. Successful. But with every second that passed, I grew more convinced that my pencil skirt, black-rimmed glasses, and blonde hair pulled back into a tight bun made me look like a child playing the part of a librarian. I quickly pulled out the bobby pins and let my hair down, tucking it behind my ears for a less obvious look.

It still didn't change the fact that I felt like a total imposter.

A fresh wave of nerves made my breathing shallow when the elevator doors opened. I gripped the handles of my black leather handbag, plastered a confident smile on my face, and started walking toward Dr. Barkley's office. My new heels—purchased specifically for this interview—clicked too loudly on the hospital floors, making me wish I had opted for my normal ballet flats instead. Since it was too late to turn back, I attempted to walk on the balls of my feet to keep the noise from echoing down the hallway, my face growing more flushed with every awkward step.

Dr. Barkley's receptionist told me to have a seat until he called me into his office. I had to force myself not to tap my foot anxiously as I waited, ready to spring up as soon as he appeared. *Slow deep breaths. You belong here.*

I *did* belong here. I had earned it.

"Ah, Dr. Bell. Come on in." Dr. Barkley poked his head out of his office, wearing a warm smile. "We'll be starting in here today."

I smiled back, finally feeling the tiniest bit of real confidence. Dr. Barkley had always been friendly. In fact, it seemed he had taken a personal interest in my success. Our first interview had been surprisingly easy, and he had let it be known he was rooting for me. As the department chief, he was the person who quite literally had the power to make or break my career at this hospital. It was a relief to know he was impressed by my work.

"Where are the others?" I asked, faltering as I stepped into the room. I had been told that this final interview would also include the assistant department chief and the assistant area medical director—two people I hadn't met yet, and who both had reputations for asking difficult questions in interviews.

Dr. Barkley gently squeezed my arm. "Relax. We'll meet them in the conference room in half an hour. It's obvious you're nervous, though you shouldn't be. You're well qualified, and meeting with them is just a formality." He leaned forward, lowering his voice. "In reality, the decision is mine, not theirs, and I've already decided the job is yours."

I relaxed—slightly. "Really?"

"Really." He gestured to the leather couch in front of his mahogany desk. "Have a seat."

I sank into the leather and felt the tension drain from my shoulders. The job was mine. Knowing that took the pressure off, and I was incredibly grateful to Dr. Barkley for it. Nerves always made me so flustered that my voice would get shaky, I would mess up my words, and I would sometimes even cry. Put me in a room with a patient and it was a different story. I loved solving puzzles and figuring out how to help people. But put me in front of a panel for an interview or make me speak at a meeting and all of that confidence disappeared like it had never even existed.

"Here," he said, heading to the liquor cabinet and pouring a shot of amber liquid into a glass before crossing to the couch and handing it to me. "Looks like you need this."

"Oh, I shouldn't." I immediately protested, putting my hand up.

"You *should,*" he said, pushing the drink into my hand and closing his fingers over mine. The smile he gave me was warm, but for the first time, a frisson of discomfort ran through me. He sat next to me, entirely too close, and casually put his arm on the back of the couch.

"I'm not really a drinker," I said, giving him an awkward smile before putting the glass on the table untouched.

He chuckled. "Are you not?"

"No," I replied. I felt hyperaware of his closeness and had to fight my body to stay seated.

He gave me an amused smile. "Want to know a little secret?"

"What?"

"I think you enjoy drinking. And I think you should enjoy that one."

"No, thank you," I replied firmly.

"Now, Allison," he said, grinning at me. "I saw you throw back tequila shots with the best of them when your group went out last week."

"That was different," I said, my face turning crimson.

"How so?"

"It's a long-held tradition that residents go to Patty's bar to celebrate on the last night." And I felt humiliated that I had to explain that.

"I'm aware," he said, giving me a knowing smile. "That's why I was there. But I'm asking why that's different than now. You were celebrating then. But this is a celebration, too, is it not?" He lifted his glass in toast. "To you, Dr. Bell, and your new position here."

"Thank you," I said, attempting to smile despite my growing discomfort. Part of me tried to tell myself that this was totally normal— two colleagues having a celebratory drink couldn't be wrong, could it? But the whole situation was starting to set off my alarm bells. It *felt* wrong, and that was enough for me. Besides, I had said no, and it bothered me that he was still pushing.

"To your future here," he said, picking up my glass from the table and attempting to hand it to me again.

"I appreciate the offer," I said, trying to make my voice firm. It occurred to me that this might be one final test before signing the contract. I'd heard other residents ahead of me talk about having to jump through unexpected hoops to get hired. Was he testing me to make sure I didn't have a drinking problem? The thought eased my mind. I understood tests. With fresh confidence, I spoke again. "That night was an exception for me. I rarely drink, and never at work. If you were there watching, you'll know I only had two shots over the course of the evening, spaced out over two hours. The rest of the night I only drank water."

His lips turned up in that same amused smile from before. "I remember."

"Dr. Barkley, if this is a test, I assure you that you can expect nothing but professionalism from me. That was one night of letting loose after we had all finished a difficult three years, but it is not indicative of my normal behavior." I smiled, hoping I had passed whatever test this was—though I wasn't ready to let down my guard completely.

"That's too bad," he said before winking at me. "I was quite taken with you that night."

My cheeks flushed with heat again. "I'm sorry?" I stammered, hoping I was hearing him incorrectly.

"The way you danced," he said, scooting an inch closer and moving his hand so it lightly grazed the back of my neck. "So free. So uninhibited. It was a completely different side of you. Gone was the uptight, smarty-pants resident always focused on her work. In her place was this different woman altogether. Wild. Free. Letting her hair down and letting the music carry her away while she danced." He lowered his gaze to my lips with lust in his eyes. "Licking the salt off the rim in a way that drove me crazy. Oh, I saw you, Allison. You can't pretend you didn't see me watching you out on the dance floor. You knew I was there, and you performed beautifully."

I scooted away, feeling shaky. "I don't know what you're talking about. I never saw you there, and I was dancing with my boyfriend. I was certainly not performing for you. That night was completely out of character and I'm embarrassed you saw it. I think I've given you the wrong impression."

"Then give me the right one," he said, chuckling like we were playing some sort of game. He leaned forward, putting his other hand on my knee. He roughly pushed my pencil skirt up, sliding his hand up my thigh.

I jumped up off the couch, my heart thudding in my chest. "Dr. Barkley, I must ask you to stop immediately." This could not be happening. Fear coursed through me as I tried to figure out what I would do if he came after me again. He was bigger than I was, and he was currently in between me and the door.

But he didn't. He leaned back, putting his arms on the back of the couch, and looked at me calmly. "You want to play hard to get? I'm fine with that. Just makes it more fun in the end. But let me make things very clear. This is your interview. You want this job? You have to earn it."

Disbelief rocked me to my very core. Could he really have said what I'd just heard?

I shook my head, embarrassed by the tears pricking my eyes. "I *did* earn it," I said, hating that my voice quivered.

He laughed, picking up the drink on the table and downing it in one swallow. "Takes more than brains to get a job working for me."

"I'll report you for harassment."

He shook his head, looking amused. "No, you won't. Not if you ever want to work in this town. I have the power to make you unhire-able and you know it."

"Not if you're reported," I replied shakily, taking a step backward.

"Nobody will believe you, Allison," he said calmly. "It will be my word against yours, and my reputation is impeccable. All I'll have to say is that I chose a more qualified candidate, but that you're making up allegations in an attempt to advance your career. I guarantee one or more of your fellow residents will happily throw you under the bus. Marcia's already proven she's willing to do anything—and I do mean *anything*—to get this job."

The truth of his words hit me like a ton of bricks. Some of my fellow residents were absolutely cutthroat, and he was right. I was a good doctor, but that was it. I had no connections in the medical field, no family lineage of physicians ready to offer me a position somewhere. I had often been too afraid to speak up and get noticed, preferring instead to work in the background.

I was a nobody, competing in a sea of qualified physicians. It had seemed like a miracle when Dr. Barkley had taken notice of me.

"You won't get away with this," I said. Tears spilled uncontrollably, just like I had been afraid they would—only instead of anxiety about public speaking, I was facing a different fear entirely.

"I have, and I will," he said, leaning forward as his face took on a hardness I'd never seen before. "You've got the rest of the day to decide. You want the job? It's yours. You can come back here and start earning it any time you want." His eyes raked over my body. "Look at that get-up. Pencil skirt and heels? That silk button-down just begging to be ripped open? You knew what you were coming here for."

He grinned again, relaxing. "Play the part of righteous indignation first, if your conscience demands it. But be aware, I won't wait long. As I said, I have a long list of candidates." He glanced at his watch. "You have until six to decide. My receptionist will let you back in whenever you're ready. Until then, I have things to do. Unless you've made your deci-sion?" He raised his eyebrows suggestively.

"Oh, I've made my decision alright." I grabbed my bag and strode out the door with the echo of his laughter ringing in my ears.

His receptionist gave me a look of empathy as I stormed out and headed straight for the elevator I'd come in on. I pushed the button for the ground floor and let out a sob when the door finally closed, leaving me alone to process what had just happened.

I couldn't believe it. It was the story of my life. No matter how hard I worked or what I did, one man could always take every bit of it away from me.

I walked into the townhouse I shared with three roommates, dropped my bag, and kicked off my heels. I leaned against the door, then slid straight down onto the floor, pulling out my cell phone to call my boyfriend, Mike.

"Are congratulations in order?" His deep voice instantly comforted me.

"No. Not at all." My voice broke again.

"What happened?" His tone became clipped.

"The interview didn't go well," I said before breaking out into a bitter laugh. "To say the least."

"Ah."

Silence echoed through the lines. I closed my eyes, wondering how on earth I could possibly explain to him what had just happened. I was so ashamed, even though I had done nothing wrong.

He cleared his throat and spoke again. "I'm sorry you had a rough time of it. But you got it over with and he'll probably leave you alone now. From what I've heard, it's just the once, and then he moves on. He has an endless supply of fresh meat."

My eyes popped open. "Wait. What? You *knew*?"

"Everyone knows." He sounded incredulous.

"I didn't," I said, shaking my head. "I had no idea what I was walking into."

"What did you think everyone was talking about when they said you had to jump through hoops to get a job from him?" He seemed genuinely dumbfounded.

"Tough interview questions?" I answered, feeling stupid.

He chuckled. "Oh, Allison. You're so innocent. Well, at least it's over now, right? Just try to forget about it. Focus on your future."

"Oh, it's over. I said no, Mike. I didn't get the job."

His voice dropped to an angry whisper. "You said no? Nobody says no to Dr. Barkley. He can ruin your future—*our* future."

"Yes, he made that clear," I said as new tears filled my eyes. How on earth could Mike have thought I would do something like that? How could he have *wanted* me to? "I threatened to report him and he said he would make me unhireable if I did."

"You made a mistake."

"A mistake?" My voice rose. "How can you even say that? Forget the fact that I'm your *girlfriend*. What he wanted is wrong. Offensive. Unethical. *Illegal*. Should I keep going?"

"Allison, all it takes is one phone call and you won't work in this city. What kind of future are we going to have if we can't even get jobs in the same place? Why not call him back? It's just one afternoon. Think of it as one last hurdle to jump through, like boards but less stressful. Maybe even a little fun, right?"

I wanted to throw the phone across the room. "You've got to be kidding me."

"I'm just saying, if you're worried about the fact that we're dating, don't. I understand. We all have to do what we have to do, right?"

"It's not right," I said, shaking my head. "We deserve jobs because of who we are and the work we've done. Not because of what we're willing to do. This is wrong on a thousand levels. Surely you know that."

"Of course I know that." His voice was cold. "But this is the way it is. If you don't play the game, someone else will."

"That's pretty much exactly what he told me." Fury unlike anything I'd ever felt before boiled up inside me. I couldn't believe that Dr. Barkley would keep getting away with this simply because everyone else seemed willing to go along with it instead of fighting to make it better. If this was how it worked, then the system was broken. And if Mike wanted me to go along with it, then we were broken too.

"So what are you going to do now?" His disappointment was clear.

"I don't know," I said. "I guess I'll have to throw out more applications."

"Good luck with that," he said. "I've got to go. I've got a meeting."

He hung up the phone and I just sat there staring at it.

. . .

I'M NOT SURE HOW LONG I SAT THERE LEANING AGAINST THE front door, but I was still in the same place when my roommate Jen walked out of her bedroom.

"Honey, what happened?" She pulled out her earbuds.

"I just got off the phone with Mike," I said, feeling oddly numb.

"Oh no. I'm sorry. I guess you heard."

"Heard what?" I looked up at her, confused.

"About Mike and Dr. Fountain's daughter." She bit her lip as awareness crept into her gaze. "Oh no. You were talking about something else."

I stood up, with a sinking feeling about what was coming. "What about them?"

Jen held up her hands. "Don't shoot the messenger, okay? But several of us have seen them together. We weren't sure how to tell you."

I closed my eyes, feeling sadness but not shock—the news made me realize why Mike couldn't have cared less if I had slept with Dr. Barkley. Dr. Fountain was over the surgical department. Mike's dream was to be a cardiac surgeon at the hospital where we had completed residency. It was a highly desired position with a lot of competition, and Mike wasn't even close to being a competitor for it. A connection to Dr. Fountain would give him an edge his performance as a resident hadn't.

"Are you sure?" I asked. The fury from earlier was gone. All that was left was deep and utter disappointment.

"Yeah," she said slowly. "I'm sure." She picked up her phone and opened her photo gallery, swiping to a photo before passing it to me. It was clearly Mike, and he clearly had his tongue down the throat of another woman.

"Wow." I was at a loss for words.

"I'm sorry. I saw them having dinner a few nights ago. I wanted to tell you right away, but we didn't want to knock you off your game while we're trying to land jobs."

"I understand," I said, knowing I might have thought the same thing in her place. "I didn't know. But it doesn't matter. It was over anyway."

"I was heading to the gym, but I can stay if you need me..."

"No, it's fine," I said, holding up a hand. "You go. I'll be okay. I have a lot of work to do."

"Work?" She cocked her head. "What kind of work?"

"Job hunting," I replied. Because after everything today, I felt like I didn't know anything anymore.

Except that I wanted to get out of this city as fast as I could.

CHAPTER TWO

Jackson

I STARED THROUGH THE GLASS AT THE SUSPECT SITTING AT my interrogation table. Legally speaking, he was an adult—but just barely. His tough-guy attitude didn't quite match his baby-face features, and I might have felt sorry for him if I hadn't seen the victim. He'd beaten his ex-girlfriend so badly she was in a coma and might not recover.

My suspect was twitchy and tired. Guilt was painted all over his face, but he hadn't talked yet. He hadn't lawyered up yet, either, so I didn't care how tired he was. We'd been here all night, and we'd stay here all day too, if that's what it took.

Sheriff Morrison walked in, whistling a tune. "You still here?" he asked, though we both knew he wasn't surprised.

"Yep. Too stupid to lawyer up, but too smart to talk."

"Been at it all night?"

"Pretty much."

He came to stand beside me, crossing his arms as he eyed the kid in the room. "Doesn't normally take you this long," he said. "You off your game this week?"

He said it mildly, and I knew he was half joking, but I winced anyway. Truth was, I was a lot off my game, but I didn't want to talk about that. "I'll get him," I said, reassuring myself as much as him.

"Are we sure he did it?"

I nodded. "I'm sure. Everything I've got is circumstantial so far, but he's the guy. She broke up with him last week and he was pissed. He's got an anger problem and two domestics on his record. Witnesses heard him threatening her less than twelve hours before her assault. His buddy gave him an alibi, said they were drinking together and rebuilding a car engine all night, but...he's the guy."

Greg nodded. "Then I have no doubt you'll get him. Need anything from me?"

I started to tell him no, but my phone buzzed. I picked it up and answered, taking the message I'd been waiting for. By the time I hung up, I felt a fresh wave of energy. It was a stimulant that worked better than coffee—though I'd kill for another cup after the night I'd had.

"What is it?" Greg asked.

"My victim's awake and talking. Said it was him *and* the buddy who alibied him. They did it together."

Greg clapped me on my shoulder. "There's your leverage. Go get him."

I WAS RUNNING ON MERE FUMES OF ADRENALINE BY THE TIME the day was over. I'd picked up the friend, and both guys had caved pretty quickly, each throwing the other one under the bus as soon as they heard that their victim was talking. I was ready for sleep and to put this particular case behind me, at least for the night. But I had one more stop to make on my way home.

The bells jingled on the door of the coffee shop when I walked in. The strong smell of espresso hit, tempting me. After all, at this point, I could probably enjoy a couple of shots and *still* sleep like the dead when I got home. But I wasn't there to risk it. I just needed to check on Anna, the owner, who'd had a little trouble of her own recently.

"Well, hey there, Jackson." Anna waved from behind the counter. "You didn't make it in for your normal cup this morning. Want one now?"

"Make it tea. Something caffeine-free. I've been up for"—I checked my watch—"thirty-six hours straight now. I'm heading home to crash."

She just shook her head. "You work too hard. You need to take a vacation."

I grinned. "Hard to take a vacation when the bad guys never seem to."

She sighed and gave me a look that said she saw right through me as she plucked a tea bag from a case and put it into a to-go cup. "Not a lot of bad guys here in Rosemary Mountain."

She was right. There really weren't. Violent crime was pretty rare here, though it had been steadily increasing as of late, a fact that had me and the sheriff both frustrated. Still, we had enough going on to keep me busy, which brought me to my real reason for being here.

"Are your new volunteers working out well?" I asked.

Some high school seniors had broken into her store after hours and had a bit of a party. No damage done, but they had helped themselves to all the espresso and syrup they could drink. I had tracked them down. Made them pay for all of it and agree to community service hours, which in this case meant volunteer work specifically to help Anna. Her husband had been struggling with cancer, and I knew she was barely keeping them afloat with the increase in medical bills. She was also in desperate need of help with the yard work and maintenance that her husband used to do.

"Yes," she said, laughing softly. "I think they've learned their lesson."

"So no more trouble?"

"None at all." She put sugar in my tea, just the way I liked it, and handed it to me. "It's on the house," she said as I pulled out my wallet.

"Don't do that," I said. "I've got it."

She stubbornly shook her head. "It's the least I can do after the way you helped me out."

"That's what I'm here for," I said, pulling out some cash to stuff into the tip jar. "That's my job."

"Well, we all appreciate how well you do it."

"How's Aaron doing?" I asked, changing the subject. I always felt a little uncomfortable when someone thanked me for what I did, though I wasn't sure why. My job gave me a lot of personal satisfaction. In a way, it felt like I was making up for all the trouble Russell had caused. Like I was putting some things right after everything he had done wrong. And I liked that. Liked that I had beaten the odds and taken a radically different path than his, despite having a bumpy start in my early years. But it still felt weird when someone else thanked me for it.

"He's having a good day," Anna said with that sweet, patient smile of hers. "Got a good report from the doctor. I think he's getting better."

"I'm glad to hear it," I said, hoping with all my heart it was true. "Tell him I said hi, will you?"

"I will," she promised.

I headed toward the door, practically counting down the minutes until I could crawl into bed to sleep for at least ten hours. But my ears perked up when I walked by a table and overheard a conversation between two town locals, Larry and Gus. Both were hotheads with a reputation for trouble, all in the name of keeping town the way they liked it.

"Yeah, you heard right," Larry drawled, nodding. "Can't believe she has the nerve to show her face here. I thought we had run that family off for good."

Gus nodded his agreement. "Takes some gumption for sure."

"Gumption? Ha," Larry scoffed. "I wouldn't call it gumption. She's probably just like her mama. Remember how that woman used to walk around holding her head up high, like none of us knew the truth of what she was? If her little girl is coming back all high and mighty, she either don't know that family ain't welcome here, or she does and she's showing up anyway. That's not gumption. That's just pure arrogance." He pointed his finger at Gus. "Somebody's going to have to put her in her place and let her know we don't abide by people like that here in our town."

I stopped at the cream and sugar station, pretending I needed to stir up my tea so I could continue listening. Who were they talking about? I hadn't heard of anyone new moving to town, much less someone who would cause a controversy.

"Aw, come on now," Gus said. "She ain't responsible for what her daddy did. Or what her mama did, neither. She was just a kid when all that went down. They wouldn't have offered her the job if she was that bad."

"I don't like it," Larry said, disagreeing. "In the end, kids always turn out like their parents. What's that saying? The apple don't fall far from the tree."

I winced, knowing he likely said the same thing about me behind my back. Most people in town had accepted me despite who my father was. Larry and Gus hadn't.

"I just don't like having another Bell in this town," Larry continued. "They're all bad seed, if you ask me. Best to root them out before they get started here again."

At that, I almost dropped my cup. *Bell.*

Allison Bell was coming home to the mountain.

The next morning, I drove straight to the station and dropped my laptop on my desk before heading to Greg's office. I knocked on his door and waited for him to invite me inside.

"Come in," he called out, not even looking up from the papers in front of him until I took the seat in front of his desk. "Oh, morning, Jackson. Hey, great work yesterday. Hope you got some good sleep last night. What's up?"

"Got a question for you."

"Shoot," he said. "And where's my coffee?" He nodded at the cup in my hand and smirked.

"Sorry," I grinned. "Your wife told me you're supposed to be cutting back."

He groaned and rolled his eyes. "Yeah. She thinks I'm"—he raised his hands in air quotation marks—"under too much stress and that reducing my caffeine might be good for my nervous system. Next thing you know, she'll be trying to get me to take up painting or meditation or something."

"She loves you," I said with more than a little envy. Greg and Janet loved each other deeply and shared one of the most beautiful relation-ships I'd ever seen.

"She does." He grinned. "And I love her. More than life itself. I even love her enough to cut back on my coffee, which as we both know is a hell of a lot of love. But you said you had a question for me. What's up?"

"Have you heard anything about someone with the last name Bell moving to town?" I was almost afraid it wasn't true. Afraid he'd tell me it was some other Bell moving here and not Allison.

He frowned and scratched his head. "Bell. Hmm. Sounds familiar." He dropped his pen on his desk, and nodded, remembering. "Yeah, yeah. I remember now. Allison Bell. Doctor. The mayor mentioned her to me last week. She's taking over Doc Rogers's old family practice."

My heart nearly jumped out of my chest. My thoughts were moving a million miles an hour, torn between excitement about her moving back and anxiety about what she might face when she got here.

"Why?" he asked, narrowing his eyes. "What do I not know?"

I shook my head. "Hopefully nothing. I heard a couple of men talking about it in the coffee shop last night. Did the mayor tell you Alli-son's originally from the area?"

Greg shook his head. "Nope, didn't mention it."

"He might not know," I said. "Allison was a kid when she lived here. Her family lived next door to me."

"Really?" Greg gave me a piercing look. He knew I had grown up in a trailer park known to house some of the rougher residents of Rose-mary Mountain. "And she's a doctor now?"

"Apparently. Her mom ended up leaving her dad when Allison turned thirteen. Just packed up in the middle of the night and was gone." I could still remember it like it was yesterday. How empty and dark life felt with her gone. How in a single moment, the only sunshine in my life had disappeared.

Anyway," I said, clearing my throat to try to mask the emotion I was struggling to hide. "One of the men didn't seem too happy about her coming back. Said someone needed to put her in her place and drive her out before she got started here. I know her dad wasn't well liked, though he seemed like a saint compared to mine. He was a drunk and a gambler though, and he didn't hold much respect from anyone. They spoke negatively about her mama, too, but that's probably guilt by association."

Greg frowned. "Well, I don't like that at all. Who was doing the talking?"

"Larry and Gus." I knew the names alone would be enough for Greg to realize why I was concerned.

"Great. Just great," Greg said, shaking his head. "Last thing we need is for Larry to have a grudge against yet another person in town. What other kind of trouble did her dad cause?"

I shook my head. "Other than his addictions, I don't know why people had such disdain for him. I had my own things going on at home and didn't pay too much attention to town gossip. You know how it was."

Greg nodded, his face grim. He didn't know everything I had been through as a kid, but he knew enough about my dad to know it hadn't been easy. He rubbed his face and muttered under his breath about not being able to get a break in this town. "Find out what you can," he finally said, looking weary. "Were you and this Allison close?"

I swallowed hard, fighting back an unexpected wave of emotion. "Like I said, we were just kids. I haven't spoken to her since she left. But Allison was the best friend I've ever had."

Chapter Three

Allison

A THOUSAND FEELINGS WARRED INSIDE ME AS I DROVE THE highway that led to Rosemary Mountain. It felt like I was seeing two realities—the real world, where the road was as unfamiliar as if I had never driven it before; and my childhood, where all the memories played against a backdrop of this very view. It felt like coming home again, in a way that brought happy tears to my eyes and a stab of pain to my chest. The memories here were the very definition of bittersweet. Childhood innocence and joy living side by side with the darkest days of my life.

But a lot had changed since I had been in this neck of the woods. The mountains were still the same, although they seemed smaller and softer than the ones that lived in my memory. The curves in the road were still familiar, curves I used to count every time my family drove back home after a trip to the city to visit my grandmother. Curves that marked the minutes until I could get out of the car, throw off my shoes, and run down to the creek to play with the friends I had missed desperately.

Everything else seemed different though. There were new housing developments, shopping centers, and restaurants on the outskirts of town. Rosemary Mountain had apparently become something of a tourist destination, a fact that triggered pride and heartache at the same time.

As a kid, I had felt like our town was isolated from the rest of the world, a poor little mountain town where nothing ever changed. That had been reason to despise it as a child and dream of the day I would leave and make my way in a more sophisticated part of the world. But then Mama and I had left, much sooner than I had ever imagined, without a chance to even prepare for it and say goodbye. The world had opened up for me. My life had improved in a thousand ways. But on nights when I longed for the stars or wanted nothing more than to splash in the creek, I suspected that the loss was greater than I ever would have predicted.

I slowed down, coasting into the city limits with a lump in my throat. The town square brought a genuine smile to my face, as it looked exactly as I remembered, only better. The old storefronts that had been boarded up when I was a kid had been revitalized and turned into something new. Here it was clear to see the benefit of tourism dollars at work.

I spied a cute coffee shop, an art gallery, and a clothing boutique I couldn't wait to explore when I had more time. Just down from them sat the clinic where I would soon be working. I drove past slowly, pleased to see the cute black shutters and white sign I remembered from my childhood. As clinics went, this one was a relic from another age. But as long as the equipment had been updated, I was actually quite happy about it. It was as far away from the hospital in Memphis as I could possibly get, and it felt like the perfect fresh start.

With a smile on my face, I turned off the main road and followed the directions to my new house—a house I'd never even seen. The clinic had been in such a rush to get a doctor in residence that they had arranged temporary housing until I could find something of my own. It made moving easy, especially since the rental came fully furnished, but I couldn't help but feel some trepidation about what the house might look like.

What I hadn't expected was the location. The address was only a few miles outside of town, but it might as well have been a million. The narrow road wound its way through lonely hills, and when I finally pulled into the driveway, I took in a sharp breath.

The house was beautiful, with a long front porch, a white-painted brick exterior, and a new black metal roof. It had clearly been redone by someone who was a fan of farmhouse-chic style, and it looked like a picture sitting there, fully surrounded by the forest on all sides. The clinic had told me it was a vacation rental, and upon seeing it, I could understand why. It was the perfect place to escape from it all and enjoy feeling alone in the woods in something much nicer than the old hunting cabins that still dotted the landscape.

But as someone who was used to living in a townhouse in the city, I felt unnerved by the isolation. It was beautiful, but the idea of staying out here alone sent a shiver up my spine.

You're being silly. I navigated Memphis every single day—a city recently ranked as the most dangerous city in the United States—and I was nervous about being alone in *Rosemary Mountain?* The town where I had run around completely unsupervised as a young girl without a single issue?

I was perfectly safe here.

The moment I opened my car door, the aroma of the mountain hit, taking me straight back to my childhood. The warm summer breeze was perfumed with pine and fresh rain and a thousand memories. I took a few moments to close my eyes and just breathe it in, basking in the sheer quiet around me. No sounds of the highway, neighbors yelling, or music blaring. No roommates arguing about whose turn it was to mop or who got the TV that night.

A new stab of homesickness hit, but this time, it was for this right here—the home I had left as a child and nearly forgotten. A completely different world than the one I had lived in the last couple of decades. A world where time stood still and people still drank sweet tea on their front porches and women could take long walks through the woods without constant worry of someone waiting to attack them. I had missed this and not even realized it.

I headed up to the porch to check out my temporary home. The door opened to a small entryway with a table holding a fresh bouquet of roses. *Welcome home,* the card said. I smiled. It was a nice touch, presumably from the rental agency.

I wheeled my suitcases inside, locked the door behind me—some habits, I knew, would linger for a long time, no matter how unnecessary they were here—and took a look around.

The place gleamed, with real hardwood floors and those same farmhouse accents. There was a study on the right that would make a perfect home office. To the left was a small dining room with a gorgeous rustic table. Stairs in the entryway led to the second floor. There was a nice kitchen in the back, more than what I would need. Finally, there was a living room, complete with a fireplace. I was impressed. The house was beautiful.

I bit my lip, wishing I could hug the child I had once been—the child who grew up "on the wrong side of the tracks" in a rundown trailer, who dreamed of someday living in a home like this. I had already lived in much nicer homes than the one of my early childhood, obviously. My mother had made sure we never lived in that kind of poverty ever again, and my Memphis roommates and I had pooled our resources to live in a nice townhouse during residency.

But this? This was all mine. And I had earned it.

Upstairs was smaller, with a single bedroom and bathroom. I frowned at that, as I had expected an extra room for guests. But did it really matter? I probably wouldn't have visitors that often. My mother had made it clear she had no intention of ever setting foot in Rosemary Mountain again, my friends would all be busy with their new jobs, and Mike...

Well, Mike and I weren't even speaking anymore.

The stab of betrayal hit again, making me feel very tired. I carried the suitcases upstairs and robotically unpacked the basics. Then I washed my face, put on a pair of pajamas, and fell deep into a dreamless sleep.

My alarm went off way too early the next morning. I

was tempted to hit the snooze button, but I couldn't. It was my first day at the clinic, and I needed to go in early to be prepared.

I dressed in the outfit I had selected in order to make the right impression—gray slacks with sensible flats, a soft-blue shell, and my lab coat—put on a touch of makeup, pinned my hair into a bun, and headed out the door, planning a stop at the new coffee shop I had noticed on the drive in.

Half an hour later, with a latte in hand, I felt prepared and even a little excited to start my new job. After all, this was the dream. My own private practice.

Sort of, anyway.

I didn't own it, and the salary was a bit lower than what I would have hoped. But it was a start. I would be an independent provider, not a resident. I could practice medicine the way I wanted, answering only to myself. I could take time to get to know my patients and really help them make positive life changes. At a small clinic, I wouldn't have to herd them though like cattle, trying to reach some big quota. It was going to be a good change. I could feel it.

Until I walked in the clinic door and felt tension so thick you could cut it with a knife.

"Good morning," I called out cheerfully, flashing a friendly smile at the receptionist, who stared at me across the room.

As I made my way toward her, she reluctantly slid open the glass separating us, rolling her eyes as she did. The woman was quite curvy and very pretty, with auburn hair cut in a cute bob, big brown eyes, and expertly applied makeup. She looked vaguely familiar and was close to my age, but I couldn't place her.

"Can I help you?" she asked in a deeply Southern voice that suggested she would greatly prefer I not need any help at all.

My smile faltered, but I took a deep breath and tried again. "I'm Dr. Bell. I'll be the new physician on site. Dr. Stone told me she would meet me here to get me set up."

The receptionist gave me a cool smile. "Dr. Stone is in the office waiting for you." She glanced at the clock. "Five minutes late. Not a great start, is it?" She shook her head and gave me a look of false sympathy. "Bless your heart." Her voice dripped with sugar and sarcasm.

Surprised, I took a step back, recognizing the "blessing" for the Southern insult it was. "Actually, I'm twenty-five minutes early. She asked me to be here at nine."

"Oh," the receptionist said, her eyebrows shooting to the sky. "I see. The rest of us have to be here at eight thirty, but I suppose that's too much of a hardship for you, isn't it? The office is straight through the doors, last doorway on the right. I trust you can find your way there on your own? Or do I need to hold your little hand and walk you down there myself?"

"I can find it," I replied, too stunned to say anything else. I blinked a few times, then turned and walked through the doors, shocked beyond belief by her unprofessionalism. This did not bode well for the clinic.

Or for me.

"Ah, you must be Dr. Bell," a sharply dressed lady said from behind the desk as I walked through the doors into the office.

"Yes," I said, grateful to see a friendly smile. "You must be Dr. Stone."

"I am. Welcome," she said, sliding out from behind the desk to shake my hand. "That's your seat now," she said, pointing to the seat she had just vacated.

"Thank you." I took her place behind the desk and put my bag on it, wishing I could have a moment alone to simply take it all in. This was the first office that was all mine. It was a moment begging to be marked in time instead of passed over so quickly.

"Your trip was alright?" she asked, gracefully taking the chair opposite mine.

"It was uneventful," I said, forcing myself to focus on her instead of running my fingers along the edge of the gorgeous maple desk. It was clear whoever had furnished the office had exceptional taste, and I was dying to explore my new space. "The house is lovely, by the way. Thank you for arranging it."

"Of course. We're glad to have you here." Dr. Stone smiled warmly.

I hesitated, then went ahead with it—no sense in wasting time. "I get the impression the receptionist isn't. She was actually quite rude."

"Ah," Dr. Stone said, shooting me a sympathetic look. "Beverly is exceptional at what she does, but if you're on her bad side, she's got quite the attitude."

"Beverly?" I asked as the name dawned on me. "Beverly Kirkwood?"

"That's right," Dr. Stone confirmed. "Do you know her?"

"We went to school together," I said, letting out a breath. "We didn't get along well."

That was the understatement of the year. Beverly had been quite competitive, furious any time I was chosen for anything over her. The final nail in the coffin was when I got my first boyfriend at twelve—a silly, innocent little school relationship—only to find out later he had been her boyfriend first and had dumped her when I agreed to go out with him.

She had been so angry she had literally slapped me in the hallway. I later found a nasty poem about me scribbled on the walls in the school bathroom, which I assumed was her work. We never made up, and frankly she was one part of Rosemary Mountain I had been glad to leave behind.

I couldn't believe I was now working with her. Worse, I was in a position of authority over her. She would never forgive me for it.

"Sorry to hear that," Dr. Stone said smoothly. "I'm afraid you have a little work ahead of you to win everyone over. May I be frank?" She leaned forward and placed her elbows on the desk, making a triangle with her arms as she tapped her fingertips together.

"Of course. I hope you will be."

She leaned her head back and tapped her fingertips together three more times before speaking, clearly weighing her words. "This position's been vacant for awhile," she finally said, sighing. "As I'm sure you know, this clinic used to belong to Doc Rogers. When he retired, he sold the practice to the hospital. We've kept it open by having a rotation of doctors take shifts here, hoping one of them would want to make it their own. None of them wanted to, unfortunately."

"Why not?" I asked, curious. "It seems like this would be an excellent opportunity for someone who wanted to leave behind hospital schedules to work regular hours, maybe start a family. I'm honestly surprised the position wasn't snatched up immediately."

She removed her arms from my desk, draping them gracefully over her legs, and nodded. "You and me both. Doc Rogers was incredibly popular and beloved by his patients, and I think that contributed to it being a difficult role to fill. His patients were—are—loyal, and they still haven't adjusted to him being gone."

"Doctors retire," I said, shrugging. "It happens. It can be hard, sure, but the patients will accept it eventually."

She nodded, and I got the feeling she hadn't told me the entire story.

"What is it?" I asked.

"Well, to be honest with you," she said, giving me a tired look, "he didn't just retire. He left due to some legal trouble. That's a complicated story," she said, waving it off, "but part of it involved handing out narcotics like they were candy."

"Gotcha," I said, nodding. "And patients are unhappy because they lost their supplier?"

"I think that's part of it," she confirmed. "When I've spoken with some of the people who have filled in here, they've mentioned that the patient population was more frustrating than they expected. I think the narcotics issue is part of what you'll be facing."

"Okay," I said. "That's something I'll keep in mind."

"Also," she said, avoiding my eyes, "the clinic is a mess. It's currently running in the red by a significant margin." She turned her gaze back to me, an unreadable look on her face. "The clinic needs someone to turn it around, and that's where you come in. One of our highly respected hospital physicians saw your CV, printed it out, and put it on my desk, telling me you were the one for the job."

I cocked my head. "Really? Who on earth?"

"Dr. Johnson," she said, smiling.

It took me a minute to place the name with a childhood memory of an emergency room doctor who had set my arm when I had broken it at age eleven. I remembered talking excitedly to him about how I wanted to be a doctor someday too and how impressed he was—or pretended to be—that I never looked away while he set my arm.

"Dr. Johnson is still here?" I asked. "Wow. That brings back some memories. He was very kind to me when I was a kid."

She nodded. "Yes, he told me he knew you as a child and that you were bright, friendly, hardworking, and determined to be a doctor from a young age. He has friends at the hospital where you did residency and has apparently kept up with your progress from a distance. He has a lot of pull at the hospital, you understand. When he picked you, that sealed the deal."

"I'll have to thank him," I said, remembering the handsome doctor who had seemed like a superhero to me. His confidence had made me brave despite the pain, and he had kept me so distracted with conversation that the whole episode had felt positive. I was touched that he remembered and vouched for me. So often, getting a good job in healthcare seemed to require those personal connections—connections I didn't have in Memphis.

"He'll be glad to see you," she said. "But..."

"Uh oh," I said, bracing myself. "You're making me nervous."

"Well," she said, shrugging. "I told you I would be frank. I've only been here in Rosemary Mountain for a couple of years and was unaware at the time of calling you that there were people in town who seemed to, well, think poorly of your family."

My face immediately went flat. It had been so many years. This could not still be an issue. Could it?

"I'm not my father," I said carefully. "I haven't even seen him since I was thirteen. He didn't raise me. My reputation stands for itself."

She raised her hands in defense. "I'm not here to get in the middle of it. Frankly, I couldn't care less about who your parents were if you can turn this clinic around and make it profitable again. The town needs a good family doctor. Without one, too many people are just using the emergency room instead. That's cost prohibitive and ties our ER docs up with things that should be handled by a primary care physician. There's also some federal funding at stake—some big money available if you help us put the right programs into place here. So we need you, but we also need you to put this clinic back in the black. If you're not capable of that, this isn't going to work."

"I understand," I said, setting my mouth in a firm line.

"I hope you do," she said gently. "I'm not sure what it's going to take for you to convince people to give you a shot. A lot of the townsfolk seem pretty set in their ways. Including your receptionist, Beverly."

"Then maybe I need a different receptionist," I suggested.

She shook her head. "Firing someone on your first day isn't going to help you make friends here, Dr. Bell. Beverly has worked at this clinic for twelve years. Win her over. Win them all over. You're going to have to."

I blew out a breath. What had I gotten myself into?

Chapter Four

Jackson

After a mostly satisfying day on the job—a quiet day in Rosemary Mountain where the biggest problem to deal with was breaking up a bar fight—I headed to the pub to grab some dinner. It beat being home alone, and I was bound to run into a buddy or two. John O'Malley, the owner, gave a hefty discount to members of law enforcement, making it one of our favorite places to eat. He considered it a good investment, as our presence also ensured he rarely had trouble from any rowdy tourists. Not that he couldn't handle it himself. The gentle giant was legendary for making troublemakers wash dishes.

"Hey, Big John," I called out, stopping at the bar to say hello before heading to my regular booth.

"Hey, young Jackson," John said, giving me a wave. "Want your usual tonight?"

"You know it."

John gave me a nod and turned to pour me a glass of the Irish red he kept on tap, while I swallowed back the cringe that always came when he called me "young Jackson." He couldn't know that Russell always called me that. It was a phrase I detested, despite knowing it was a term of affection from John. He'd shown me nothing but respect and kindness since I'd returned to Rosemary Mountain a few years back.

I leaned against the bar while I waited and turned to face the room, scanning it automatically. But my gaze stopped when it landed on a face that was both unfamiliar and so familiar I'd know it anywhere.

Allison Bell.

Gone was the girl I had once known, yet somehow, I'd still know her anyway. She had grown up into a beautiful woman. That blonde hair that had always lit up a room was a tad darker now. Tonight, it was loose around her shoulders. Simple and chic. But I still remembered when she used to wear it in pigtails and how fun it had been to chase her, tugging on them when I beat her in hide-and-seek.

John placed my beer down. "Something caught your eye over there?" he asked mildly, never one to miss a beat.

"Just an old friend," I said. "Haven't seen her since we were kids. It brings back a hell of a lot of memories." The best ones. In fact, the only good ones from my life back then. The ones that were all painted golden from Tennessee sunshine and Allison's hair.

"You should go say hi," he said, raising his eyebrows.

"I think I will." I grabbed my beer and walked her way, feeling suddenly nervous. Would she even remember me? Those years might not have meant as much to her. She had been my lifeline, but she might have only seen me as another trailer park kid, one in a hundred sad stories. God knows we had no shortage of those in my neck of the woods.

Her eyes stayed focused on her tablet. As I approached, she scribbled notes to herself with an electronic pen. I stopped right in front of her table.

"Allison Bell," I said, unable to stop the grin that appeared from just saying her name. "Never thought I'd see you again." I shoved my free hand into my pocket to stop from reaching out and tugging on those golden locks.

Shock filled her eyes first. Then a huge smile broke out on her face.

"Jackson Sharp. Oh my goodness! I almost didn't recognize you. You're all grown up now."

I grinned again. "So are you. And it's Jackson Ford now. Adopted," I explained at the confused look on her face.

That look of confusion changed to relief and understanding. "Wow. We do have a lot to catch up on then. A new last name, huh? Lucky you." There was a flash of pain in her eyes, making me think her own last name had already caused some discomfort. "So, Jackson *Ford*, what has it been, fifteen years?"

"Try closer to twenty," I said, laughing.

"No way. I'm not that old," she teased. "Sit down! Catch me up on everything. Gosh, it seems like yesterday, doesn't it? But so much has changed. And apparently in a good way for you," she said, gesturing at my deputy's uniform before closing the tablet and tucking it into her tote bag.

I accepted the invitation, sliding into the booth across from her. It was hard to believe that we were both really here all these years later.

"Yep," I said, nodding as I braced my elbows on the table. "Things turned out okay for me. Not long after you left town, I got put into foster care again, for good this time. Probably saved my life. Ended up getting adopted by some great folks—you'd love them. Moved to Nashville, where they were from, but came back to the mountain a few years ago. Draws you back, you know?"

"Apparently," she said with a sheepish smile. "Whether you mean for it to or not."

"Looks like things turned out well for you, too," I said, raising my glass in a toast. "Rumor has it you're a doctor now."

She flushed up prettily. "I sure am. Finally finished my residency this year."

"So it's true you're taking over Doc Rogers's old practice?"

She nodded. "For now, at least. I got the call just when I was looking for something new, so I said yes. But"—a shadow crossed her face—"I'll admit I didn't give it a lot of thought before accepting the position. I'm not sure it was the best idea."

"Interesting," I said, raising my eyebrows. "Rough adjustment?"

"Something like that." Her face became a mask. Then she changed the subject. "So, do your adoptive parents live here now too?"

I shook my head. "Nah. They're still in Nashville. Miss them like crazy. But the city never felt like home, not like this place. So when the opportunity came for me to move back here, I took it. Those years I was gone, I never stopped missing the mountain. Never stopped thinking about all those places we used to wander around until it got so dark we had to go home. We had some good times, even then, didn't we?"

"We did," she agreed. "Goodness, I hadn't thought about any of that in years. But when I stepped out of my car here and smelled the forest, it took me right back." She shook her head, smiling. "Remember that little clearing where we used to catch lightning bugs? And the creek where we'd go fishing when we played hooky from school?"

"I remember that creek well," I said, a smile playing on my lips. "How could I forget? That's where I caught you and Sarah-Lee skinny dipping." I placed my hand reverently on my chest. "That's one of my core life memories, Allison."

She threw her head back and laughed, making a sound that took me right back to that clearing, where we'd run around barefoot, laughing like we didn't have a care in the world. Like we were normal kids—for a little while at least.

"I had forgotten about that," she said, turning red even while she was laughing. "Sarah-Lee was furious. Where is she, anyway? Is she doing okay?" Allison cocked her head, curious.

"Still here in Rosemary Mountain," I answered, unable to stop the look of sadness from crossing my face. "Married now. I don't see her often, unless a neighbor's called me to come out. Her husband takes too much after her old man, and she takes too much after her ma to do anything about it."

Allison's face fell. "I hate to hear that."

"Yeah. I've tried to get her to leave him and press charges. She won't. Same old, same old. You know how it goes. Maybe someday I'll get through to her. But if you're asking about her, I guess you didn't stay in touch with anyone from around here?"

She shook her head. "No. We 'needed a fresh start,'" she said, rolling her eyes and using air quotes. "Mama didn't want me keeping in touch with anyone from here." Allison's eyes grew sad and her voice softened. "I wrote to you once. Borrowed a stamp from a friend at school and mailed you a letter to let you know where I was. But I never heard back, and I wasn't sure if it was because you didn't get it or if Mama intercepted your reply."

"I never got it," I said, swallowing back the lump that formed in my throat even now. "Either Russell didn't give it to me or I was already in foster care when it arrived."

"I'm sorry. I missed you, you know."

"I missed you too." More than I could possibly say.

"Mama said cutting off all contact was for my own good, but really, I think it was for hers," Allison explained. "She wanted to pretend like that chapter of our lives never even happened. I always thought she was so strong, but now that I'm older, I look back on it all and think she was really fragile. She couldn't handle it."

I understood exactly what she meant. "Fresh starts can be a good thing," I said.

"Yeah." She was quiet for a moment. "But I felt like I abandoned you."

"You were still a kid," I pointed out. "It's not like you had any choice about moving away or any way of keeping in touch if your mom didn't want you to. Besides, it seems like it worked out well for you. I mean, you're a doctor. That's no small thing. I'm proud of you, Allison."

"Thanks," she said, flushing again with those pretty pink cheeks that reminded me of the girl she had been. The girl I had once dreamed of running away with so we could get married and have a houseful of kids —kids we'd actually love and take care of. Kids that wouldn't feel the need to prowl the woods for hours at night just to stay away from us. Kids who'd feel happy and safe with parents who loved them. That was before I realized that, with Russell's blood running through my veins, I could never risk having a family and repeating the cycle.

"So when do you start work?" I asked, deliberately changing the subject.

A troubled look crossed her face. "Today was my first day, actually."

I studied her. "Didn't go well?"

She let out a breath and shook her head. "Not exactly."

"What happened?"

"I think I'm in over my head," she admitted. "I'm still so new to this. This is my first time to really practice on my own. I've always had backup—more experienced providers to bounce ideas off of or to double-check what I'm doing. I don't know, Jackson. I thought I was ready for this, but I feel like little Allison Bell again. Like I went right back to my childhood, and I'm just playing dress up. And that's about how everyone treated me today. The few patients who even came in, anyway. Apparently, people started canceling their appointments as soon as they heard who was taking over."

I frowned. "I'm sorry to hear that."

"Plus," she said, sighing, "Beverly, my receptionist, hates me. My nurse didn't even show up today, so I had to room the few patients who came by myself. On top of that, I've already made an enemy of one of them. So all in all, it was a rough start for sure."

"An enemy?" I asked, my senses coming on guard. I hadn't forgotten Larry's attitude about Allison's return.

"One of my first patients was there for refills," she explained. "Doc Rogers had been prescribing him a ridiculous number of narcotics, and the interim physicians who handled things until I got here just kept refilling them. I refused to do the same."

"Good for you," I said, meaning it.

"I offered him a lower dosage and help getting off of them altogether in time, but I couldn't in good conscience prescribe what he wanted. Honestly, I'm surprised the combination hadn't killed him already."

"Yeah, we've been fighting an uphill battle here with opioids. Doc was only part of the problem. Did the patient agree to the lower dose?"

She shook her head. "No, he stormed off with a few choice words about how a 'pretty little girl' like me needed to watch myself. Said he would find a real doctor to take care of him and that someone needed to teach me my place around here." She shuddered. "It kind of shook me up, honestly."

I pulled out my wallet and gave her my card. "He's probably all talk. Just blowing off steam. But if you ever have any problems, you call me. My cell's on there."

She looked at the card, her face lighting up as she studied it. "Gosh, it's still hard to believe you're in law enforcement. I bet your daddy wasn't thrilled about that."

I chuckled, even as I felt the shadow pass over my face. "No, he's not. Thinks of me as a traitor. Doesn't matter. I avoid him and he avoids me." *Mostly.* Ever since Russell had found out I was back in town, he'd taken to occasionally harassing me, just to show me he still could. It was happening more and more. And for some reason, I kept letting him get away with it.

Her eyes got soft. "Well, I'm awfully proud of you, Jackson. You know, I thought of you a million times after we moved away. Hoped somehow things had gotten better for you or that you had gotten away from him. I'm glad you did."

"I thought of you, too," I said. I opened my mouth to tell her how much her friendship had meant to me and how much I owed her for giving me strength to hang on through the dark times. But before I could, her cell phone rang.

"Oh!" Her eyes went wide in shock when she saw the screen. She bit her lip, staring at it like she was debating whether or not she should answer.

"Need to take that?"

She kept staring at it. "I don't know." The call ended before she had a chance, and relief flashed through her eyes—until whoever it was immediately called again. She sighed. "I probably should answer. I'm sorry."

"It's fine," I said, standing to leave. "It was really good seeing you, Allison."

She gave me a long look. "It was really good seeing you, too, Jackson. Maybe we'll run into each other again soon." She reached over and squeezed my hand. Then she answered the phone with a look of regret.

But not before I saw the name *Mike* on the caller ID.

CHAPTER FIVE

Allison

I WAS SHOCKED TO SEE MIKE'S NAME ON MY CELL PHONE
screen. I hadn't spoken to him since the day he had practically encour-
aged me to sleep with Dr. Barkley for a job, which had hurt even worse
than finding out about him and Dr. Fountain's daughter. After Jen had
left that day, I called and left a voicemail letting him know we were
done. It was the coward's way out, but it hadn't seemed to bother him.
He had never even taken the time to call me back.

Part of me knew better than to answer the phone. But the other part
of me knew I would worry until I found out why he was calling.

"Hello?"

"Allison." His voice came through, strong and confident. "It's been
too long."

"It's definitely been a while," I agreed, flooded with mixed feelings
over hearing his voice again. On one hand, it filled me with warmth to
hear the familiar way he said my name. We'd been friends, then more,

since med school, and his absence in my life after being part of it for so long had felt strange.

On the other hand, hearing his voice brought the hurt right back.

"I'm sorry I didn't call you," he said. "I didn't know what to say."

"It's fine," I lied. I would never let him know it had crushed me that I hadn't even been worth an explanation.

"Darnell told me you moved," he said, a trace of hurt leaking through his voice. He paused for just a moment. "I was surprised you would leave without saying goodbye at least."

I bit my lip, forcing out a breath. "Mike, what's the point? We're over."

"I know," he said. He took a deep breath, letting silence feel the void. "It's complicated. Look, I just want to say that I'm sorry for the way things went down. I got in over my head, and you know the pressure my dad put on me to land something prestigious. I was playing the game. I'm sorry it hurt you."

"Okay," I said, not knowing what else I could possibly say. It wasn't as if I was going to let my feelings out. How could I? I didn't even understand them. Because while the whole thing definitely hurt, it was also a relief in some ways. He had been a great friend during med school, but I had never been completely comfortable with our relationship turning romantic. Truth be told, there had always been some red flags with him—things I'd been willing to ignore in exchange for having a partner who knew what residency life was like and didn't expect more from me than I was able to give.

"I miss you, Allison."

My stomach clenched. "You don't get to say things like that anymore."

"Can we not be friends?" he asked. There was a bit of sadness in his voice. It tugged at my heart, reminding me of what I used to feel for him.

I sighed. "Honestly? I don't know."

"Can we try? Allison, I could really use a friend right now."

I closed my eyes, unable to block out the pleading in his voice. "We can try," I finally said.

"So, uh. Tell me about your new job." It was clear this was as awkward for him as it was for me.

For a brief moment, I considered ending the conversation, preferring to go back to the one I was having before Mike had interrupted. My eyes automatically sought out Jackson, but he was at a new table, having an animated—and hilarious, by the looks of it—conversation with a gorgeous redheaded woman who appeared to know him quite well.

Other than Jackson, who was obviously occupied, I didn't have a single friend in town, and the only thing waiting for me was an empty house. So I tried to shake off the past and take all the emotion out of the conversation.

But I couldn't. "I'm sorry, Mike," I said. "But I need to go."

When I left O'Malley's, the late summer sun had already slipped behind the mountains, letting darkness wash over the woods. I shuddered involuntarily as I pulled my car up to the lonely farmhouse. "This is Rosemary Mountain," I reminded myself aloud, forcing my voice to be steadier than I felt inside. "It's perfectly safe. Much safer than Memphis. You just need to get used to it again."

Still, I put my pepper spray in one hand and my keys in the other before getting out of the car.

"Doesn't anyone here believe in garages?" I muttered to myself. This house was from the days when Rosemary Mountain was still a tiny mountain town with homes built by people who didn't have many resources. A carport was a luxury back then. This house didn't even have that.

Pulling into a garage and closing it behind me would have felt so much safer than walking exposed to the front porch. If I decided to make this move permanent, a garage would be at the top of my wish list.

As I stepped out and closed my car door, something swooped down above my head, making a screeching noise. I shrieked, unable to help myself, and took off running to the relative safety of the porch before it registered that I was running from a bat. I shook my head, feeling my heart pound in my chest.

"It's just a bat," I said aloud, attempting to reassure myself. But my voice seemed so small here, surrounded by the vast forest. My hands shook as I put the key in the front door and turned it, practically falling in as soon as it opened. I closed the door behind me and locked the deadbolt before flicking on the lights and letting out a sigh.

I was home—in more ways than one. And I wasn't going to let a creepy house, angry patients, *or* a rude receptionist send me running back to Memphis.

CHAPTER SIX

Jackson

I ATE A QUICK DINNER AT THE PUB, SHOVELING DOWN BITES of food in between quick exchanges with the host of people who stopped by my table to chat. Despite being alone, I was never lonely in Rosemary Mountain. Everyone knew everyone else in this small town, and most people here had an appreciation for their law enforcement.

A few years back, I had returned to town as a stranger, hiding my past association behind my new name. I knew people were unlikely to recognize a kid who had been a nobody here years before. But when events forced me to tell the truth of who I was, the townsfolk had still accepted me—in fact, to my surprise, they had embraced me even more warmly. I was a local, one of them. I belonged. They called me a hero for changing my life and walking a different path than my father.

The same should be true for Allison, and I hated that it wasn't. It bothered me that her first shift had been so rough. Bothered me even more that I couldn't fix it all for her.

I made up my mind to take a closer look into what had happened when her family left town. Information was power, and maybe if I at least understood what some people held against her, I could do something about it.

With that in mind, I went to pay my tab only to find it had already been taken care of.

I whistled as I walked to my truck, my thoughts drifting back to those childhood memories of Allison. I was so distracted I almost didn't notice the footsteps trailing behind me in the shadows.

Almost.

"What do you want, Russell?" My hand automatically went to my service pistol as I spun around to face him.

Russell moved into the light, grinning as he dropped his cigarette onto the ground and stamped it out with his boot. "Been a long time, young Jackson. Is that any way to greet your pa?"

"You're no pa to me," I replied, crossing my arms. When Russell came around, it was always the same song and dance.

He shook his finger. "Your blood says different. Don't matter how long you try to deny it. That's Sharp blood running through your veins, and it'll get you in the end." His grin turned sly. "Oh, what a story that will be, won't it? When the town hero finally falls. Good cop gone bad. You'll see, boy. Blood don't lie."

I kept my face straight, even though the words cut me like a knife. They always did. I suspected that's why he repeated them to me so many times. He knew the quickest way to hurt me was to remind me that I came from him.

"What do you want?" I repeated.

"Money," he spat out, glaring at me. He hated asking me for money. Hated that I had worked diligently to cut off as many of his illegal activities as I could. It hadn't been easy. He was as slippery as an eel and conniving enough to keep himself out of any serious trouble these days. But the people he worked for weren't always as smart, and I had managed to take down some of his biggest "patrons," seriously cutting into his ability to earn income by doing their dirty work.

"Get a job," I told him. "A legitimate, legal job."

He narrowed his eyes. "Not likely, now is it? Those days are good and over now. No one wants to hire the disgraced father of the town hero. Wouldn't want to get on the *detective's* bad side, now would they? That's just asking for you to go poking around in their business."

I shook my head. "You're wrong. If you want legitimate work, I'll help you find it. There are people who owe me favors. They could hook you up with something. You show up, work hard, actually live with a little integrity for once, and before you know it, you'll have something you can put on a job application for something better."

He just sneered. "I'm too good to start at the bottom, and I don't want your favors."

"No, you want my money. Well, that's not happening. Russell, you want to change your life? I'll help you. But no handouts."

"You owe me," he growled. "If it wasn't for you, I'd still be sitting high on the hog. You can't destroy a man's livelihood and then force him to starve."

"No one is forcing you to starve," I said evenly. He wanted me to pity him, and I did—but for different reasons. I wasn't going to give an inch. He wouldn't get a dime from me, just an opportunity to change his life. "I've already told you, if you want work, I'll get it for you."

He spat on the ground. "Don't say I didn't give you a chance, boy. You'll get what's coming to you. One way or another. Maybe it's time for me to speed up the downfall of the town hero." His eyes glinted with the sick pleasure he took in torturing me.

His words sparked the same fear and nausea in me that they had as a kid. But I wasn't a kid anymore, and I'd never let him see he could still affect me that way. I stood my ground, arms crossed, face stony until he slunk off into the shadows.

But that night, the nightmares of my childhood came calling once again. I woke up drenched in sweat, my heart racing, like I had so many times before.

Because like Russell knew, I'd never really be free.

·   ·   ·

The next morning, I felt rough when I headed into work. Seeing both Allison and Russell in one night seemed to have brought my childhood back in a way I'd thought I was past. The nightmares had never totally gone away, but they hadn't been this bad in years. I hadn't slept more than thirty minutes at a time all night.

Sheriff Morrison stopped at my desk on the way to his office.

"You okay, Jackson?" he asked, giving me a thoughtful look. "Are you coming down with the flu or something?"

"Uh. Maybe." I nodded, deciding to go with it. "Yeah, maybe that's it."

"You look awful," he commented, tapping on my desk. "Why don't you go on home for the day?"

"I'd rather work, sir."

"You've got to take some time off sometime, son. There's only so many vacation days you can roll over each year before you start losing them. It's been a quiet week. None of your cases are that pressing." He peered at me again. "Why don't you go see a doctor?"

At that, my ears perked up a little. "You know, you might be right," I said, shrugging. "I guess it wouldn't hurt to get a professional opinion."

He nodded and tapped my desk again. "Exactly. Make an appointment before I call Fiona up here to doctor you herself."

"You wouldn't," I said, chuckling. Fiona, our town herbalist and midwife, was a bit of a character. In her defense, her teas and tinctures worked remarkably well, and I'd asked for her help more than once when I was fighting off an illness. But there was nothing she could do for me today, and I had someone else in mind to see.

"I will if you don't take some damn time off and take care of yourself," he warned. "Now, go on." He picked up the stack of papers on my desk. "I'll handle or delegate anything urgent. Everything else will be waiting for you when you're feeling better."

"Thanks," I said.

Looking at Greg, I couldn't help but be struck by the difference between him and Russell. Sheriff Greg Morrison was my boss, and I wouldn't forget it. But the truth was that he was more of a dad to me than my own biological father was.

Greg had taken me under his wings, mentored me, given me a promotion to detective, and put me in charge of his new investigative unit. He and his wife had practically made me part of their family, inviting me to their gatherings any time my work schedule prevented me from going back to Nashville to be with my parents for the holidays. When I had to confess the truth of my identity, Greg had my back and supported me publicly, minimizing the fallout with the rest of the sheriff's office. He was always looking out for me—unlike Russell, who seemed intent on making my life miserable.

Greg nodded. "Take care of yourself. There'll be plenty of work when you're feeling better." He disappeared down the hallway to his office, carrying my work with him, whistling as he went.

I grabbed my phone and looked up the number for the clinic. "Hey, Bev?" I asked when the receptionist picked up. "It's Jackson Ford. Listen, do you have any appointments available today?"

Chapter Seven

Allison

I WOKE UP THE NEXT MORNING WITH FRESH ENTHUSIASM FOR my new job. Seeing how Jackson had changed his life and made a place for himself here in Rosemary Mountain made me believe I could too. While I wasn't at all certain I wanted to spend the rest of my life here, my contract committed me for at least two years. It was up to me to make sure they were happy ones.

But all of my enthusiasm drained away the moment I walked through the clinic doors and saw Beverly give me the side eye from where she was whispering to a scrawny man in wrinkled blue scrubs. She looked at the clock and raised her eyebrows.

"Yes, I know, I'm three minutes late," I said, forcing myself to not roll my eyes as I held up the packages I was carrying in my very full hands. "I stopped to buy coffee and donuts for everyone, and it took longer than I expected."

"Yes, well, you should know Anna's extremely busy in the mornings and you need to call ahead for large orders," Beverly said, those overly groomed eyebrows still arched as high as she could possibly get them.

"Three coffees and a dozen donuts is hardly a large order," I said before realizing it was pointless to argue. "I'm putting these in the breakroom. Help yourselves."

I carried them myself, along with my purse and the heavy medical bag that was about to take my arm off, since neither of them offered to help. I knew I needed to introduce myself to the man, who was presumably the nurse who hadn't shown up the day before, but I couldn't even begin to do that until I got some relief for my arms.

Thankfully, he followed me down the hallway to the breakroom, which gave me a chance to chat with him—though I was seriously annoyed he didn't offer to carry anything.

He did at least hold the break room door for me, which I appreciated.

"Hi," I finally said when I had slid the coffees and the box of donuts onto the table. "I'm Dr. Bell." I held out a hand to shake.

"I know," he said, cocking his head and ignoring my hand. "Don't you remember me, Allison?"

I searched my childhood memories for his face and almost said no, but then the recognition finally dawned. "Oh my goodness. Danny?"

"That's right." He grinned at me.

"Danny Rogers. I can't believe it." I shook my head.

When I had accepted the job in Rosemary Mountain, it had never crossed my mind that I would be working with people I had gone to grade school with. I had forgotten what a small world this town really was. Danny Rogers, of all people. I blushed, wondering if he would remember the fact that he had been my first kiss. Boyfriend number two, at age thirteen. We had technically still been "going steady" when my mama had moved us away in the middle of the night.

Funnily enough, I hadn't even thought to write him a letter the way I had with Jackson.

"I couldn't believe it, either," he said. "I remember back then you used to talk about wanting to be a doctor someday, and it looks like you did it."

"I did," I said. "You talked about that too, though!" In fact, it was the only reason I had agreed to be his "girlfriend." As Doc Rogers's nephew, he had access to all of Doc's medical textbooks and sometimes helped out in the clinic, which I had thought was ridiculously cool back then.

"Yeah," he said, his face changing from a smile to something a bit darker. "Well, plans don't always work out for everyone. Went to nursing school instead."

"RN?"

"LPN," he said, obviously growing more uncomfortable by the second.

"That's great," I said, realizing I had stuck my foot in my mouth. "I'm so glad to have you on the team here."

"Yeah. Hey, listen, can I take you out to dinner tonight? Catch up, for old time's sake? I mean, we never technically broke up, so I think that means you're still my girlfriend." He winked at me before laughing awkwardly.

I felt like a deer caught in the headlights. "Well, Danny, I don't know. I mean, I *just* got out of a relationship, and I'm just not ready to…" I felt myself babbling and clamped my mouth shut. *You're his boss,* I reminded myself. It was inappropriate for him to even ask. I didn't have to give any excuses or justify saying no.

"Right," he said as his face turned bright red. "Well. I'm just going to grab a coffee." He reached around me and grabbed a cup. Then he fled the room.

THREE HOURS LATER, ANY ENTHUSIASM I'D HAD FOR THIS JOB was completely gone. In fact, I was poring over my contract, looking for a loophole that would allow me to leave without notice. Not that I'd do it. Once I committed to something, I saw it through.

But with the day I was having, I wanted to at least know what my options were.

I jumped when my office door flew open. My cheeks flamed when I saw Beverly's smug smile. She had caught me with my head in my hands, feeling totally defeated—and the look on her face told me she liked it.

"Hi, Beverly. I'd appreciate it if you'd knock in the future. Can I help you with something?" I asked, forcing a smile on my face.

"You told me to let you know when your patients are checked in," she said in that falsely sweet Southern accent of hers.

My first four patients of the day had sat in their rooms for nearly half an hour past their appointment times, simply because nobody had bothered to tell me they had arrived—or update their status on the electronic health record I kept eyes on while in my office.

"Yes, thank you. I'll be right there."

"I wouldn't keep this one waiting," she warned. "We take care of our own around here, and Detective Ford is a town VIP. Frankly, I'm surprised he's here at all." She sniffed, looking at me in disdain. "But since he is, don't screw it up."

I bit my lip, fighting back all the retorts I wanted to give her. Beverly was a snake, but unfortunately, she was a snake who seemed to have more job security than I did at the moment. Thankfully, the mention of Jackson was a balm that helped me keep my cool.

"Oh, Jackson. Good," I said, nodding. "Let me pull his chart and I'll be right in."

She raised her eyebrow at the use of his first name. I felt a tiny bit of guilt at using him to gain some leverage with her, but I had a feeling he'd understand and approve.

THERE WAS ALMOST NOTHING IN JACKSON'S CHART OTHER than his required annual physicals for work. He wasn't on any medications and seemed to never get sick. The note for today's visit said he was feeling rundown. He had seemed fine last night. Had something happened? Maybe a virus that had hit him in between now and then?

Or...was it possible he was here just to see me?

I leaned back in my office chair, gazing at the ceiling as I let my mind wander there. Jackson was...attractive. To say the least. It had caught me off guard the night before. All these years, he had lived in my memories as a kid. Blond hair, blue eyes, long limbs tanned by the sun. Wiry and athletic, always climbing trees or balancing his way across the boulders in the creeks. He had been a gorgeous little boy—when he wasn't black and blue from the bruises his father loved marring his face with. But he had been a boy, nonetheless. A boy frozen in time in my memories.

The Jackson I'd met last night wasn't a boy. That wavy hair had darkened some since he was a kid. He wasn't skinny anymore—he was built to impress, with that little bit of sexy swagger that came from wearing the uniform. Those blue eyes were still bright though, and when he grinned—well, that grin took me right back to the best days of my childhood. The days when it felt like I might actually reach the clouds if he pushed me hard enough on the swing. The nights we stayed up giggling, scaring ourselves silly with ghost stories that weren't half as terrifying as the ghosts he lived with at home.

My heart ached just thinking about those days and the closeness we had shared. It had been completely platonic. Just two kids trying to make it in a crazy world. After all, he was younger than me, so even when I hit the boy-crazy stage, I hadn't put him in that category. But I had known he had been half in love with me in that innocent, childlike way.

After seeing him again, I couldn't help but wonder if maybe there was a spark of that left.

I opened the door to the exam room and saw Jackson sitting on the table, wearing a polite smile as Beverly openly flirted with him. She was wearing a skin-tight dress cut deeply enough to show off her ample cleavage, and she knew how to strike a pose on my stool to put her curves on perfect display.

"*Finally,*" she said before looking at Jackson and rolling her eyes like they were in on some sort of joke together. "I'm so sorry, Detective. I'm afraid our new *doctor* hasn't quite figured out how things work around here."

"Hey, Allison," Jackson said, a boyish grin lighting up his face. It was so much better than the polite smile he wore for her.

"Hey, Jackson." I gave him a smile back, hugging my tablet to my chest. When Beverly made no move to leave, I looked at her pointedly. "I've got this, Beverly. And the phone is ringing up front."

She just rolled her eyes again and huffed off.

"Wow," Jackson said, raising his eyebrows. "I've dealt with a couple of coworkers who didn't like me, but man. This is a whole new level."

I just sighed and let myself plop onto my stool like I was at a bar with my best friend instead of a new physician in a professional clinic. It was wrong to be so casual with a patient, yet, with Jackson, it felt right. Like it would have been weird for me to wear my professional mask in front of him. How could I? He had known me since we were kids. Despite the years that had passed, I suspected he'd see right through it anyway.

"It's been a rough day," I said.

"Wanna talk about it?" His eyes were filled with genuine concern.

I shook my head. "No. Not here anyway. Besides, you're the one who's sick." I cocked my head as I did a visual scan. He looked perfectly healthy from where I was sitting. "What's going on? You seemed to be feeling okay last night."

He gave me another grin. "Aw, I'm probably fine. I didn't get a lot of sleep last night, so I looked a little rough this morning. The sheriff's worried I'm coming down with the flu or something. Says it's going around."

"It's not really flu season, but maybe," I said. "Let's check you out."

I moved to take his vitals and he gave me a weird look.

"Danny already did that," he said.

"I know," I said, sighing again. I'd realized quickly that I'd have to double check Danny's work, because he'd entered incorrect information on every patient of the day. I wasn't sure if he was completely incompetent or if he was just having a bad day. "But I'm going to check you over myself."

"Okay," he said, swallowing hard.

I pulled out the thermometer and scanned his forehead. "No fever," I said, showing him. "Let me look at your throat." I checked out his throat, eyes, ears, and nose, and I listened to his heart and lungs. "Any symptoms other than the difficulty sleeping? Sore throat, body aches, anything?"

"Nope," he said, shaking his head.

"You seem perfectly healthy," I said, shrugging. "I don't even see any reason to swab you for the flu."

"I told you, I'm fine. Sheriff Morrison probably just saw this as a great way to force me to finally take a sick day before I lose them. Besides," he said before clearing his throat. "I decided I didn't mind having an excuse to see you again."

"Oh really?" I asked, feeling my own heart rate pick up. This was entirely unprofessional. I shouldn't have been feeling, well, *anything* while examining a patient. But standing so close to Jackson suddenly had my mouth going dry.

"Really," he said, grinning. "We never got to finish our conversation last night. Are you free for dinner? I'd love to continue catching up."

Now I was the one swallowing hard. On one hand, there was nothing I wanted more than to go to dinner with Jackson. He was a friendly face in a town where I hadn't seen many of them. I felt completely comfortable with him, like our friendship had never missed a beat. On top of that, I was attracted to him in a way I really shouldn't have been.

But there was the problem. For one thing, I had just turned Danny down, and things had been awkward there ever since. If he saw me go out with Jackson after I'd told him I had just gotten out of a relationship, it would make things even worse.

Plus, like Beverly had said, Jackson was a town VIP. Getting involved with him only to have a public breakup—because in small towns like Rosemary Mountain, *every* breakup was public—would worsen my reputation. I knew that, no matter the true circumstances, the public would decide I was the one at fault and hate me for breaking his heart. It would be the final nail in the coffin.

"I don't know," I said slowly. "Jackson, I got out of a relationship recently, and—"

"Whoa," he said, holding up his hands. "I didn't mean on a date. I'm talking about dinner as friends."

"Just friends?" I asked.

"Sure." He flashed that grin at me again and I thought I saw a little challenge underneath it.

"Okay," I agreed, despite knowing it was still a bad idea. "Why not?"

"What time do you get off work?" he asked.

I just laughed. "Whenever the work is done." I checked the schedule. "Looks like my last patient is at four twenty. Assuming everything goes well, I should be wrapped up here by five. I'll want to grab a shower. We could meet around six thirty?"

"Sounds good," he agreed. "You name the place."

"Is Marco's still in business?" I asked, my mouth watering at the thought of the pizza from my childhood.

He laughed. "No, it's not. *That's* a long story. But we have a new pizza place now. It's not Marco's, but it's not bad. It's right off the highway, on the north side of town."

"Sounds perfect," I said with a smile.

Pizza was safe. Pizza was friendly. Pizza wasn't a date.

Even if part of me sort of wanted it to be.

CHAPTER EIGHT

Jackson

WHEN I LEFT ALLISON'S CLINIC, I SAW RUSSELL DISAPPEAR behind the building across the street. My body immediately tensed. I threw my shoulders back and marched across the street to confront him. But when I rounded the corner of the old brick building, the alley was empty. He had disappeared into thin air.

Typical.

When I had first moved back to the area, he had practically been a ghost, content to stay in his trailer on the outskirts of town and make his contacts come to him to arrange work. I'd never had to see him unless I sought him out deliberately, needing information—or to reassure myself he couldn't touch me now. My uniform, badge, and age had formed the kind of protection I hadn't had as a kid, an invisible shield that even he didn't dare cross.

But lately, he had been showing his face more and more, and I had the feeling he was up to something. Of course, this was Russell—he was always up to something. And as I stood in the alleyway, watching carefully for movement, wondering when he might reappear from wherever he was hiding, I felt the certainty in my bones. He was messing with me. The only question was why.

It was a conflict of interest for me to investigate him, so technically speaking, I should report my suspicions to the sheriff. But I felt as dumb as rocks telling Greg I was getting freaked out just by seeing Russell in town. That was only going to land me a psych review. Before I went to him, I needed something solid. Something worth presenting.

So I'd keep it to myself for now.

"You might as well show yourself," I said, feeling silly as I spoke to the empty alley, but I made sure my voice didn't show it.

Nothing.

I gave it another minute. Then I finally turned and walked away, knowing it would eat at me the rest of the day.

While I waited for Allison to arrive at the restaurant, I told myself my excitement was about catching up with an old friend. After all, that's how it had to be. Even if my own resolve to stay single had wavered a bit when I'd asked her to have dinner with me, she had made it clear she didn't want more than friendship. That was perfect. It kept us both exactly where we should be.

There was something special in having a friend who had known me in my old life. Nowadays, pretty much everyone knew me as Jackson Ford, and even the ones who knew my past hadn't really known me as a kid. They might know my father and sympathize with me because of it, but it was only an interesting piece of my story to them. It wasn't my identity.

Allison was the strongest link to the good parts of my childhood, and there was something special about getting that link back.

As long as I could remember, my life had been divided into two parts: life before I was adopted and life after. The *before* part of my life felt so far away that, in some ways, it felt like it had all happened to somebody else. Seeing Allison again reminded me that it hadn't. That those parts of my life were really mine, too.

Which was good and bad at the same time.

She had brought the good memories back, but between reconnecting with her and the recent sightings of Russell, the dark parts of my past were feeling uncomfortably close. The worst part of it was how quickly Russell could erase the years between us, turning me from a confident member of law enforcement to a scared kid with a broken heart. Part of me wondered if getting close to Allison was a mistake. If maybe I should put as much distance between the past and my future as I could.

But when she walked in—looking slightly hesitant as she glanced around, until she saw me and her face lit up—I realized she had a completely different effect on me than Russell did. Instead of making me feel like a weak little kid without resources, I felt stronger when she was around. More confident. Ready to face anything.

And I wasn't quite sure what to make of that.

"Sorry I'm late," she said breathily as she slid across from me into the booth . "My last patient of the day went long."

"Complicated case?" I asked, signaling the server for another menu.

She rolled her eyes. "Yes and no. Not really complicated, medically speaking. But I had another patient come in on too many prescriptions. She's mixing narcotics with benzos and sedatives, and frankly, I'm surprised it hasn't already killed her. I told her I couldn't continue the prescriptions as written, but that I could help her safely taper down. She didn't take it well, though she did eventually agree to try something different. I think it helped that her husband was there and he took what I was saying seriously."

I sighed. "I'm sorry you have to deal with that. A lot of people loved Doc Rogers for the wrong reasons."

She hesitated, then spoke again. "I'm thinking of starting a medication-assisted treatment program, where I can prescribe safer alternatives and help with the withdrawal process. It's something I haven't done personally, but I know there's been some success with other clinics. There certainly seems to be a need for it here. There's also some grant money available for the program, which would help the clinic get out of the hole."

"That's a great idea," I said, giving her an encouraging smile. "That would do a lot of good."

"Right?" she asked, agreeing with me even though it was clear she was still looking for affirmation. "I think it would be a really good thing for the community, to help the ones who are reliant on painkillers by still giving them relief but in a way that doesn't get them high. Plus, the program would require drug testing in order to get the prescription. So it's built-in accountability and motivation to stay off everything else."

I nodded, though I felt the need to damper her excitement. "It's a good idea and definitely worth a shot. But it could be a hard sell. Rosemary Mountain has grown a lot since you last lived here, but it's still your typical small town in most ways. And you know the issue with small towns in Tennessee."

"Yep. But things can change."

I fought to keep the look of doubt off my face. "I hope you're right. It always feels like we're fighting a losing battle there, and sometimes I wonder if it's a battle even worth fighting."

Her eyes softened, not with judgment but with empathy. "I imagine it does feel that way working in law enforcement. It's the same on the medical side. But sometimes you reach people. It's those times, the ones where you get someone to turn their life around and actually show up to live it, that make all the stress worth it in the end. It's a gift to them and their families. If you save even one, it's worth it. Right?"

I looked at her and saw the little girl she had been for just a moment. That same serious look in her eyes, that fragile bravery. I had always thought of her as a princess—the warrior kind who would fight dragons if necessary to protect her people. The woman sitting across from me right now seemed exactly the same.

"You're right," I said, knowing she was thinking of her father. Unlike mine, hers had never gotten involved in drugs. That I knew of anyway. But he had his own addictions and she had lived her own kind of nightmare because of it.

She took a little breath and smiled like she had needed my affirmation. It was a funny thing. I knew—because people were talking already —that everyone saw her as this ultra confident know-it-all who had come back to town thinking she was better than everyone else.

I saw the truth.

· · ·

The server—a teenage girl with stringy hair, a face full of acne, and an attitude suggesting she'd rather be literally anywhere than here—arrived, interrupting my thoughts. She slapped two plastic cups down on the table hard enough to make me wince.

"Soda machine's over there. Self-serve. If you want beer, I'll have to get Shelly to bring it to you."

"I'm good with soda," Allison said, gently sliding her cup out from the teenager's hand, which was clamped down on the top of it.

"Same," I said.

"Great," the teenager said without a single trace of emotion. "What kind of pizza do you want?"

"She might need a few minutes to look—" I started, but Allison shook her head.

"I looked at the online menu over my lunch break," she said. "I want to try their Happy Hippie pizza. Want to split a large half and half? If not, I'll order a small."

"We can split," I said, grinning. "But make my half pepperoni." I handed the menu to the teenager, who turned and walked away without a word.

"Pepperoni," Allison said. "Apparently some things never change."

"You can't top pepperoni, so why try? It's the perfect pizza."

"As your new doctor, I might gently suggest you try a slice of mine and get some vegetables into your life," she said. The twinkle in her eyes let me know she was teasing. Mostly, anyway.

"Don't worry," I said, patting my stomach. "I had a healthy lunch of fish and vegetables."

"Did you really?"

"Yep. Fried catfish, French fries, fried okra, and fried green tomatoes."

She closed her eyes and shook her head, but she was fighting back a smile. "I see I have my work cut out for me."

"I'm afraid so."

She opened her eyes, meeting my gaze, and a sense of wonder hit me. How was it that I already felt this comfortable with someone I had only reconnected with yesterday? Talking with people was part of my job, and I was good at it. Good at connecting with ease, getting people to open up and think of me as a friend. It was why I was better at my job than a couple of my coworkers who liked to hold themselves apart and act superior because of the badge.

But this was different. I wasn't just acting comfortable. I felt a deep sense of comfort, like I had known her my whole life. We had spent most of our lives apart, in completely separate worlds. It didn't make sense that this kind of connection would come back so easily. But it had. And it felt like I had found something I had searched for my entire life.

"Where'd you go?" she asked, cocking her head. "You look like you've drifted off deep into thought."

"I guess I had," I admitted. "I was just thinking how nice this is. How easy it feels. How it's like I've known you my whole life."

"We sort of have," she chuckled, but a little bit of worry crossed her face. "This is great, Jackson, and I love that we reconnected. But I do just want to be clear that I meant it when I said I only want to be friends. I've thought about it a lot, and I just don't think it's a good idea for us to get involved."

I held up my hands. "I get it, Allison. I was being serious when I said that's what I wanted, too." I hesitated, then leaned forward and lowered my voice, deciding to open up to her in a way I hadn't opened up to anyone. "I don't do relationships. Ever. It's a rule of mine. And your friendship means too much to me to screw things up with a fling, so. Just friends. For real." I shrugged.

She gave me an interested look. "Why do you not do relationships?"

I couldn't stop the rush of negativity that flooded me from thinking about it. "You knew Russell."

"Yeah," she said in a questioning tone, like she didn't understand where I was going.

"And you're smart enough to know how these things work. He was the way he was because of his dad. His dad was the way he was because of his dad, and so on and so on in a long chain of miserable, broken people. I decided a long time ago that the chain stops with me."

"But, Jackson," she said, her eyes narrowing, "you don't have to stay single to stop the chain. You've already broken it. Look at you and the life you've chosen. You're nothing like him."

I shook my head. "That's different. But I'm not going to be a husband or father. I wouldn't be any good at it. My real dad—the one who adopted me—was awesome. He had the patience of a saint. But I don't." I shrugged, even though the pain of it all still ate at me. "Russell's blood runs through my veins."

"That doesn't mean anything," she protested.

"As a doctor, you know enough about genetics to know that isn't true," I said, raising my eyebrows.

She blushed but didn't contradict me this time.

"I work harder than anyone knows to be different than him." I dropped my gaze and took a long drink from my soda, trying to swallow back the hurt that always came when I remembered the things he said. I couldn't take the risk of putting myself in a situation that might prove him right.

"But—" she started to speak, but I interrupted her.

"Besides," I said, trying to wave her off and change the subject to a less painful one. "I work long hours in a job that can be dangerous. That's not fair to a wife and kids, either. When I was a kid, I remember how my mom would sit and wonder when Russell was coming home. *If* he was coming home. How we'd make it if he didn't. I'm not going to put anyone through that."

"Whatever happened to your mom?" she asked quietly.

I looked down at my straw. "She took off. Pretty sure she was the one to make that last report, the one that landed me in foster care for good. But she didn't hang around to see what happened. Just left. I never saw her again."

"I'm sorry, Jackson."

I shrugged, even though it still hurt. "She probably saved my life. Can't really blame her for protecting hers by disappearing. My folks helped me track her down when I turned eighteen, but she'd died a couple years before that. But enough about the past. The point of all that was to say I don't do relationships. I'm married to my job, and that's the only commitment I'm looking for. So you don't have to worry about me trying to blurry up the lines of our friendship."

When I looked up, Allison was looking at me with that same empathy. I could tell there were a million things she wanted to say, but she seemed to settle on just one.

"I get it," she finally said. "I do. It's a different thing altogether, but I know how hard residency was on my last relationship. When you're working long hours and the job comes first, it's really difficult to make something work. And I know how I avoid making a habit of anything that could be addictive, because of my father, even though I've never struggled with addiction myself."

"So we understand each other," I said. "Neither one of us wants a relationship. But we could both use a friend."

She smiled. "Yeah."

"We'll make a pact." I grinned, knowing it would bring back memories of the pact we had made as kids on our final night together.

Sadness flooded Allison's face. "I'm sorry I broke it."

"You didn't," I said, shaking my head firmly. "You're not the one who made the decision to move away. Besides, the pact held. We're still friends, right? And now that we've found each other again, we'll keep it.

Allison grinned, her sadness lessening at my words. "You're right. We're adults now. Nobody can separate us."

"Exactly. So we'll shake on it." I stretched my arm across the table, waiting with my hand open.

She put her tiny hand in mine and I swore I felt electricity snake up my arm, like something incredible had just happened and the world had somehow changed. But I ignored it, kept my customary grin on my face, and shook.

"Friends," I said.

"*Best* friends," she corrected.

"Forever," I said, repeating the words from our youth.

"Forever."

CHAPTER NINE

Allison

PIZZA WITH JACKSON TURNED OUT TO BE EXACTLY WHAT I'D needed. I had debated canceling all afternoon, torn between wanting to hang out with him and knowing it was a bad idea. I was attracted to him, but the more I thought about it, the more I knew getting involved romantically was a terrible idea. If I wanted any chance of staying here permanently, I needed to establish trust with my patients. A failed relationship with the town hero would ruin any chance of that.

So I had picked up my phone to cancel three times but couldn't bring myself to send the message. He had said it wasn't a date, and it was possible I had imagined the challenge in his eyes.

Once we got any potential awkwardness out of the way by putting it all on the table and agreeing to keep things platonic, any last concerns about spending time with him faded. We had reminisced all night about some of the best memories of my childhood—things I would never dream of doing now, like when we bribed a teenager into driving us up the mountain so we could sneak onto Old Man Murphy's property.

There had been a rumor that if you made it into his barn at midnight on the night of a full moon, you'd see him turn into a werewolf. He hadn't —in fact, his fully human self had chased us out of his barn with a pitchfork, yelling about how he'd take the law into his own hands if we rascals didn't stop harassing him. As adults, we knew we had been one hundred percent in the wrong for that one. But back then, it had been a bigger thrill than any rollercoaster or theme park the rich kids had ever experienced.

I was giggling so hard I snorted my drink up my nose before we finally let the conversation wind down so we could say goodnight.

"Come on," Jackson said, pulling out some cash and tossing it onto the table as a tip for the teenager who was staring at us from the kitchen doorway, obviously willing us to leave. "I'll walk you to your car."

"Such a gentleman," I said, teasing him as I grabbed my purse.

"That's how we do it in Tennessee, ma'am." He deliberately thickened his Southern accent and tipped a pretend hat toward me.

I laughed, but this time it was half-hearted. "Not every man in Tennessee is a gentleman."

His eyes narrowed. "Everything okay?"

"Yeah." I shrugged it off. "Long story."

"I've got time," he said, falling into step beside me as we walked through the restaurant toward the exit.

"Yes, but I don't have the emotional energy to tell it. Not tonight. Tonight has been pure fun, and I needed that."

"I did too."

I looked up and saw he was looking at me fondly, almost the way a big brother would look at a little sister. But my reaction to his platonic affection wasn't the relief I'd expected. A wave of regret rolled through me before I squashed it down. We had a pact, and it was better this way. Fewer complications.

Besides, this friendship was a balm for my wounded soul, and I wanted to protect it.

He pushed the door open to the dark parking lot.

"Wow," I commented, "I hadn't realized it had gotten so late."

He chuckled. "No wonder they were ready for us to leave."

"I'm parked over there," I said, pointing to my car before realizing how silly it was. There were only three vehicles left in the lot—mine, a white truck that was obviously his, and an older, beat-up car that could only belong to the girl serving us. Jackson was a detective; he would have instantly realized which car was mine.

He didn't comment on it though, just motioned for me to lead the way. But then his steps faltered, and I felt him tense beside me.

"What is it?"

He paused for a moment, then continued. "Nothing," he said. "Just thought I caught a glimpse of movement. Probably a stray dog or something."

"Probably," I agreed. But a quick glance at his face told me he wasn't entirely convinced. The relaxed Jackson had disappeared, and something oddly familiar was etched into his features. There was tension there, and irritation. Worry. It was a look I remembered well.

"Everything okay?"

He glanced down at me and relaxed his face, though it appeared to be a deliberate effort. "Yeah," he said. "Long story."

"I've got time," I said, repeating the phrase he had used on me.

"Another night. Tonight was fun. Next time, we'll pour out all our sorrows to each other." He reached to open my door and instantly frowned when it opened for him. "Allison, you should lock your car."

"I thought I had," I said, confused. "It's such an automatic thing, I can't imagine I forgot it. Maybe I'm already slipping back into old habits now that I'm out of the crime capital of the United States."

He reached for his pocket and pulled out a flashlight, leaning into my car to check the backseat.

"That serious, huh?" I asked, feeling my eyebrows knit in concern.

"Crime happens here too," he said, pulling out of the car and turning back to me. His face was different again—this time, a mixture of worry and sorrow.

It hit me that he was speaking from experience and it affected him in ways he didn't ordinarily show. "I guess you've seen the worst of it," I said, my voice soft, "with what you do."

He nodded. "We may not be Memphis, but don't let your guard down, Allison. People get hurt here too. Did you lock up your house today?"

"Yes," I said, nodding.

"Good." He hesitated, then reached out and gave me a quick hug, letting go before I even had a chance to return it. He looked down at me with an unreadable expression on his face. "I'm really glad you're back. I've missed you."

"I missed you, too," I said, recognizing the words to be deeply true. I hadn't thought of Jackson in years before moving back here, but it was true just the same. Reconnecting with him was filling up a piece of me that I hadn't realized was missing.

"See you soon," he said, standing back so I could get inside the car. He closed the door gently, then stood watching as I backed out, still glancing to his right every so often in search of the shadow that had changed him.

THE FAMILIAR FLUTTER OF NERVES ABOUT PULLING UP TO AN empty house hit the moment I turned my car into the long driveway. Jackson's words echoed in my mind. But there was nothing to get worked up over. I had locked up before leaving home, and I'd remembered to leave lights on both inside and out. And really, despite Jackson's concern, the odds of anything happening here had to be something like one in a million.

Crime happened everywhere, yes, but it was almost never random. It was personal. While I wasn't exactly beloved in town yet, my only real enemy was Beverly, and it wasn't as if she was the kind of person to murder me in my own home. She was content with barbed words and mild sabotage at the clinic, making me miserable in hopes I would leave.

So I told myself nerves were silly, grabbed my bag, and headed into the door with false confidence—only ducking once when the bat swooped overhead again.

I let myself into the house, which was already starting to feel like home. It hadn't taken long to discover the pleasure of living alone. The place was as tidy as I had left it, without Jen's dirty laundry strewn across the living room. There was no annoying music blasting, no soap operas streaming on the TV. It was blissfully quiet and peaceful—until my cell phone buzzed.

Mike. I stared at the name on my caller ID, shaking my head. I had said we could try to be friends, but honestly? I wanted space. He needed to respect that.

I ignored the call, locked the door behind me, and dropped my bag on the entryway table. All I wanted now was a long soak in a hot bath. I went upstairs and started running the water, filling the garden tub with a ridiculous amount of bath salts. Then I went to my room to grab a set of clean pajamas.

Once I'd lowered myself into the bath, I laid my head back, closed my eyes, and felt a smile form on my face. This was heaven. A quiet house, a nice bath. Even better, this sweet relaxation was following an evening with Jackson that had filled my soul with goodness.

Jackson.

The thought of him and his sweet smile conjured images of him being across from me in this very bath, lazily stroking a hand up my leg, and leaning forward for a kiss...

My eyes popped open and I sat up straight. *That* was out of line for a platonic friendship. But it didn't mean anything. It couldn't. Seeing him had been comforting and pleasant, and my mind had simply associated those feelings with the comfort of the bath. It meant nothing, and it wouldn't happen again.

In the middle of my internal lecture, I heard a noise that caught my attention. I held my breath, listening. It almost sounded like scratching noises, like...like something—or someone—was scratching at my door.

Images of all the horror movies Mike had forced me to watch flooded my mind.

The noise stopped, and I breathed again, lying back in the tub. It was probably a branch. Was it windy? Not that I remembered. But it could have been a stray cat or something. Or even my imagination. Perhaps my brain was inventing a distraction from the uncomfortable lecture I was giving myself about Jackson. That was entirely possible.

I took a deep breath and closed my eyes, attempting to sink back into a zen state. But as I did, I heard the noise again.

I sat back up, my heart pounding. This wasn't going to work. As silly as it might be, I couldn't relax until I knew for sure what was causing that noise. Once I figured out what was responsible for it, I could get back into the bath and ignore it. But until then, I would just keep spooking myself.

I reluctantly left behind the warmth of the tub, quickly drying off with a towel before slipping into my fluffy pink robe. I padded barefoot into my room to check those windows first. The trees grew close around the back of the house, and a tree branch scratching the window was the solution I was hoping to find.

Even if logic suggested I would have heard the noises the night before if that were the case.

Still, I methodically checked all the upstairs windows, feeling a pang of disappointment when I realized they were all clear. The trees grew close, yes, but not *that* close. There weren't any branches within a foot of any of the windows.

I slipped my cell phone into the pocket of my robe before heading downstairs. I didn't hear the noise anymore, and I hoped that meant it was an animal that had been scared away. A stray cat would make sense. Maybe a previous tenant here had even fed one, invited it in sometimes, and it was just looking for its next meal. There were raccoons in the area too, and there could be one looking for food—or even a squirrel trying to make a home somewhere.

I looked out all the windows and saw nothing. There was really nothing left to check except the two doors, but the idea of opening them felt like a mistake. Unless it really *was* a stray cat, in which case I felt terrible about the idea of it being alone and hungry. I stood in the hallway, paralyzed with indecision, waiting to hear the noises again. They never came.

Finally, I gave up. It had likely been an animal, but whatever it was was long gone. I should have stayed in the bath like a reasonable adult. Now, the moment had passed, and I might as well just turn on a TV show—for entertainment, I lied to myself, despite knowing I would simply feel safer with some background noise.

Chapter Ten

Jackson

I woke up bright and early the next morning to squeeze in a run before I headed in to work. Running was more than good for my body; it gave me time to let my mind wander. It was usually during that time that I would think of an angle I hadn't yet considered and crack whatever case I was working on.

When Sheriff Morrison had started an investigative division, more than a few people had laughed at the idea. We were a small county with a small budget to match. Detectives were for big cities, everyone protested. It would be a meaningless title here in Rosemary Mountain, where there was supposedly nothing to investigate—nothing that required a deputy's full attention, anyway.

But they had been proven wrong, and as they had begun to realize just how useful I could be, I had gotten busier and busier. Sure, most of my investigations were for minor, petty stuff. A lot of them were drug related. But we had worked a few homicides, and I had even helped out on a high-profile case involving a senator from California. I was proud of my work and grateful the sheriff had seen fit to pick me for the responsibility.

But today as I ran, my mind wasn't on my official cases. I couldn't stop thinking about how Russell kept popping up. Last night, when I had walked Allison to her car, someone had slipped behind the building into the shadows. I didn't get a close look, but my gut said it had to be him again. He was following me—and had potentially broken into Allison's car while we ate. But why?

He had asked for money, but I had made it clear I wouldn't give it. He had too much pride to keep pushing for it. If he was ready for me to hook him up with a job, he wouldn't go slinking around in the shadows.

The words he'd spoken to me last time came back. *"You'll get what's coming to you, boy."* When I was a kid, those words had meant there was going to be pain—and lots of it.

But things were different now. Truth was, I knew he was at least a little afraid of me. He had to fear that, if he ever gave me the chance, I'd gladly give him a taste of his own medicine. That's what he would do in my shoes. Revenge was Russell's middle name, and like he always said— his blood ran through my veins.

He was getting older, and a lifetime of drugs and alcohol had left him looking thin and frail. I, on the other hand, had turned to exercise as the very best free therapy, so I would easily outmatch him in a fight— especially now that I regularly trained with Cole Hawkins, a special forces veteran and martial arts expert Greg had brought on to train all of his deputies. The local news had done a special feature on Cole's training sessions with us. Russell would have heard about it. He had to know he didn't stand a chance against me in a fight these days.

He was probably just trying to scare me.

I hated that he still could.

I kept my guard up all day, knowing that if Russell really did want revenge, he'd probably try to get it by cutting my brake lines or something equally cowardly. Something hands off that he could do without getting caught. That or he'd offer to trade jobs with someone younger and fitter, maybe get me called out to a situation that was really a trap.

I was deep in thought when Greg stopped by my desk.

"Earth to Jackson," he said in a voice that showed amusement instead of annoyance.

"Sorry," I said, looking up from the paperwork I hadn't even really been seeing. "What's up?"

"Were you planning on going to the dance at town hall tonight?"

I shook my head. "Not really. Why? Need me to clock some extra hours?"

"Well, sort of," he said, looking pained. "I was actually hoping you'd go to the dance, make an appearance."

"Are you not going?" I asked, suddenly curious. Sheriff Morrison thought it was important to attend as many events as possible to show that he was part of the community and working to make it better for everyone.

He shook his head. "Janet's got a bad cold. I want to stay home and take care of her, but I had already promised the mayor I would call out the raffle winners. I'd owe you one if you covered for me."

"No problem. I'll handle it."

"Thank you." He breathed a sigh of relief.

"Tell Janet to feel better soon."

"I will. And seriously, I owe you one."

He moved away from the desk and my mind drifted again. Did Allison know about the dance? She might not, since she had just gotten to town and wasn't really in the know yet. But it would be a great opportunity for her to start showing up as a member of the community and building rapport, just like Greg had.

But I didn't want to invite her in a way that would make it seem like I was asking her on a date. Even though we had made our pact the night before, inviting someone to a dance was different. In fact, I had made a point of *always* attending these things alone so I didn't give anyone the wrong impression.

We didn't have to go together though. I could just shoot her a message and let her know about it. I grabbed my phone before I over-thought the whole thing.

Jackson: Hey, has anyone told you about the dance at town hall tonight?

Allison: Oh my goodness, are they still having those things?

Jackson: Yep. Every quarter.

Allison: Wow. Some things never change. Well, to answer your question, no, I didn't know about it. Why?

Jackson: Might be good for you to make an appearance. Greg—Sheriff Morrison—was an outsider too. Replaced Sheriff Joe Hemsworth. Remember him?

Allison: Ah, good old Sheriff Joe. Of course I remember him.

Jackson: Then you know he was as beloved as Doc Rogers. Greg faced the same kind of battle you are, but he's gained acceptance and respect. Part of how he did it was showing up at every town function he could, proving he cared about the community.

Allison: Ugh. I always hated those things. But you're right. What time does it start?

Jackson: Six.

Allison: Will you be there?

Jackson: I'll be there.

Allison: Then I'll see you tonight. 🙂

I STARED AT MY PHONE FOR A MINUTE. IT WASN'T A DATE. WE weren't even going together. But her little smile when I said I'd be there felt more important than it should.

As a kid, I'd been half in love with Allison Bell.

As an adult, I couldn't let that happen again.

Chapter Eleven

Allison

I took a deep breath when I pulled up to the town hall. The parking lot was already nearly full, suggesting these dances were still as popular as they had been when I was a kid. Based on the stragglers who'd arrived late, it appeared this was a tradition held by the older crowd. Jackson and I might be the youngest in attendance by a few decades.

After a quick pep talk, I forced myself out of the car and slipped through the door, grateful when nobody seemed to notice me. I went straight to the punch bowl to get a drink, just to have something to do with my hands. Jackson was right—town events were important. If I ever wanted to be accepted here, I needed to be part of the community. But I felt entirely out of place, and the long-forgotten but still familiar sounds and smells were bringing back memories I'd rather forget.

It was in this same building that I had first realized what the town thought of my father. I couldn't have been older than six or seven at the time. Mama had always told me he was "sick." In my sheltered way, I had thought I was being a good daughter and taking care of him when he asked me to pour him another glass of gin. "It's his medicine," Mama would say. "The only thing keeping him alive."

I hadn't realized until much later that those words had been laced with a sarcasm she only dared hint at in his presence.

But here, in this room, everything had changed. I had been so excited to go to the town dance in my new party dress. New dresses were a rare thing indeed, and technically speaking, this one wasn't new at all —it was a hand-me-down from an older girl who lived in the nice part of town. But it was new to me, and I had never felt so beautiful as when I tried it on the first time.

First off, it was *blue,* not yellow like most of my hand-me-downs. Cerulean blue, a color that seemed so utterly perfect I couldn't believe it. The full skirt draped the ground—the dress was probably two sizes too big—but it made me feel just like Cinderella when I twirled. Mama pinned the dress up so it appeared to fit me everywhere else, but I begged her to leave it long, like a ball gown. She agreed, with misty eyes that reminded me she, too, had once been a little girl who'd dreamed of being a princess.

Even then, it had struck my heart with pain to realize how unfair life could be. We all dreamed of being princesses. But she had grown up to take care of a sick man. She was always tired and sad, and she had started working late at night to help pay the bills.

"What's wrong, baby?" she had asked as she watched my face fall.

"I just wish you had a princess dress, too, Mama," I said.

Grief washed over her face, but she quickly replaced it with a reassuring smile. "My princess days are over. But nothing makes me happier than seeing you become one. No sadness, sweetheart. Tonight, you go to the ball. Just think of me as your fairy godmother."

"Okay," I said, giving her the smile I knew she wanted.

Mama curled my hair and pinned it up so it fell in ringlets around my face, and she even let me spritz myself with her fancy perfume that smelled like roses. She told me I would be the belle of the ball and to just watch—everyone would be smiling for the princess.

I was a bundle of nerves on the way into town, both because of how excited I was for the dance and because of how terrifying the drive was.

Dad sipped his flask the entire time, apparently without a thought in his head about the danger he was putting his family in as he whipped around the mountain curves, unable to keep the car in its proper lane. I just reminded myself of what he always said—he was sick and trying his best.

When we finally arrived, I walked into the room, beaming from ear to ear, looking around eagerly to see everyone's reactions. But instead of smiles, I heard the loud whispers about how the town drunk had somehow managed to make it in one piece and how pathetic it was that he couldn't even buy his daughter a dress that actually fit her.

It was like everything in my brain suddenly shifted. I didn't have all the pieces of the puzzle yet, but I knew suddenly that the picture of my life looked nothing like I'd thought. For the first time in my life, I felt shame. And I no longer wanted anyone to notice me.

I didn't dance that night. I slipped away from my family, choosing to watch the dancing from a distance. From a hidden corner, I watched the more respectable families lead the festivities, and I realized there were divisions in Rosemary Mountain I had been blind to. I found myself wishing I came from a different family. Then I felt ashamed I would wish for such a thing.

Nobody looked for me. Nobody except Jackson, that was. Jackson had come with his mother. Knowing full well how the town saw them, thanks to Russell, they had slipped in quietly. His sharp eyes somehow spotted me in my hiding spot, and he made a beeline for where I was.

We hid under a table and watched the dancers, making up silly stories about ridiculous things happening in their homes too. It eased some of the new heartache I was feeling to pretend that old Mrs. Miller had been late because Mr. Miller had gotten angry and hidden her high heels. Or that the mayor couldn't eat any cake because his wife had scolded him for growing a belly so big that, when he got dressed for the evening, his button had popped off and hit her in the eye.

We made things up about other people to take the sting out of them talking about our families. And it worked.

We also stuffed ourselves with as much cake as we could stomach, knowing we didn't get such things often at home. And that night, we went from being neighbors to best friends, a friendship that would get me through the rest of my years in Rosemary Mountain—until the day mama finally got her head on straight, left my father, and started a better life for us both.

Why on earth had I returned here to relive the chapter of our lives we both preferred to pretend had never happened?

I shook off thoughts of the past when I spied Jackson standing at the front of the room, looking incredibly handsome in his uniform. Relief flooded my body at the sight of him. He was waiting patiently while someone—probably the new mayor—welcomed everyone to the dance and explained the rules of the raffle.

Jackson's eyes met mine from across the room and his mouth turned up in a little smile. I took a deep breath, suddenly knowing everything would be okay. I wasn't a young girl in a ridiculously over-sized dress who needed to hide anymore. I was an adult with a medical degree. More importantly, I had a friend in this room, a friendly face who was truly happy to see me. The same friend who had gotten me through these dances before.

Jackson made a beeline for me when the mayor was finished with him. Our eyes stayed connected as he walked across the room, slipping through the crowd to join me on the outskirts.

"You look nervous," he murmured, pouring himself a cup of punch.

"I am," I admitted. It was hard to ignore all the curious glances. Everyone knew everyone else in this town, and despite having been born here, I was now considered an outsider. I'd expected some of the town busybodies to accost me, wanting to find out what, exactly, my connection was to Rosemary Mountain as well as all the personal details they could wrangle out of me. But strangely, none of them had. Either the town was changing and people were keeping to themselves more or everyone already knew who I was and had decided to shun me.

Based on the looks and whispers, I was pretty certain it was the latter.

"Come on," Jackson said, placing a hand under my elbow and drawing me out from the back of the room. "I'll introduce you to people. You can't just hide out back here. It's like you're flashing a neon sign that you want everyone to leave you alone. And they're doing it."

"Maybe you're right," I admitted. I hadn't considered how it looked that I had come in and stayed in the back, not speaking to anyone else. Jackson was obviously a pro at navigating the social aspect here. I needed to take a lesson from him.

"I know I'm right," he said, looking down at me with a warm smile. His confidence helped me relax, knowing he had my back. "It's time for you to own the fact that you're home and should be treated as a respected member of town."

I swallowed hard. "I don't know, Jackson. I'm still a Bell. Based on how everything's gone so far, it's hard to imagine anyone just immediately accepting me like that."

"Don't worry," he said, flashing his grin at me. "You're with me. Gives you street cred."

I just raised an eyebrow and fell into step beside him as he took me to meet the mayor.

An hour later, I squeezed Jackson's hand and mouthed *thank you* to him. He had made the rounds, introducing me to nearly everyone in the room as Dr. Allison Bell, and people had responded more warmly than I had expected. A few people even asked about my mother and said they hoped she was doing well. Nobody mentioned my father, a fact that made me incredibly grateful. By the time Jackson was finished making introductions, I was actually starting to enjoy myself.

But the highlight of the night was getting to meet Dr. Johnson again and thanking him for giving me a chance. He was older now—mid-sixties probably—but somehow just as handsome as ever. He knew me before Jackson even had a chance to introduce us, and he beamed as he shook my hand.

"Allison Bell. Of course. I'd know you anywhere. You're the spitting image of your mother." His eyes seemed to linger on me with a trace of feeling.

"Thank you," I said, pleased with the compliment. And pleased again to be associated with my mother rather than my father.

"How's the clinic treating you?" he asked. He cocked his head and gave me a look of interest, letting me know he wasn't asking simply to be polite.

I moved my head back and forth in a noncommitted way. "It's going alright," I said carefully.

He raised his eyebrows and leaned forward conspiratorially. "You can be honest with me, Allison. I know that clinic has a reputation for being difficult."

"Really?"

He nodded. "But I believe in you. You can turn it around. And if I can be of any assistance to you, don't hesitate to ask."

"Thank you," I said, beyond grateful to have another ally in the medical community. If I was going to change things, I'd need all the help I could get.

I started to tell him about my idea for a drug treatment program, but mid-conversation, an elegantly dressed woman pulled him away for a dance.

At almost the same time, a gray-haired lady leaning heavily on her walking cane approached Jackson. "Young man, you owe me a dance," she said, wagging her finger at him.

"I did promise, didn't I?" he replied, smiling as he held his arm out for her. "Be right back," he told me.

"I'll be here," I said. "And I get the next dance."

His eyebrows shot up. "Absolutely."

I STAYED ON THE SIDE, WATCHING HIM SLOWLY WALTZ THE fragile lady around the room. She couldn't have been more than four feet tall, and he had to stoop over to dance with her. But she was grinning from ear to ear, and the sight made me smile. Jackson wasn't just good at managing the community. He genuinely cared about them, and it was sweet to see.

"I wouldn't get your heart set on that one," said a voice beside me.

I looked and was surprised to see the woman who had just pulled

Dr. Johnson away for a dance—a dance that apparently hadn't lasted long. I automatically glanced at her hands and noticed an over-the-top diamond wedding ring on her finger.

"Oh, Jackson?" I asked. "We're just friends."

"Good," she said, nodding. "Because Jackson's a good man, and he could do a hell of a lot better than a Bell." She turned on her heel and walked away.

My face flushed hot and pain squeezed my heart. Her cruel comment was humiliating—a reminder of who I was and always would be in the eyes of everyone here.

When Jackson returned, he frowned at me. "What's wrong?"

"Nothing," I said shakily. I smoothed down the front of my dress, trying to get myself under control. "Who is that?" I asked, pointing at the woman who now had her back toward us.

He glanced over. "Red dress?"

"Yeah."

"Penny Johnson. Dr. Johnson's wife. Why?" he asked, giving me a strange look. "Did she say something to you?"

"It doesn't matter," I said, glancing back toward the direction she had walked.

She was staring at me, her lips set in a thin line.

"It matters to me," he said, following my line of sight with a puzzled look on his face.

"Forget it." I gave him a reassuring smile. "I want that dance now."

Chapter Twelve

Jackson

Penny Johnson had clearly upset Allison. She had been fine until I left to dance with Mrs. Steinbeck, but she was back to being embarrassed and awkward when I returned. She shook it off quickly though and insisted she didn't want to talk about it. She just wanted to dance, and I couldn't say no.

But when the dance started, part of me wished I could have.

Allison stepped forward and put one hand in mine and the other on my shoulder. I slipped my arm around her waist as we started to move in time with the music, a soulful ballad about finding love that would last a lifetime. In some ways, it felt familiar—we'd been dance partners at plenty of town dances before. But that was Allison the kid.

This was Allison the woman.

I'd done a great job of keeping things light and friendly all night. But with her in my arms, gazing up into my eyes, I couldn't keep an easy smile on my face. Couldn't hide the fact that everything within me was at war.

I couldn't pretend not to notice how incredible she smelled or how amazing it felt to be this close to her. How I wanted to pull her even closer and feel her body pressed up against mine. How I wanted my hands in her hair, to press my lips to her pretty mouth.

How I wanted this song to be about us.

All things I could never have.

My no-relationship rule wasn't going to change, and Allison was way too important to ruin everything by crossing the boundaries of friendship for a fling. So I'd have to squash those feelings down tight and keep things safe and platonic for both of us.

But that was hard to do while holding her this close. It felt wrong to avoid her eyes, but when I looked down at her, everything I was feeling threatened to spill out of me in a mess of words I knew I shouldn't say. So I closed my eyes and gave myself the rest of the song to pretend that things could be different.

As soon as the song ended, I made a lame excuse about needing to leave so I could get to work early the next day.

"Really?" she asked, disappointment clear on her face. "It's still so early."

"Yeah," I said, tugging at the collar of my uniform. "Sorry. I've been in this all day and I'm ready for a shower and some sweats." Though in reality, it wasn't the uniform making me uncomfortable—it was the way she looked in that blue sundress. An innocent, classy sundress that had me thinking all sorts of thoughts that weren't classy at all.

"Hey, I get it," she said. "Thanks so much for introducing me to everyone and helping me get established here. I'm glad you made me come."

"I'm glad, too," I said, staring down into those gorgeous blue eyes. They looked up at me with so much trust, so much affection. Things I knew I could lose in a heartbeat if I didn't get out of here before I acted upon the feelings she was bringing up in me.

"See you soon?" she asked hopefully.

"Soon," I promised.

I walked outside and nearly ran straight into Russell. "What are you doing here?" I demanded, not at all in the mood to deal with him.

"I'm a citizen, same as you." He smirked. "Don't I have the right to come to town events?"

"No, you don't." It wasn't true, of course. I just didn't want him anywhere near Allison.

A challenge rose in his eyes. "I do," he said. "Unless you're about to cross the line and try to deny me my rights?" He threw his glance toward the open door like he was searching for someone inside. But then he looked back at me with a sly grin on his face. "I feel like I'm in the mood for a dance, young Jackson. Might want to go inside and find me a pretty young thing to dance with tonight. Take her home, show her a real good time."

My pulse skyrocketed. "You need to go home. Now." I crossed my arms and stood my ground.

He studied my eyes. Maybe he saw I was edgier than normal, because in a move that was totally unlike him, he backed down.

"Fine, I'll go," he said, scowling. He spit in the grass beside my feet. "No one worth talking to in there anyway." He stalked off, away from the entrance.

I sat alone inside my truck, keeping guard, until the party started breaking up and I saw Allison leave. It wasn't until I saw her safely pull her car out and head toward home, unfollowed, that I breathed a sigh of relief and went to get the rest—and space—I desperately needed.

Seeing Russell again had me shaken up enough that I didn't get that rest after all. My night was marked by nightmares, and I woke the next day feeling even more exhausted than before. I kept to my routine but felt like I was constantly looking over my shoulder, just waiting for him to pop out of the bushes somewhere.

It wasn't like him to walk away without a fight. That meant he was saving the fight for later.

But nearly an entire week passed uneventfully, without trouble or even a sighting of Russell. And despite my intention to put some space between us, Allison and I wound up meeting every night for dinner. It felt okay though because we had to keep them short. She was having a busy week meeting with hospital administrators, trying to get the clinic set up the way she wanted, and setting up her house at night. The quick dinners felt casual and had established a routine of easy friendship.

So it was no surprise when she texted me Thursday evening about getting together again.

Allison: Today has felt like the longest day ever. I know it's a little early, but I can't look at charts anymore. Want to grab dinner?

Jackson: I could eat. I'm still at the station, finishing up a report, but I'll be done in about ten minutes. What sounds good?

Allison: Something light. Sandwiches or a nice salad? Is there anywhere that serves anything like that?

Jackson: Honey, you're in the fried food capital of the world.

Allison: LOL, I've noticed. But I'm craving something healthier. Besides, in school they told us we should set a good example for our communities, be seen eating healthy and all that. That we have a responsibility and a standard to live up to.

Jackson: LOL. And I'm guessing you wrote that down in your notebook and took it as gospel, didn't you?

Allison: ...well, yes.

Jackson: I knew it. You're in luck though. There's a cafe downtown called Luna's. Best soup, salad, and sandwiches around. Even has vegan options. Sources a lot of their stuff from local growers.

Allison: Wow. Go Rosemary Mountain. Meet you there?

Jackson: I'll be there in twenty.

. . .

SHERIFF MORRISON LEANED ON MY DESK AS I POCKETED MY phone. "What are you grinning about?" he asked, eyebrows raised.

"Just joking around with an old friend about restaurant options here in town."

He grinned. "Would this be a female friend? Rumor has it you've been seen taking the same woman out every night this week."

"Yes, but she's *just* a friend," I clarified. "It's Allison Bell. We talked about her."

"Ah," he said, nodding. "The new doctor in town. You guys reconnected, huh?"

"Yeah. We've been catching up. She has her work cut out for her here, trying to win over everyone who still thinks Doc Rogers should be practicing."

Greg snorted. "Good luck to her. I've been here for, what, three, four years now? And there's still a handful of people who tell me how much better things were when Joe was in charge."

"Ah, yes," I said drily. "You mean when they had a sheriff willing to look the other way on anything they did behind closed doors as long as he could keep up the impression that this was a quiet little town where nothing bad ever happened. Speaking of which, Allison has an idea."

"Oh yeah? What's that?"

"She mentioned that a lot of her patients are still on too many prescription drugs. She wants to start a medication-assisted treatment program, help get them clean."

Greg's face beamed with approval. "That would be great. I was just doing some reading about how that's working in another small town with a similar demographic to ours. It's not a perfect solution, but the stats are good. If there's anything she needs from us, or if she wants us to help with public education, let me know. We might be able to work something out where, if we arrest anyone who's using, we could offer some sort of deal contingent upon program compliance. Might actually help people change their lives for good."

"That's similar to what I was thinking. Glad to know you're on the same page."

"I like this girl already. Any chance this 'just friends' thing is temporary?" He winked at me.

I knew he was rooting for me to find someone and settle down. He had recently gotten remarried and declared it to be the best decision he had ever made. He wanted the same for me. But I couldn't bring myself to admit to him all the reasons it wouldn't be.

I shook my head. "Nah. We've already talked about how we don't want to mess up anything by having that possibility on the table." I paused for a minute, deciding to open up just a bit. "When I was a kid," I said, glancing around to make sure we were alone, "she meant a lot to me. Might even be the reason I'm still alive. You don't screw that up by screwing around."

He nodded. "I understand. Sounds like you two have your heads on your shoulders. Either way, I'm glad she's back. I appreciate anyone who wants to make a positive difference in our community, and I'm glad you've got a good friend in her."

"Me too." It meant more than I could say.

"Hey," he added as he turned away. "You're coming to dinner tomorrow night, right?"

"I'll be there," I said, nodding confirmation. Once a month, Greg and Janet hosted a Friday night dinner for their family, and they included me in the count.

"Bring Allison," he suggested. "If she's having a hard time making friends, Daphne and Willa would be good for her. You know they'll immediately make her part of the group."

"That's a good idea," I admitted, even though I knew if I showed up with her people would automatically assume we were a couple, and it might lead to some awkward conversations.

Still, he was right—Daphne and Willa were both close to Allison's age and would make her feel welcome. That would give her two good girlfriends here, and since they were both pretty popular in the community, having them as friends would give her some automatic credibility.

Although part of me wasn't quite ready to share her.

"It's settled then," he said. "I'll tell Janet to add another place setting to the table. Now go on and get out of here. That paperwork will wait until morning and you know it."

"Yes, sir," I said, giving him a salute.

He just laughed and headed out the door.

And with a smile on my face, I grabbed my stuff and followed him.

"THIS PLACE IS ADORABLE," ALLISON SAID, HER FACE lighting up as she took in all the details of the historic home-turned-café. "You said Luna owns it?"

"Yeah. She bought this place and turned it into a restaurant about a year ago."

Allison shook her head. "It's so fun to see how people we were in school with turned out. I remember how Luna loved to play with the miniature kitchen at the children's library. Now she owns a restaurant of her own."

"Yeah." I grinned. "And I can remember you walking around with the toy stethoscope."

Allison's face broke into a smile. "I did! You're right. I don't remember what you used to play with though. Do you?"

"Nah," I said, shaking my head and keeping my grin on, even though a flicker of pain hit my heart. "I don't think I was ever much into toys."

Allison looked like she could see right through me. "Yeah, probably not," she said, but the sadness in her voice told me she had remembered the same thing I did—how I had learned early on that if Russell picked me up and saw me playing with anything at all, he'd find a way to humiliate me for it in front of all the other kids.

The toy kitchen was women's work. The doctor set was ridiculous because I was too stupid to ever become one. Books? I was a sissy, wasting precious time reading dumb fairytales.

The only thing he would have been happy to have me play with were the toy guns, but only if I was the bad guy. And that was the one thing I had been determined to never be. If he had caught me playing the role of a cop? He'd probably have called me a traitor and killed me that night.

"Anyway," I said, deliberately changing the subject. "Luna did a great job with the project. She really kept the character of the old house.

You can rent out the top floor for meetings or events. The bottom is open for lunch and dinner as a café. It's been pretty popular, especially with the tourists."

"I can see why." She peered at the counter. "Lobster bisque? Fresh mozzarella with toasted hazelnuts, balsamic glaze, and truffle oil?" She clapped her hands like a little girl. "Everything sounds incredible."

"Thank you," Luna herself said, walking in just in time to catch Allison's excitement.

I watched the surprise on Allison's face as she took in the sight. Luna had grown up into a stunning woman who liked to dress like she was heading to dinner at a castle or something instead of running a restaurant in Rosemary Mountain. She always knew how to make an entrance, that was for sure.

"Hey, Jackson," Luna said, giving me a smile.

"Hey, Luna. Remember Allison from school?"

Luna turned to Allison, keeping her face cool, though I noticed the quick flicker of surprise in her eyes. "Allison Bell, right?"

"That's right," Allison replied with a warm smile. "It's great to see you after all these years. Congratulations on the restaurant! I can't wait to try it."

Luna shrugged and held up a graceful hand as if it was nothing. The red jewels on her bracelet sparkled in the light. "Thank you," she said. "I hope you enjoy it. Welcome back to the mountain. I've heard you're taking over the family practice on the square?"

"I am," Allison confirmed.

"Good luck. You'll need it," Luna said, raising her eyebrows. She turned her body away from us to address the girl behind the register as we moved up to the front of the line. "The detective eats on the house tonight. Come see me sometime, Jackson." She squeezed my arm, then gave me a wink as she turned and headed up the stairs to the top floor.

"Ohhh," Allison whispered. "Someone has a crush on you."

I just laughed and gave my order to the girl at the counter. "And whatever she wants," I said, gesturing to Allison.

The girl hesitated. "I think I can only give you yours for free."

"That's fine," I said. "But I'm paying for hers."

"You don't have to do that, Jackson," Allison protested.

I shook my head, feeling annoyed that Luna had comped mine but not Allison's. I'd rather it have been the other way around or not get comped at all. Luna had always been nice, but her behavior tonight confused me. "I get to eat for free more often than you'd think, and sometimes I'd rather pass it on to someone else."

Allison hesitated. "Okay. If you're sure. But I'm getting yours next time."

"Not necessary." I passed my card to the girl checking us out. "Order whatever you want," I said, turning back to Allison. "I just saw my favorite table open up, and I'm going to grab it before someone else does."

Allison laughed. "Okay. Be there in a sec."

Chapter Thirteen

Allison

I gave the girl my order and retrieved Jackson's card, then went in search of him. He was seated at a corner table in one of the front rooms.

"So why is this your favorite table?" I asked as I dropped into the chair across from him.

"Because," he said, lifting his hand to point at the wall behind him with his thumb. "I've got a wall at my back. I can see the side entrance from this window"—he pointed at the window to his right—"and when someone walks in the front, this wall pretty much hides me from their view. I can see them, but not vice versa. It's a great tactical position."

I stared at him for a second before bursting into laughter. "Wow. That's definitely a cop answer. I thought it would be something like how it has the most comfortable chairs, or the best lighting, or how you always get lucky if you take a date to this table."

Jackson winked. "I don't need a special table to get lucky."

"I bet you don't. In fact," I said, raising my eyebrows, "I'm pretty sure you could get lucky just by walking upstairs right now." I laughed to let him know I was teasing, even though truthfully I was feeling an odd jealousy.

Odd because I had never felt any kind of jealousy when fellow residents would flirt with Mike. Jackson and I weren't romantically involved, I definitely didn't have the right to feel this way. But it had started the moment Luna had staked her claim on him, and this conversation was making it ten times worse.

Jackson had the decency to blush. "Just so you know, Luna and I have never—"

I interrupted him. "You don't owe me any explanations. We're friends, right? What you do is your business." Even if it was making me feel something I had no right to feel.

"Right," Jackson said, clearly uncomfortable as well. "But still. Luna and I have always just been friends. Completely platonic."

"So no girlfriend then? I mean, clearly. That was a stupid question," I stammered. "If you had a girlfriend, you wouldn't be out with me. Plus, you already told me you don't do relationships." I felt mortified. Why was I suddenly acting so awkward? I needed to shake this off.

"No, no girlfriend," Jackson said slowly. "What about you? Do you have someone back in Memphis?"

I bit my lip. "No. Not anymore."

"What happened?"

I took a deep breath. "Well. We haven't exactly talked about why I ended up here, but here's the short version. I was up for a position with the hospital system where I did my residency. Only, the department chief expected me to sleep with him in order to get the job."

"What?" Jackson's jaw dropped.

"Yeah. Obviously, I refused. Then I made the mistake of threatening him with HR." I sighed. "It was stupid. I should have known he had way too much power for that. He threatened to destroy my reputation and make me unhireable in Memphis." I shook my head, still feeling the disbelief of how it had all worked out. "My boyfriend at the time— Mike—actually told me I should have just done it. He apparently knew what was going to happen at the interview and didn't even warn me."

Jackson blinked like he was having trouble comprehending my words. "I'm sorry, did you say your boyfriend actually wanted you to sleep with a superior to get a job?"

I nodded. "Yeah, he did. Turns out, the reason I only saw Mike once every couple of weeks was because he was also dating the daughter of a different department chief. I had no idea until that day."

Jackson shook his head in disgust. "I'm so sorry."

I sighed, then did something that surprised even me. I smiled. "It's okay," I said, meaning it for the first time. "It's odd. We were together all through residency, but I don't miss him at all. He didn't love me, and I know now that I didn't love him." The certainty of it felt like a gift.

"Well, good. I'm glad you're okay."

"After that," I continued, "I decided I was just...tired of it all. Tired of the politics, the striving, the cutthroat environment. I wanted a fresh start somewhere quiet and peaceful. I started sending out my CV that night, and Dr. Stone called about this job shortly after."

"As far as the other guy goes, is there anything I can do? Are you still thinking of filing a report?"

"I don't know," I admitted. "I mean, it's just my word against his. I don't have proof of anything. He, on the other hand, has people willing to speak out against me because of what he can offer them in return."

Jackson put his elbows on the table and clasped his hands together, resting his chin against his knuckles. His eyes were thoughtful. "He's probably done this to other women. If we found others willing to speak out, we might be able to do something about it."

I smiled softly. "Thank you."

"For what?"

"For believing me. For wanting to help. For not saying I was stupid about the whole thing. Everyone seemed to think I should have just done it. Small price to pay for a career, right?"

"No," he said, shaking his head. "No, it's not."

"Exactly. Not to me, anyway. But." I smiled, surprising myself again. "Other than having a receptionist who hates me and an incompetent nurse, I'm starting to think it all worked out for the best."

"Oh yeah?"

"Yeah. I think I ended up exactly where I'm supposed to be."

. . .

DINNER WAS FABULOUS IN EVERY WAY. MY IRRATIONAL annoyance at Luna aside—how was it possible for a woman to be so insanely beautiful? And why on earth did she have to like Jackson?—I had to admit, she knew what she was doing when it came to her restaurant. The meal would have easily stood up next to some of the best award-winning restaurants I had ever been to. And sharing the meal with Jackson made it even better. I felt so comfortable with him, and it was lovely to have someone to decompress with at the end of the day.

So when Luna swept over to our table in her long red dress—placing a hand on the back of Jackson's chair—to ask how everything was, I told myself the reason I found it annoying wasn't because I wanted a romantic relationship with him. It just reminded me of the reality that our friendship had an unknown end date. He was an attractive, popular man. Despite what he had told me, he wouldn't stay single forever. Someday, some girl would convince him to give a relationship a try, and he'd be so in love with her that he would say yes.

And then our dinners would be over.

The thought nearly broke my heart. But it was just my personality, I assured myself. I was a woman of routine. I got into habits and then struggled with change. Dinner with Jackson had somehow already become a regular part of my new life, and of course it would be difficult when that routine had to change.

Difficult? my inner voice whispered, mocking me. *Don't you mean it will rip your heart out and shred it to pieces?*

I sighed. It was true. I'd been attracted to him from day one, and we had gotten way too close. I was playing with fire. Maybe it would be better to end our dinners now, before I lost my heart completely.

No. I would not fall in love with him. We had an agreement.

And if the sight of Luna looking down at him with adoration in her eyes was making me crazy, it was only because it was rude of her to intrude on our date.

I mean, our conversation.

Okay, maybe I did need to take a step backward.

When Luna finally left and Jackson apologized, I did my best to be totally cool. "Don't worry about it," I said, waving him off. "Seriously, I can be your wingman. I'm good here with this fabulous meal. Do you want to be alone with her? It's fine."

"No," he said, looking at me like I was crazy—which, admittedly, I was feeling. "I told you. There's nothing whatsoever between us."

"She's gorgeous," I said.

A funny grin spread over his face. "Maybe *you're* the one who wants to go chase down Luna. Is there something you're not telling me, Allison?"

"What? No!" I sat back, shocked, as he died laughing.

"I'm teasing you," he said. "But seriously. Let's drop it, okay? I'm not sure why she's being so friendly tonight, but I'm not interested. Now, what were we talking about before she came over?"

"Movies," I said. "Specifically how you've never seen any films based on Jane Austen's novels, and how I need to remedy that."

"Oh. Right," he said with a look of regret. Or pain. Or both.

"I own all of them," I said, enjoying the distress on his face. "We could get takeout and start with *Pride and Prejudice* tomorrow night. Or *Sense and Sensibility,* which is my personal favorite."

"Actually," he said before clearing his throat as a look of relief flashed across his face. "I have plans."

"Oh," I said, feeling an unwelcome disappointment. "No worries. Some other time."

"Yeah. Rain check on the movie. But listen, I meant to talk to you about tomorrow. Sheriff Morrison and his wife, Janet, are hosting their monthly dinner party. He asked me to invite you."

"Really?" I was surprised. "Why? I haven't even met him."

Jackson moved his head back and forth like he was trying to figure out how to explain. "Sheriff Morrison—Greg—is kind of a mentor. Almost like family. He knows you're important to me and also that you haven't had a chance to make other friends here yet. Plus, you can meet Daphne and Willa. They're both really sweet. You'll love them."

"Oh," I said, feeling a little uncertain. Big groups of people were never my thing.

On the other hand, Jackson would be there, and that felt safe. Comfortable. And tempting.

"It's a small group," he said, almost like he could read my thoughts. "Some of the best people you'll ever meet. Oh, and Fiona will be there."

My breath caught. "Fiona? You mean Fiona Flanagan?"

"That's right," he said, grinning.

"Oh my goodness." I felt my whole face light up. "I haven't thought about her in years. She has to be getting on up there in age."

"Early seventies," he confirmed.

"Wow. That's hard to imagine. I can only think of her as the vibrant, eccentric woman she was."

Fiona had practically been a legend. Herbalist, midwife, mountain woman, and one of the biggest personalities in town. I had been half afraid of her as a kid, thanks to the rumors that circulated around school about how she was a witch who knew black magic and could turn you into a frog with just a few words and a point of her finger.

But she had always been very kind to me, especially when my mother got pregnant again and then miscarried. It was a horrible day that stood out in my memories, a day when my mother cried so hard I worried she would die from the grief. I would never forget how gentle Fiona was with her, how she wouldn't leave even after everything was done. She stayed for three days, sleeping on our couch and taking care of everything, until she knew my mother was going to be okay.

"Oh," Jackson said, interrupting my thoughts. "She's still as vibrant and eccentric as ever. Maybe even more so."

"She has to be getting frail though, in her seventies."

He scoffed and shook his head. "Not a bit. Emerson—you'll meet him if you come—likes to say she's too damn stubborn to grow old and feeble. I think he's right."

The thought made me smile, and suddenly I wanted very much to go to the dinner party. "I'd love to come," I said, "if you're sure the sheriff doesn't mind."

Jackson grinned. "It was his idea. They'll be disappointed if you don't."

"What time and what's the address?" I asked.

He hesitated. "How about I just pick you up? They live in the valley, outside of town. We can ride together."

"Okay." I fought back a smile, reminding myself that this would not be a date. We had made a pact, for goodness' sake! No matter what feelings I was having, I had to stick to our agreement.

As I walked through my front door that night, my cell phone rang. When I pulled it out and saw Mama's name on the caller ID, my face lit up—until I remembered our last conversation. To say she had been against my move to Rosemary Mountain was the understatement of the year. We hadn't spoken since I had told her it was my life and I couldn't talk to her until she accepted that. It was the longest we'd ever gone without speaking. So I was a bit nervous when I answered.

"Hey, Mama."

"Hi," she said in a measured tone of her own. "I was just calling to see how things are. It's been a little while since we've talked."

"Yeah," I said, unable to stop from sighing as I put my purse down on the entryway table and locked the front door behind me.

"I guess you're pretty angry at me?"

"No," I said, feeling instant guilt. "I'm not angry. I just wish you understood that I'm capable of making my own decisions, and this was the right one for me."

She was silent for a moment. "Are you lonely out there?"

"No," I said. The answer came quickly, and it surprised me how true it was. Despite everything, I felt less lonely here than I had in Memphis, surrounded by people.

"Are people being nice to you?"

I hesitated, unsure of how much to tell her. Of course she would be worried. She had endured my father's reputation, and she worried it would be the same for me, even after all this time. I wasn't about to let her know she was right.

"Yes," I said, giving her a half-truth. "The director of the clinic has been great. And I went to the town dance last week and reintroduced myself to a lot of people. Some of them said to tell you hello and that they hope you're well."

"Sure they do," she laughed, a trace of bitterness marring the words.

"I can't believe they're still having town dances. I guess they're stuck in the last century."

"I guess so," I said, trying to keep my voice light. "But it was fun. You remember Jackson from next door? He's a detective now, working for the sheriff. Can you believe it?"

Mom paused for a minute. "That cute little blond boy you ran around with?"

"Yes," I said, laughing. "I'll have to tell him that's how you referred to him."

"Do you...see him often?"

"Pretty often, yeah. It's been a blast catching up with him."

"Allison." I could hear the warning in her voice.

"What?"

"You have absolutely no business cozying up with a man like that. You know how his father was. And after all these years, Jackson's still living in that awful town. Detective or not, that tells me all I need to know."

"Mama, we're just friends," I said, shocked by her outburst.

"You better be."

I closed my eyes and pictured her face, the same one she used to scold me as a child. Eyes narrow, lips in a tight line, her face white with anger.

Jackson didn't deserve that.

"He's a good guy," I said, wanting to defend him. "He's nothing like Russell. He was adopted a few years after we left town, and he only came back a couple of years ago. And did you not hear the part about him being a detective? He's practically the town hero."

"That's not saying much." Disapproval seeped through the phone's connection. "But, changing the subject," she said, brightening her tone. "Guess who called me today."

"Who?"

"Mike."

My alarm bells instantly went off. "What? Why did he call you?"

"He said you're not answering his phone calls. You two were so great together. I think you've taught him a lesson. Why don't you call him back?"

"Why don't I call him back?" I asked, raising my voice. "Mama, he cheated on me *and* said I should have slept with a superior to get a job. I don't really ever want to speak to him again."

She let out a breath. "He's sorry about the other girl. It was a mistake, Allison, and one you should forgive him for. He was only trying to get a better position so he could take care of you."

I shook my head, dumbfounded. "Are you hearing yourself right now?"

"And he never said you should have slept with that man," she continued, ignoring me. "You completely misunderstood him. He explained everything to me. He loves you, and he'll be an excellent provider."

"*I* will be an excellent provider for *myself*," I said, unable to keep the edge out of my voice. "Or did you forget that I have a medical degree, too?"

"What I know is that you have a lot of student loans," she said. "He comes from money. No student loans for him, and he'll earn far more in his specialty than you ever will as a mountain town family doctor. He wants to give you everything, Allison. Why on earth would you throw that away over a misunderstanding?"

I couldn't believe what I was hearing. "So you're taking his side? Over mine?"

"There's no need for sides," she said, soothing. "He just wanted me to talk to you. Tell you to come back. He's worried about you, and he misses you. *I'm* worried about you too. You don't belong there. Mike said he'll use his connections to get you something in Memphis."

"I'm not going back." My tone made it clear there was no room for discussion.

"You will," she said, like a promise. "You can be as stubborn as you want right now, but you'll see. That town has a dark side. I only hope you get out before you get hurt."

With that, she hung up the phone.

Chapter Fourteen

Jackson

FRIDAY FLEW BY. I ATTRIBUTED MY GOOD MOOD TO THE FACT that I had closed three cases that day, even though I knew at least half of it was because I was looking forward to seeing Allison again. I had long been the fifth wheel at Greg and Janet's dinners. Fiona and I were the only two single people regularly included. Allison wouldn't be there as my date, but it still felt good to bring someone with me.

Allison texted that I'd need to pick her up from the clinic, as she wouldn't have time to run home after work to change. When I got there, ten minutes after they should have closed, I heard the muffled sounds of an argument from inside. I pulled the front door open, ignored Beverly completely, and strode straight through the door that separated the waiting room from the clinic.

Allison was in the hallway with a man towering over her, cussing her out. Her shoulders sagged with relief when she caught sight of me.

I walked straight to the man and tapped him on the shoulder. "What seems to be the problem?" I asked, my tone clipped. I was inwardly seething at the way he had been speaking to Allison, but I was good at my job, and part of that meant staying calm in the face of pressure.

The man—Frank Cross, as it turned out, a man I'd arrested twice for DUI and once for domestic assault—turned around and immediately flushed with embarrassment. "Oh, sorry, Jackson," he said. He shook his head and rolled his eyes, jerking his thumb toward Allison. "The new girl here is refusing to give me the medicine I need. I've been in every day this week asking for refills and she won't give them. I'd like to file charges. That's got to be a crime, right? Medical neglect or something?"

I bit the inside of my cheek, willing myself to keep it under control. "If by 'new girl' you're referring to *Doctor* Bell, I'm assuming there's probably a medical reason she's not filling the prescriptions you're asking for. Doctor?" I addressed her, making sure I modeled the respect she was due.

She took a breath. "That's right. As I've tried explaining to Mr. Cross every time he's come in, his prescriptions aren't appropriate for his condition. They're also highly addictive and have a plethora of potential side effects with long-term use. I've offered other combinations that are less dangerous, I've offered help getting into rehab, and I've offered referrals for procedures that would likely eliminate the pain he's feeling so that the meds aren't even necessary. Mr. Cross," she said, her face softening. "I know this is hard, but we're talking about your life. You can't continue like this."

Frank's face reddened again. "You don't know what the hell you're talking about," he hollered, jabbing her with his finger. "I've been getting by just fine, and I'll keep getting by if you'll just do your damn job and write the scripts!"

"That's enough," I said, stepping in between the two of them. "Frank, you're out of line. At this point, Dr. Bell could press charges against *you*."

Frank stepped back, shocked. "I didn't do nothin'!"

"You're verbally harassing her, and I just saw you jab her with your finger," I said evenly. "You're crossing the line, Frank, and with your history, no one's going to go easy on you. Now, according to Dr.

Bell, she's offered you three alternatives. Which one will you be taking?"

His face turned even more red. "I'll tell you which one. None of them! I'm going to go find me a real doctor. Kept coming here out of loyalty to Doc Rogers, but it ain't worth it anymore. I don't know what they were thinking, hiring a Bell. Bells are no-good trash. Ain't never done anything good for this community. You're probably just like your mama," he said. Then he snarled at Allison as he kicked the metal trash can in the hallway.

It was getting harder and harder to keep my professional demeanor. "It's time for you to leave," I said. "And, Frank?"

"What?"

"I don't ever want to hear you speaking about Dr. Bell that way again, you hear me?"

"It's a free country," he said. "I'll speak about her anyway I want."

"Not in front of me, you won't."

The warning in my eyes must have made him realize I was serious. He spun around and walked out, muttering under his breath the whole way. I followed, keeping him in sight until he was out of the building. Then I locked the door behind him.

When I turned around, I saw Beverly smiling smugly. I walked over to her, my arms crossed. "Beverly, the next time a staff member here— *any* staff member—is being verbally harassed, you need to call for law enforcement immediately. You know Frank has a reputation for getting hot under the collar, and he's desperate for narcotics. That could have escalated into a dangerous situation quickly. I'm disappointed you were content to sit here and watch the show instead of helping your colleague."

Her mouth dropped open, but she was too shocked to say anything. Which, frankly, I was glad about.

I walked through the doors to the back of the clinic and started looking for Allison, who had disappeared from the hallway. I found her in an exam room, typing on her laptop. Her hands were shaky, her smile even more so when she looked up at me.

"Just a sec," she said with a bit of a wobble in her voice. "I just need to document all of that in his chart. Then we can go."

"Take your time," I said. I crossed over to the exam table and hopped onto it, studying her from across the room.

She was the ultimate professional, but it was clear the scene had gotten to her. I got the sense it was important for her to complete her routine though, to document whatever she needed to so she felt like she had a little control over the situation. Or maybe I was projecting my own feelings onto it. Either way, I waited for her to finish before checking on her.

"Okay," she finally said, closing the laptop. "I'll grab my things and we can head out."

"You want to talk about it first?"

"Not really," she said, shaking her head and then letting out a breathy sigh. "Two years."

"Two years?"

"That's how long my contract is. I'm less than a month down. I'm not sure I'm going to make it." She gave a tired laugh, looking more weary than I had seen her since she had come back.

"You'll make it," I said, though a new unease hit me. I had never thought about her contract being temporary.

Two years was a long time, but what then? She had said this was where she was supposed to be, but that didn't mean she was supposed to stay forever. Of course not. Allison was smart and ambitious. She wouldn't be content settling into a small-town clinic and passing out narcotics like they were candy. She'd want more for her life.

Which meant, in two years, I'd likely lose my best friend all over again.

I forced thoughts of Allison leaving out of my head as we drove out to Greg and Janet's house. Peace settled into my heart as the familiar sight of the valley came into view. Once she'd gotten out of the clinic, the weariness had vanished from Allison too.

"I wish I would have had time to change," she said, glancing down at herself. "Do you think this will be okay for dinner?"

I looked over at her in the passenger's seat, trying to notice the clothes themselves instead of the way they highlighted her perfect figure.

But the more I tried *not* to notice, the more I did. It was a simple, professional outfit—a light-gray skirt with an ivory top and a little sweater over it. It reminded me of something a librarian might wear—a very sexy librarian, though clearly, that wasn't the look Allison was going for.

"Um." I cleared my throat, turning back to the road in front of me. "You look great."

"I get nervous meeting new people," she blurted out.

I looked back over at her. "They'll love you."

"I'm trusting you," she said, giving me a tentative smile. "I could use some friendly faces in town."

"Well, you're about to meet the best of the best," I said, trying to reassure her as we pulled in and parked. "Trust me."

"I do," she murmured softly.

Two simple words that hit me like a brick. I felt honored to have her trust—and determined to keep it by not screwing anything up.

I hopped out and opened the truck door for her. She was clearly still nervous as we walked up Greg's long driveway. The encounter with Frank had made us late, and my truck was at the very back of the line.

"There's a lot of people here," she said, eyeing the vehicles.

"Not too many," I said. "Greg and Janet, of course. Daphne—she's Janet's daughter and Greg's stepdaughter—and her husband, Emerson, and their daughter, Eileen. Fiona, who you already know. Willa, Daphne's best friend, and Cole, Willa's fiancé."

"Oh." Allison's eyes got big, and she lifted a hand to her mouth. "Willa. Of course. I just realized who you're talking about. She was all over the news. I don't know why I didn't put two and two together."

"You've had a lot on your mind," I said.

"That's the truth."

The front door flew open, and Fiona's familiar form stepped into the frame. "Hurry on up, Jackson!" she called. "And introduce me to that pretty girl you've got with you!"

"Sorry," I apologized below my breath. "I told Greg we're just friends, but there may be some assumptions."

"It's fine," Allison said, waving it off. "Why, Fiona Flanagan!" Her face lit up as she stepped onto the front porch. "You haven't aged a day!"

"Well, my my!" Fiona peered at her. "I heard we had a certain *Doctor*

Allison Bell back in town, but I can't hardly believe my eyes! You've grown up into a real pretty young lady, and successful too!" Fiona grabbed her into a strong hug. "I'm real proud of ya and so happy you're back."

"Thank you," Allison said when Fiona released her. "It's really good to see you too." Happiness shone in her eyes, making me even more glad Greg had invited her.

"Come meet everyone," Fiona said, waving her in. She turned to whisper to me. "I took care of the punch. Don't tell Janet."

"Your secret's safe," I promised, putting my hand over my heart.

Fiona winked at me and turned around, leading the way.

"What does she mean?" Allison whispered.

"She probably means she spiked it," I answered under my breath. "She's always adding whiskey to everything."

Allison's eyes grew worried. "Does she have a drinking problem?"

"Nah," I said, waving her off. "More like a Janet problem. They love each other, but they're like oil and water. Fiona likes poking at her and loosening her up."

"Gotcha," Allison said, relieved. "That sounds like the Fiona I remember."

"You two stop whispering back there," Fiona complained. "Makes it too hard to listen in on what you're saying. Daphne, this is Allison Bell! I've known her even longer than I've known you!"

"Any friend of Fiona's is a friend of mine," Daphne said, stepping forward to say hello. She gestured to the adorable baby on her hip, a tiny thing with solemn eyes and a headful of red hair, just like her mother. "This is little Eileen."

"Eileen," Allison said, recognition dawning on her face. "Wait. You must be Eileen Sullivan's daughter. Except, Jackson said Janet is your mom. I'm sorry. I'm all mixed up." Confusion and embarrassment clouded her features.

"Both are right," Daphne said in the soft voice she always used when speaking of her late mother. "Eileen was my mom, but my father remarried after she died. Janet raised me."

"Oh, I see," Allison said. "You look so much like her."

"You knew her?" Daphne's face lit up.

Allison nodded. "Not well, but I do remember her. She volunteered at the library. She was always very sweet." Her voice was soft, like Daphne's.

Daphne's eyes grew misty, and she pulled Allison into a hug. "I don't have any memories of her, so I always enjoy hearing other people's. We'll have to talk sometime."

"I'd like that."

"Come on. Mom and Willa are in the kitchen," Daphne said, dragging Allison away from me. But Daphne turned around and gave me a knowing smile and a nod of approval as she did.

I felt my face go red. I'd have to correct a lot of assumptions, it seemed.

"Hey, man," Cole said, coming over to shake my hand. "Good to see you."

"You too."

"This is the first time you've brought a girl to a family dinner." He gave me one of his serious looks. Of course, Cole was almost always serious. Willa was the only one who ever seemed to make him laugh.

"She's just a friend," I repeated, knowing it was a phrase I was going to have to repeat a hundred times.

"Sure she is," he said, crossing his arms.

Emerson meandered over to join us. "Leave him alone, Cole," he said, punching him lightly on the shoulder.

"Aw, come on," Cole complained. "You didn't leave me alone when I was denying my feelings for Willa, now did you?"

Emerson grinned. "That was different."

"How?" Cole demanded.

"I don't know," Emerson said, laughing. "It just was. Maybe it's more fun to tease you than it is to tease Jackson."

Cole rolled his eyes. "Come on," he said, turning back to me. "What's the deal?"

"There's no deal," I said. "Allison and I have known each other since we were kids, but we're just friends. We made a pact and everything." I attempted to laugh it off.

"A pact?" Emerson asked, now suddenly curious. "To just be friends?"

"Best friends," I said, nodding.

Emerson and Cole exchanged looks and started cracking up.

"What's so funny?" I asked.

Cole shook his head. "It'll never work."

"Ten bucks says they'll kiss before the Fourth of July," Emerson said.

Cole scoffed. "I don't take bets I know I'll lose."

Chapter Fifteen

Allison

Despite my initial unease, I quickly felt more comfortable than I had in a group setting in a very long time. The party was held on Greg and Janet's back deck, which had an incredible view of the mountains. Between the view, the smell of burgers on the grill, and the ice-cold sweet tea, it was the perfect summer party, made even more lovely by the fun and laughter of everyone attending.

This group of family—because that's what they were, even though only half of them seemed to actually be related in any way—clearly loved each other and had a "the more the merrier" mentality when it came to me. It was also clear by the exchanged looks and smiles that they assumed Jackson and I were dating, something that made him more uncomfortable than it did me.

In fact, I liked the idea more than I should have, considering I was the one who had initially insisted our friendship stay platonic.

Being in this group of happy couples, I felt an ache in my soul I'd never expected to feel. It wasn't that I missed Mike. I didn't. And it wasn't exactly loneliness. I felt completely welcomed and part of the group, not at all like the outsider I'd expected to be. In many ways, Jackson took care of me the same way the other men took care of their partners.

But there was something different there, something I rarely got to witness up close. There was a tenderness, a trust, a communication that went beyond words. I saw it with Greg and Janet, in the tender touches they shared almost without noticing as they went about their hosting duties. I saw it in Daphne and Emerson, in the little smiles and exchanged glances that hinted of conversations and chuckles to come. And I saw it in Cole and Willa, with the way he was so clearly her protector, even though she didn't need one anymore.

They all had something I had only seen in the elderly couples who came to their doctor's appointments together, unwilling to even spend that time apart after a lifetime of loving each other. I had never seen it in my parents during their marriage, nor in the several marriages my mother had after.

I certainly hadn't experienced anything like it in my own life.

The scientist in me wanted to study it, to dissect it and find out exactly what made them different from those of us who always seemed to get it wrong. What secret had they unlocked? And was it something someone like me, someone who had never had a healthy marriage modeled, could ever dream of replicating?

I didn't know. But when Jackson lightly touched my shoulder and offered to take my empty plate, I started wondering if it might actually be possible for two people like us to learn from this group that had embraced us.

Maybe it was rebellion against my mother or annoyance that we had jumped into our pact so quickly, but I felt a trace of sadness that we couldn't even find out what we were capable of together. I tried to dismiss it as a ridiculous thought. Nothing had changed. Dating Jackson was still a terrible idea that would threaten my place here when we broke up.

But looking around at the couples we were with, I had to wonder if breakups were inevitable after all. What if... What if, when you found someone like this, someone who was your best friend and who was truly committed, you just made it work? Not out of forced obligation, not because you were trapped without options, but because...

Because you just couldn't imagine life without that person.

"What are you thinking about?" Jackson whispered, taking his place back beside me on the deck.

The sun was just starting to slip behind the mountains, creating a beautiful pink glow in the sky. Janet had flipped a switch, turning on twinkle lights that were strung across the pergola on the deck. It was a beautiful night, and for the first time in a while, I felt totally content.

"Nothing really," I said, smiling at him. I couldn't exactly tell him I had been sitting there contemplating whether we had a chance of creating this ourselves, either together or with someone else.

Especially when it was the together part I kept thinking about.

"I hope you're having fun," he said. "I know our group can be a lot."

I laughed and glanced around. Daphne and Willa were both giggling over some story Fiona was telling, while Janet shook her head in disapproval. Cole, Emerson, and Greg had retrieved cigars and were lighting them up on one side of the deck. Little Eileen was bouncing in her bouncer, guarded closely by an older-looking German Shepherd who never seemed to leave her side.

It was perfect.

"I'm having a great time," I answered sincerely. "I really appreciate you guys including me. Daphne, Willa, and I are having a girls' lunch together next week."

"Good," he said, smiling in approval.

My phone buzzed and I pulled it out of my pocket automatically, frowning when I saw Mike's name on the screen.

Jackson raised his eyebrows. "Is that the ex?"

"Yeah," I said, rolling my eyes and hitting the "end" button on the call.

It didn't matter. He immediately called again.

"Listen," I said, glancing back at the party. "Maybe I should take this. I've been ignoring him, but he just keeps calling. He even called my mom this week. I think he's going to keep it up until I tell him to stop. I'm just going to slip inside real quick."

"Take all the time you need." He gave me a look I couldn't quite read, but that almost seemed to have a trace of regret in it.

"Thanks," I said, giving him a half smile.

I answered the call and walked inside.

"Mike," I said when I had closed the door behind me. "I'm only answering to tell you to stop calling. I know I said we could try to be friends, but honestly, I just can't. Please. Give me some space, okay?"

"Allison." His voice was broken. "I'm sorry. I screwed up in ten thousand different ways. Is that what you want to hear? Because I did, and I know it, and I'm sorry. But I miss you."

I shook my head, even though he couldn't see it. Because I couldn't say the same. "What do you want?" I asked again, sighing.

"I want you. We were together for three years. Can't we fix this?"

I paced the room, trying to figure out how to explain it. "No, Mike, I don't think we can. We were together, but let's be honest, it's not like our relationship was that great, was it? We barely saw each other, and neither of us even minded."

"I thought it was perfect," he said.

"No," I said, looking out the window at my new friends. "It was easy. And easy was what we both wanted then. But I don't think it's what I want anymore."

He was silent on the other line.

"Besides, aren't you dating Dr. Fountain's daughter?" A tiny bit of the anger tried to flare, but the truth was, I cared too little for it to even matter that much.

"Not anymore."

"What happened?"

"Dr. Fountain picked someone else," he said, his voice hollow.

I stopped my pacing and sighed. "So the only reason you were dating her was because of him." It wasn't a surprise, not really. But with me gone, I had expected him to continue on with her anyway. After all, the photograph I had seen suggested they had chemistry. Or something like that.

"Of course it was," he said, his voice earnest. "Allison, you're the one I want. You always have been. My whole family misses you. They're giving me hell about screwing this up."

I couldn't help a tiny smile. I had liked his family—more than I had liked him if I was being honest. "I'm sorry," I said.

"Can you not forgive me? I just needed to play the game. Get an edge. You know how the world works."

I stared out the window again at the little group on the deck and realized he was wrong. "We get to decide how the world works," I said softly. "And I choose a different kind of world than the one you live in."

I hung up and walked back to my new friends.

Chapter Sixteen

Jackson

"You okay?" I murmured under my breath when Allison rejoined our group. All these years later, I could still read her like a book. The phone call had upset her, and it wasn't a big mystery as to why. Mike needed to leave her alone.

"I'm fine," she said, sighing in a way that let me know she really wasn't. "I don't know why he's still trying."

I toyed with a loose thread on the pocket of my jeans. "Trying. You mean trying to get you back?" It bothered me more than it should. I told myself it was because I was the kind of guy who stood up for women and got pissed off when someone was harassing one. I'd feel the same if it were Daphne or Willa.

But it wasn't Daphne or Willa, and the truth was, my feelings for Allison were completely different than what I felt for them. Even if I had to deny it to my dying day.

She nodded. "Yeah. He wants to get back together. My mom's even on his side, which she let me know when she told me to take him back."

"Ouch. I'm sorry."

She shook her head, her lips in a flat line. Then she sighed in defeat. "Am I being stupid? He says this is how the world works. But when I look at everyone here tonight, I can't help but think he's wrong. *This* is how it should work. Can you even imagine Emerson or Cole being disappointed that Daphne or Willa refused to sleep with a man to get a job?"

I snorted, unable to help it. "If someone backed either one of those women into a corner like that, I'm pretty sure I'd have to arrest Emerson and Cole both. The man would be lucky to make it out alive."

"Exactly. Is it ridiculous that I want that?"

"Ridiculous that you want your man to protect you? No, I don't think so." I toyed with the loose thread again, knowing I was veering into dangerous territory.

"Does it make me less of a feminist?" she asked, suddenly looking at me with worry in her eyes. "I mean, I've always believed men and women are equal. I went to medical school, for goodness' sake. I did that on my own. But now I want my partner to go all caveman on me? What's that about?"

This time, I couldn't help it. I laughed out loud, not caring if anyone looked our way. "First of all, we're talking about a situation where a man tried to force you to sleep with him in order to get a job you should have been hired for based on professional merit. I don't think you have to turn in your feminist card for wanting your partner to be outraged over that. Second of all." I turned my head and raised my voice. "Hey, Daphne?"

"Yeah?" she asked, looking up from where she was dishing up a piece of cake for Eileen.

"What would you do if Emerson went to a job interview and the chief was a woman who demanded that he perform, um,"—I looked at Eileen and stammered as the girl's innocent eyes caught mine—"non-job-related *duties* in order to get the position?"

"Hmmm..." Daphne pondered that as she placed Eileen in a high chair and gave her the cake, inviting her to go to town. "Before or after I marched up there and punched her in the face?" She glanced at Greg and Janet and saw the disapproval on her mom's face and the exasperation of a sheriff who knew she wasn't joking. "Sorry," she said, laughing.

"See?" I said, turning back to Allison. "Sometimes it goes both ways."

"Maybe you're right," she said, smiling for the first time since the phone call had swept her happiness away.

"For what it's worth, I want to punch this doctor in the face myself, and I'm not even your boyfriend," I said.

Her eyes twinkled. "I guess I wouldn't mind getting a slap in myself, now that I think about it. Thanks, Jackson."

"Anytime."

WHEN THE NIGHT WOUND DOWN AND I DROVE ALLISON BACK to town, she asked that I drop her off at her house instead of the clinic where her car was.

"You sure?" I asked.

"Yeah," she said, yawning. "It's been a long day and I don't like to drive at night when I'm tired. Besides, it's only a couple of miles from my house to the clinic and I could use some exercise in the morning. I'll get up early, jog to get my car, then go back home and get ready for my day."

"I don't mind picking you up in the morning," I said. "I'll be going into town for work anyway, and your place isn't out of the way."

She looked over at me and smiled. "Thanks. But this will force me to get the exercise I've been neglecting ever since I moved here."

"The offer stands tomorrow if you wake up and decide you don't feel like it."

"I appreciate it. And you." She turned her head to gaze out the window. Soft moonlight cast a glow around her golden hair. She was stunning, almost fairy-like as she seemed to get lost in her own thoughts, looking out at the night sky.

"What are you thinking about over there?" I had to know.

She turned back toward me with a sad little smile. "I was thinking about Mama," she said.

"What about her?"

"How sad it is that she's never had anything like what I saw tonight. She's been married four times since she left Dad. Never for love. Each marriage has been to someone a little more successful than the last, someone who can offer her a little more. She's bought herself security, but never happiness. Not like what those couples tonight have, I'll tell you that," Allison said, shaking her head. "That's something different altogether."

"They're an exception," I agreed. "Lucky devils."

She laughed out loud. "That's the truth." Then she got quiet again. "You ever wonder if people like us might find something like that someday?"

I swallowed hard. "No. I try not to wonder about that at all."

She glanced over at me like she wanted to say something, but she didn't. Then she turned her head back to the window, sitting quietly as we drove to her house.

I had a hard time not getting lost in my own thoughts. Truth was, I'd found myself wondering about that same thing tonight, though I'd never admit it to Allison. Having her there had made it the most fun dinner party I'd experienced. She'd fit in with our group so well, and it had felt nice to be part of a couple—even if we weren't. I'd enjoyed taking care of her the way the other men took care of their partners, and it had been too easy to imagine what it might be like if she was mine.

I'd never ask, but I was dying to know if any part of her had imagined having that with *me*.

When I pulled into Allison's driveway, the first thing I noticed was that the front window was open. I frowned, not wanting to lecture but needing to say something. "Allison, it's not a good idea to leave your windows open. Even if it's not Memphis."

But Allison was frowning too. "I didn't," she said. "I've never opened that window."

"Stay here," I said, instantly going into cop mode. I slid my service weapon out of its holster. "I'm going to check it out. Give me your keys."

Her face was pale as she pulled the keys from her purse. She handed them to me as I swung out of the truck. I stuffed them into my pocket and headed toward the front, weapon in hand.

Chapter Seventeen

Allison

My heart was pounding as Jackson approached the door. I hadn't thought to check the locks on the windows. Raccoons— or even bears, for that matter—were sometimes ingenious when it came to getting into things. Was it possible an animal had opened my window and gone inside in search of food? Maybe the same animal I heard scratching at my window before? As much as I dreaded cleaning up whatever mess a wild animal might have made inside, I hoped with all my heart it was as simple as that.

Jackson turned his face toward me, making eye contact as he frowned. He pointed to the doorknob and made a motion with his hands indicating that it had been unlocked before he got there.

My heart sank. A raccoon might open a window, but it would go out the same way—if it left at all. Only a human would open a window in order to unlock a door.

I reached over and made sure the truck doors were locked, sinking into my seat even as I strained my eyes to catch a glimpse of Jackson. He had gone inside, and from what I could see through the open front door, he was methodically clearing rooms with his gun raised.

I was beyond grateful he had brought me home tonight. I probably would have run straight inside, thinking only of the bat, never even noticing the window. Someone could have been inside waiting for me. My body went cold at the thought.

Time stretched slowly as I waited for Jackson to return. When he came back outside, he didn't come to the truck—not right away, at least. He used a flashlight to look around the house, disappearing again as he slowly made his way around the back. When he finally returned and opened my truck door, his face was grim.

"Whoever it was is gone now," he said flatly. "Nothing is visibly disturbed, but I'll need you to walk me through and make sure you don't see anything missing. I'll dust for prints, though the odds of that turning up anything are slim. Are you completely sure you've never opened the window?"

"One hundred percent," I confirmed.

"Any chance you left the door unlocked?"

"No," I shook my head. "Locking up is so ingrained in me after living in Memphis that there's no way I would have left without locking that door and double-checking it."

"You left your car unlocked the other day," he pointed out.

I frowned, feeling defensive. "I told you I don't know what happened that night."

He looked at me and sighed. "I'm sorry. I don't mean to question you. I'd just rather this be a mistake on your part than a break-in. You shouldn't have to go through that."

"Story of my life," I said, attempting a smile. But he didn't smile back. He just held my gaze, like he could see right through me.

"You ready to go look around?" he asked, his voice softer than before.

No. Not even close. But I swallowed hard and nodded. "Let's do this."

· · ·

Jackson had me lead him through the house. He was mostly quiet, but he would occasionally ask questions, verifying if something was normal. I was glad he was there, as his presence was the only thing giving me a sense of safety after everything that had happened. But it felt wrong that his first time at my house was walking through it like it was a crime scene. A friend coming over for the first time should be fun, relaxing. It should have been a dinner party or a game night. Or even the Jane Austen movie night I had threatened him with.

Not this.

But we both pretended it was the most normal thing in the world for him to go through my house room by room as I checked to make sure nothing was missing.

It was easy enough, since I had always shared a home and didn't own many so-called valuables. Very few people would be interested in stealing medical textbooks. As far as I could tell, everything of mine was still there.

When we finished and he had dusted for prints, Jackson stood in my living room, arms crossed, with a look of frustration on his face. "I don't like it, Allison. It seems like someone broke in just to look around. Nothing's gone. Nothing's out of place. But they also didn't bother to hide the fact that they were here. They could easily have closed the window and at least locked the bottom lock before leaving. You might have second-guessed whether or not you had set the dead bolt. Whoever was here didn't care if you knew about it."

The thought sent chills up my spine. "Why?"

"I don't know," he said, shaking his head.

"Any luck with prints?" I asked hopefully.

He shook his head again. "The window and door had both been wiped clean. So he didn't care if you realized he was here—maybe even *wanted* you to know—but he took the time to wipe away the evidence of his identity."

"So we've got nothing?" My heart sank.

"It's still a clue," he said. "I suspect that means he knows his prints are in the system."

"Does that narrow it down quite a bit?" I asked, biting my lip.

He winced. "Not as much as you'd think. But some."

"What now?"

"We file an official report. I want to find out where Frank Cross was tonight, after the incident at the clinic." His eyes softened. "I'm going to find out who did this, Allison. I promise."

I shook my head. "Don't make promises you can't keep. That's one of the first things we learn in the medical field. If there aren't any prints, this could be a dead end and we both know it. You shouldn't promise me differently."

"I'll find him," he said firmly.

His confidence made me smile. "Okay. You'll find him. Or her." Another thought crossed my mind, one that felt infinitely less threatening. "Any chance this is a Rosemary Mountain busybody just wanting to poke around in my business?"

He nodded, finally showing me that grin that had been missing since we arrived at my house. "Honestly? Yeah. It's possible. A few years ago a family moved to town and came home to find one of the neighbors in their house. The woman had broken in just to look around and see what remodeling they had done. She was flabbergasted that they had a problem with it."

Something in me loosened, shifted. "Then I'm going to hope it's as simple as that. After all, whoever it was didn't take anything and didn't stick around to hurt me. So maybe it's nothing?"

His face darkened again. "I hope so."

I cocked my head. There was something he wasn't telling me. "What are you hiding from me, Jackson?"

"Nothing," he said, his face becoming a mask. "Just don't let your guard down, okay? Not until we know for sure. Promise me."

"Okay," I said, swallowing hard. "I promise."

He helped me clean up the mess from where he had attempted to get fingerprints. I delayed him leaving as long as possible, trying to keep him engaged in conversation in an attempt to feel normal. When he left, I would be alone in the house, and there was a fear inside me that I knew would come out to play the minute I was alone.

Jackson seemed to sense it, because when we finally finished and I walked him to the door, he lingered. "Are you going to be okay here tonight?"

"Of course," I said, even though I could hear the doubt in my voice.

"Allison," he said, reaching up to touch my face softly. "It's okay if you're scared. I don't mind sleeping on the couch."

I started to assure him it wasn't necessary, but I paused. What if I didn't have to be brave just yet?

"Really?" I asked, hesitant. "I know you have to work tomorrow."

"Yes. So do you, and you don't even have a car here. I don't really like the idea of you jogging alone tomorrow after this. Let me stay, Allison." His face told me he was dead serious, that he truly wanted to keep me safe.

I wrapped my arms around myself to keep from wrapping them around him. "Okay," I said. "If you're sure you don't mind. I had completely forgotten about my car, but after this, I don't want to jog to the clinic." I shivered. "And here I thought I was going to leave the gym behind and get back to exercising in nature now that I'm out of Memphis."

"You will," he said. "Just not tomorrow."

"Not tomorrow," I agreed.

Jackson retrieved some things from his truck while I busied myself setting up the couch for him. The house had only come with basic linens, so I pulled one of my pillows off the bed, along with an extra blanket I had found in the linen closet. It wasn't a particularly nice setup, and I felt so guilty I almost offered to take the couch myself. But I knew it was pointless to offer—Jackson was a gentleman who would never let me give up my own bed.

Besides, the thought of sleeping down here so close to the window where the intruder had come in was terrifying. What if he came back tonight? The very idea conjured images in my imagination that gave me fresh chills. When Jackson came back inside, he rushed over to me.

"What's wrong? What happened?"

"Nothing," I said, shaking my head as I came back to earth. "I was just imagining how bad it could have been if...if things had been different." I put my hand on his chest, feeling somehow more stable when I felt his heartbeat underneath it. "I'm hoping this was nothing more than someone with curiosity and boundary issues, but I admit I'm more freaked out than I realized. Thank you for being here, Jackson."

"Always," he said as he reached up and squeezed my hand.

"I'll have to figure out a way to repay the favor."

He laughed as he plopped down onto my couch. "You could always get your girlfriends to go skinny-dipping with you again and give me a heads-up as to when and where. Give me another one of those core life memories."

"Jackson! That's terrible," I said, tossing the pillow at him, even though I was grinning from ear to ear.

"You asked," he said, winking.

"I'm too old for skinny-dipping," I retorted. "Although I'm sure if you asked Luna…"

He threw the pillow back at me. "Not even funny."

"Sorry," I said. "You're right. I shouldn't tease you about her."

"No, you shouldn't," he said, though he was smiling.

I tucked my hair behind my ears and sighed. "I guess I should head to bed." Even though I knew there was no way I would be able to sleep.

He looked at me for a long minute. "I don't know about you, but I'm not sleepy yet. How about that Jane Austen movie you promised me?"

"Really?"

"Really." He grinned. "Especially if it comes with hot cocoa."

"Believe it or not, I can manage that," I said, laughing. "It's one of the few things I always keep stocked."

"I know," he said. "I cleared your house, remember? Saw the tin sitting in the pantry. Looked fancy and expensive. I always buy the cheap stuff that comes in envelopes. Easy peasy."

"Oh no," I said, shaking my head. "None of that fake chocolate and corn syrup here. You're about to get treated to decadent organic cocoa with real cream and sugar. You'll never be the same."

"Might even make the Jane Austen movie worth sitting through."

CHAPTER EIGHTEEN

Jackson

WITH THE BEST DAMN CUP OF HOT COCOA I'D EVER HAD IN hand, I tried to appear relaxed and into the movie Allison obviously adored. But my mind was a million miles away.

This whole thing stunk of Russell. I wouldn't mention him to her until I was sure, but he was my number-one suspect. It was exactly like him to break in here and look around just to show me that nothing of mine was off-limits to him.

Not that Allison was mine. But we'd hung out publicly almost every night since she'd arrived in town. Half of Rosemary Mountain had probably jumped to the conclusion that we were together, no matter how often we denied it. Russell would make that assumption, too. And if he wanted to get back at me, he might strike out at her.

First thing in the morning, I would go to Greg and tell him everything. It was one thing when Russell was just harassing me. It was another thing altogether for him to involve Allison. And considering the conflict of interest, I couldn't investigate this alone. Maybe not at all, depending on how Greg decided to handle it. It might be out of my hands completely come tomorrow.

Though that sure wouldn't stop me from looking into things in my off time. Or spending as much time as possible with Allison to make sure she was safe.

Part of me wanted to rush out to find Russell right now and demand that he tell me where he had been tonight. But I knew that was a rash decision. The worst thing I could do was leave Allison alone right now. Partly because it was clear as all get-out that she wouldn't know how to defend herself if whoever this was broke back in again. And partly because I had seen the fear on her face when she thought I was leaving. She had put on a brave front, pretending she was blowing the whole thing off as a nosy neighbor. But the truth was in her eyes. This had shaken her more than she wanted to admit.

When she said she was going to go to bed, it was clear as day she was too nervous to actually sleep. So I'd sit here and watch every Jane Austen movie there was with her until she was relaxed enough to actually rest, if that's what it took.

But it only took thirty minutes for her to fall asleep, curled up in a tight ball on the other end of the couch. I couldn't bring myself to wake her, so I covered her with the blanket she had brought for me, turned the TV off, and stretched out on the rug beside the couch.

I stared at her for a little while, wondering if this was what it was like for couples like Willa and Cole. Feeling so comfortable and safe with your partner that you just relaxed and fell asleep easily.

Allison wouldn't know this, but I had never spent the night with a woman before. It was a firm rule I had with dates. No sleeping over. The nightmares that still occasionally plagued me were too humiliating. I would never want a date to witness that.

Yet here I was, volunteering to spend the night at Allison's house, and not even bothering to make sure we were in separate rooms. Somehow, I knew I wouldn't have nightmares tonight. Not with her right there. I had stayed to make her feel safe, but something about her presence made me feel safe too.

The floor was hard, but the pillow smelled like her. And before long, I was deep into the most restful sleep I'd had in years. Instead of nightmares, my dreams were sweet—and they all featured a certain golden-haired beauty curled up beside me.

I woke the next morning to Allison's surprised cry. "What is it?" I asked, jumping up.

"I'm so sorry!" she said. "I didn't mean to fall asleep here. Did you sleep on the floor all night?"

I stretched out, popping my back and neck. "Yeah. It's fine."

"It's not fine," she said, giving me a stern look, "and based on the sounds your body is making, I'm the worst doctor in the world for making you do that."

"You didn't make me." I rubbed my hand over my face, trying to wake up. "You were sleeping so peacefully I couldn't bring myself to wake you." I opened my eyes to see her smiling at me.

"That's sweet of you," she said. "But next time? Wake me. And sit up, with your back to me."

I gave her a confused look but did what she'd said. She immediately put her hands on my neck, startling me.

"Good grief," she said. "You're ridiculously knotted up. Jackson, I'm so sorry. Let me see if I can work some of these out for you." She went to work kneading the knots in my neck with her thumbs, providing both pain and relief at the same time.

"Um. Thanks," I said, reminding myself that she was a doctor who probably didn't think twice about putting her hands on her patients. I, on the other hand, had just spent a night enveloped in her incredible scent, sleeping close enough to her that I had to stop myself from reaching up and pulling her down on top of me, and now her hands were doing magical things to my neck.

She trusted me, and I'd die before breaking that trust. So I jumped up, away from those hands I wanted on me more than I could possibly say. "Coffee," I said, struggling to speak. "Need coffee."

She gave me a weird look. "Oh. Yeah, of course. I'll put on a pot. Are you one of those people who can't even string a sentence together in the mornings without it?"

I nodded, even though it wasn't true at all. I loved my coffee, but I often went on my morning run before I had my first cup. Caffeine deprivation wasn't the reason I was flustered beyond belief this morning, but it made a damn good excuse. An excuse that didn't break our pact.

I FOLDED UP THE BLANKET AND HID IN THE BATHROOM LIKE A coward while Allison made coffee. The guilt was killing me. I had to get over these feelings she was stirring up in me.

Was it just because I couldn't have her? I thought it over as I did my best at brushing my teeth with some toothpaste on my finger. As an adult, I'd never really wanted a relationship. Never imagined a future with anyone or thought about what it might be like to set up house and start a family. Those dreams had died for me a long time ago.

But all of a sudden, my brain was trying to convince me I wanted the American dream after all. Was it because she was off-limits?

No. It was because she was her.

I sighed, splashing my face with cold water. "You need to get over this," I warned my reflection in the mirror. That kind of life wasn't meant for a man like me, and I'd made Allison a promise. I wasn't going to mess things up now.

I just had to survive coffee, breakfast, and driving her to the clinic. Then I could get some space and finally think straight again.

ANY RELIEF I EXPECTED TO FEEL WHEN I DROPPED ALLISON off at the clinic was short-lived. I missed her like crazy the minute she was gone. When she climbed out of my truck, waved goodbye, and shot me a little smile over her shoulder as she disappeared into the clinic, it felt like the world had suddenly gotten darker and colder all at once, as if the sun had disappeared behind the clouds.

Allison was my sun. And that was a very dangerous thing.

But I had work to do, and while I hated that the work involved her, I was glad to have a distraction. I drove straight to the office and went right to Sheriff Morrison's door.

"Come on in," he called out.

"Morning, Sheriff."

"Morning, Jackson," he said with a smile. "Enjoyed meeting your friend last night. Sweet girl. Daphne and Willa both gave her their stamp of approval. Bring her to our get-togethers anytime."

"Thanks," I said before clearing my throat. "But I actually need to talk to you about something official."

"Oh?" he asked, leaning back in his chair. He put his hands behind his head. "Go on."

"Last night, I took Allison back to her house. Her window was open and the front door was unlocked."

His smile turned to a frown. "Sit down."

I took the seat across from him and waited for him to speak.

He studied me for a moment. "Any chance it was her being absent-minded?"

"No," I said, shaking my head. "First, she's not the type. Second, she moved here from Memphis. Locking up is second nature to her. Third, the window frame and doorknobs had both been wiped clean."

"Ah," he said, grimacing. "So no luck with prints at all?"

"None. And nothing was missing or out of place."

"Suspects?"

I sighed. "There's a few people who come to mind. Yesterday, Frank Cross was harassing her at the clinic because she refused to prescribe him the opioids he wanted. I basically pulled him off of her and told him to go cool off."

Greg nodded. "That's a good place to start. He's got a temper, and if he's desperate, he may have gone searching her house in hopes she had a supply there. Had the clinic been broken into as well?"

I winced, realizing I had missed something crucially important in my desperation to get away from Allison that morning. "I'll check," I said, pulling my phone out to shoot her a text.

She replied almost instantly.

"Clinic was fine, according to her. But I can swing by and take a look around, see if there's any signs of disturbance she might not have noticed."

"I'll do it," he said breezily. "I'm headed over that way in a little while anyway." He grabbed a notepad and scratched down some notes to himself. "Any other suspects come to mind?"

"Well, if you remember, I heard Larry and Gus talking about her before she moved here. Larry acted like he wasn't too happy and wanted her to leave."

Greg mused. "Breaking in without actually damaging anything doesn't seem like his style. He's more the type to make a show of it. Jail time has never been much of a deterrent for him, so I can't see him bothering to wipe his prints. But maybe."

I nodded, knowing he was right. "It's a long shot, but she also has an ex who wants her back. He called her at the party and apparently even called her mom, trying to get her to put in a good word. He wants her to move back to Memphis. From what she's told me about him, he seems like a real prick."

Greg's mouth went flat and he shook his head. He leaned back again and put his pen in his mouth, chewing on the end of it. I knew to sit quietly while he thought things through. "Alright," he finally said. "So let's say, hypothetically, it's the ex. He might not want to hurt her, but maybe he thinks he can scare her into running back to him. In that case, I still think he'd make it more obvious though. Mess some things up, make it look good."

"Unless he wasn't trying to make it obvious. Maybe he forgot about the window," I said, shrugging. "Maybe it wasn't a show at all, and he just wanted to do a little snooping. See what she's up to, make sure she hasn't moved on with someone else." Even as I said it, it was clear I wasn't convinced. The ex was just another person we'd have to rule out.

"Yeah," Greg said doubtfully. "Like you said, long shot. I'm not really seeing it. But still something we'll have to check into."

"Yeah," I said, swallowing hard. "Then there's Russell."

Greg leaned forward, putting his elbows on the desk. His face turned hard. "Russell? What does he have to do with this?"

"I've caught him following me a few times," I said, shifting awkwardly in my seat. "Wants me to give him money and I won't do it. He's made some vague threats."

"Why are you just now telling me this?" Greg's voice was gruff, his normal cool gone.

"What was there to tell?" I lifted my hands in frustration. "My dead-beat dad wants money and is running his mouth. What's new?"

Greg made a face, giving me the point. "Has he made any direct threats or tried to lay a hand on you?"

"No." I knew Greg was asking more as a father figure than as a sheriff. "Nothing like that. You know his style. He's too smart to come after me directly. But threaten someone I care about? Well, that's as Russell Sharp as it gets."

"Was the window closed when you picked Allison up yesterday?"

I shook my head. "I picked her up at the clinic. She hadn't been home since that morning. It could have happened anytime between eight a.m. and nine thirty p.m."

"Any clues on site?"

I reached into my pocket, pulling out an envelope to hand him. "Just this. Found it out back, behind her house. Can't be sure it was from yesterday, but..."

He sighed as he took the clear plastic bag and stared at the cigarette butt inside. "That's Russell's brand."

"Yeah, it is."

He placed the bag on the desk. "You know it's a conflict of interest for you to investigate this."

"Yes, sir."

"I also know you're the best detective I have and that you aren't going to have any peace of mind if I assign this to a lesser one."

I nodded, grateful he understood.

"So, I'll handle it myself," he said in a tone that made it clear the matter was closed. "If there's anything else I need to know, you come to me right away. Don't approach Russell. Let me handle that. I'll keep you in the loop. Anything else happens, you call me. Got it?"

"Got it." I stood up to leave.

"And, Jackson?"

"Yeah?" I turned back to him.

"Keep your girl safe."

I nodded, feeling a lump form in my throat. "I will, sir."

Chapter Nineteen

Allison

I went through the day with a smile on my face despite the events of the night before. I had expected to be shaken up. Instead, I felt happy. Calm. Safe.

In fact, yesterday felt like it had happened a million years ago, having been far outshadowed by everything that happened after. Jackson had stayed with me. He had volunteered to watch a movie he clearly had no interest in just so I didn't have to go upstairs and sleep alone. And he had slept on the uncomfortable floor to keep from waking me.

Pact or no pact, one thing was clear. Jackson was a completely different kind of man than Mike, and I was beginning to think my decision had been made in haste. It was still a terrible idea to date the town hero and then break up. But breaking up might not be inevitable after all.

That is, if Jackson felt the same way about me that I was starting to feel about him.

That was the one thing that made me pause. He might not be interested in me at all. He also seemed to be set on remaining single, believing against all evidence that he wasn't capable of being a good husband or father. My heart ached just thinking about it.

Russell had really done a number on him, and I knew those wounds weren't likely to heal quickly. But surely he could see that he would never make the same mistakes. He was a good man, deserving of every good thing in life. That might not mean a wife and kids for him, but if he wanted it, he shouldn't deny himself the chance.

OTHER THAN HIS QUICK TEXT ASKING ABOUT THE CLINIC that morning, I didn't hear from him all day. By midafternoon, his absence had left a hole in my day that hadn't existed prior to the renewal of our friendship. I had never been one to keep up with my phone—work always got one hundred percent of my focus. But I missed him.

So I sent him a text asking if he wanted to meet for dinner. He didn't reply. But twenty minutes later, when I heard Beverly loudly saying hello in the sugary tone she seemed to reserve for Jackson, I smiled. Unable to stop myself, I got up from my office chair and headed straight for the lobby.

Unfortunately, it wasn't Jackson waiting for me there. It was Sheriff Morrison.

"Oh, hello, Sheriff," I said, reaching out to shake his hand. "What can I do for you today?"

"Call me Greg," he said warmly. "I'm actually here—" He stopped, glancing at Beverly and Danny, who were both hanging close by, pretending to work so they could overhear our conversation. "Could we talk in your office?"

"Of course," I said, ignoring the glare Beverly shot me. I led him down the hallway and opened my office door, gesturing for him to enter. "Have a seat."

"Thanks." He slowly walked into the room, taking a look around as he did. "Nice office. I see Doc left his furniture."

"Did he? I wondered who had furnished it." I walked to my desk and sat with what I hoped was calm elegance, despite my anxiety about why Greg was here. I wanted him to get to the point already, not make small talk about my office.

"Yeah," Greg said before finally taking a seat. "Looks almost the same as when he was practicing. But I see you've added some touches of your own." He pointed at the succulents I'd placed in the window and the photographs on my desk.

"So," I said, still wanting to skip past the pleasantries. "What can I do for you?"

"Jackson told me about the trouble at your place last night," he said, interlacing his fingers in his lap and tapping his thumbs together. "I'm here to follow up on that and to see if you've noticed anything out of place here today. One of our theories is that a disgruntled patient may have been looking for narcotics. Jackson told me about the incident he witnessed with Frank Cross yesterday."

I tilted my head. "Is it typical for a sheriff to investigate? I thought that was Jackson's job."

Greg's mouth lifted in a smile he appeared to be fighting. "Jackson's got a conflict of interest, seeing as you two are close. And I'm the only one he'd trust with someone who's important to him."

"I see," I said as my heart soared. If I was important enough to Jackson that Greg wouldn't assign him to my case, well, that meant something.

"So have you noticed anything out of place today? Any sign that someone was here who shouldn't have been?"

"Not a thing," I said, shaking my head. "We aren't a pharmacy, though. It's not like we have narcotics on site."

"No samples or anything?"

"Not currently. When I inventoried what we have here, it was just the basic stuff you'd keep on hand for emergencies and some expired samples of migraine medications and beta blockers. Nothing like what Mr. Cross was looking for." I rapped my pen on my desk and mentally reviewed my day, trying to remember if anything at all had felt odd. It hadn't, but would I have even noticed? I had practically floated through my day with thoughts of Jackson on my mind. My patients still got one hundred percent of my focus when I was in the room with them, but otherwise, I hadn't been the most observant version of myself.

"Mind if I look around?" Greg asked. "See if I notice anything you might have missed?"

"Please, be my guest. Do you want me to walk with you?"

"Not yet," he said, standing. "I'll holler for you if I need to ask you any questions. No more problems with Frank or anyone else today, right?"

"None," I said, feeling fresh relief over it. "I haven't heard from him."

"Good deal. I don't want to scare you, but Frank has a tendency for violence," Greg warned. "I'm not here to tell you what to do, but my recommendation would be that if you're going to stick to your guns and not prescribe what he wants, you should send him somewhere else. Because he's not going to back down."

"I understand," I said, nodding. "I plan to call him first, talking to him over the phone for safety, and offer him the protocol I think would help. If that conversation goes as badly as the office visit, then I agree with you and will be firing him as a patient."

"Good," Greg said, nodding. He headed toward my doorway, but I stopped him.

"Can I ask you something?" I said tentatively.

"Of course."

"I haven't heard from Jackson today. I texted him and he never wrote back, which isn't like him." I took a deep breath, suddenly feeling very silly to be asking the sheriff about this and not knowing how to begin to explain. "Things were a little weird after last night and I was just wondering..."

Greg gave me a sympathetic look. "He got a tough case this morning. Child abuse. Pretty awful situation. You know about his childhood, right?"

"I do," I said.

Greg's eyes were still kind, but his face had turned dark. "Then you know Jackson's going to give everything he has to this case. But this kind of thing eats at him more than anyone knows. He'll probably be a mess for a few days."

My heart sank. Not for myself, but for Jackson. I hadn't even thought about how his job could trigger the past like that for him. It made me realize how selfless he was, that he would continue causing himself pain and bringing up those terrible memories just to make things right for someone else.

"He might try to shut you out," Greg warned. "Jackson comes across as the sunniest, happiest person in my office. But don't let it fool you. He still carries a heavy burden. He just refuses to let anyone else close enough to see it."

"I won't let him shut me out," I said, willing it to be true.

Greg smiled. "I knew I liked you."

"You're leaving early." Beverly's voice, as smug as ever, echoed down the hallway as I locked up my office and headed toward the exit.

"I need to run by the post office before it closes. Feel free to leave early too," I said, attempting to be friendly. "You and Danny both," I added, trying to catch his eye.

He'd been awkward with me ever since I'd turned him down, which was less than ideal considering I needed to be able to rely on him in the clinic.

"We're done with patients for the day," I continued. "No need for you guys to hang around for another twenty minutes. Go ahead and lock up, head home before the five o'clock rush." I laughed, thinking they would get the joke—there wasn't a five o'clock rush here, unlike Memphis, where traffic could be completely gridlocked as everyone tried to leave work at the same time.

But neither of them even cracked a smile.

"Absolutely not," Beverly said with that same smugness still in her voice. "*Some* of us get paid by the hour and can't afford to jet off early whenever we feel like it, now can we? Besides, we have a responsibility to be available should anyone call for a last-minute appointment."

"We don't schedule appointments after four twenty," I pointed out. "So they would have to wait until tomorrow anyway."

"Still, they might want to know they have a slot scheduled, right? Goodness, I'm glad *some* of us still care about our patients."

I clamped my lips and took a deep breath, refusing to argue. "You're right," I said, forcing myself to play nice. "You're a blessing to the clinic."

Danny spoke up. "Um, since you won't be here to see patients, is it okay if I knock off early? I have some stuff to do." He glanced at Beverly, who glared at him.

"Of course," I said, giving him a bright smile.

He sighed in relief and grabbed his bag, hitting the door before Beverly had a chance to pick her jaw up off the floor.

"Call me if you need anything," I said, feeling like I had won some sort of victory. "Have a good night, Beverly."

She gave me one of her classic fake smiles and bustled out of the room, acting like she had important work to do and couldn't waste time saying goodnight. I just shook my head and walked out.

After stopping at the post office to drop off a package of local goodies for Mama—a peace offering of sorts—I drove through a fast food drive-through on my way home. It wasn't the healthiest choice, but I felt emotionally exhausted after a day that had turned out to be as draining as every other day at the clinic. I wanted comfort food, a hot bath, and TV.

Going back to my house without Jackson felt a little unnerving, but I reassured myself all would be fine. Other than a quick text telling me he was working late, I hadn't heard from him. But it was okay. Like Greg had said, Jackson was in the middle of a big case. I couldn't depend on him to be around every night. And nothing had really been wrong the day before anyway. It really might have been as simple as someone poking around out of curiosity.

Still, I added a voice memo to my phone to order a taser to carry for self-defense. I hadn't bothered in Memphis, as I wouldn't have been allowed to carry it inside the hospital anyway, and walking to and from the parking garage to the hospital doors was the most unnerving part of my routine there. But here, I could carry it in my own clinic, and it would make me feel safer when I eventually started jogging again.

I pulled up in my driveway, eyeing the house. Nothing appeared to be out of place. No windows open this time, no movement anywhere.

Still, I sat there for a good five minutes, watching everything carefully before making my approach.

I stuck my keys through my fingers as a makeshift weapon and walked up to the door, my heart pounding in a way it never had before for something as simple as coming home. A quick test revealed that the front door was still locked, a fact that made me sigh in relief. Everything was okay.

Safely inside with the door locked behind me, I moved to the kitchen, humming to myself as I pulled out a plate and dumped my burger and fries onto it. The sight of the sad meal made me instantly regret my choice—tired or not, I should have taken the time to get something better. This didn't even look appetizing.

I went to the fridge, thinking I could at least throw together a salad or something to add a little nutrition to the meal. Then I froze, as I heard a creaking noise from upstairs. My heart pounded as I gripped the refrigerator door.

You probably imagined it. Still, I didn't move. I stood frozen, adrenaline coursing through my body, straining my ears to listen.

Nothing. See? It was your imagination. Everything's fine.

Just as I began to relax, I heard another creak.

Then another.

Footsteps, slow and deliberate, came from my bedroom above.

I grabbed my phone and keys and ran for the door.

Chapter Twenty

Jackson

I WAS STANDING IN THE SHOWER, TRYING TO WASH AWAY what had been an emotionally brutal day, when my phone rang. "Damn," I muttered, turning the water off and grabbing a towel. My parents normally called on Sunday afternoons to catch up. If my phone rang at night, it could only mean one thing—something was wrong and I was about to clock some overtime. Again.

I stepped out of the shower and grabbed my phone off the bathroom counter, frowning as I looked at it. Allison's name was on the caller ID. She normally texted. Worry coursed through me as I wondered if something else had happened.

"Hey," I answered, holding the phone between my shoulder and ear as I dropped the towel and grabbed my clothes.

"There's somebody in my house." Her voice was strained and full of fear.

"What?" I almost dropped the phone as I yanked up my jeans.

"There's someone in my house," she repeated. "I came home and was about to eat when I heard footsteps upstairs."

"Get out, now," I directed her. I reached for my wallet and gun, shoving the wallet in my pocket and the pistol into the waistband of my jeans.

"I'm out," she said. "I'm in my car. What should I do?"

"Have you called nine-one-one?"

"No. I called you." Her voice sounded so afraid, so helpless. A shot of warmth flooded my heart that she would call me first, that I would be the one she turned to without even thinking.

"We're going to hang up. I'm on my way, okay? But you need to call nine-one-one. Someone might be on patrol closer and can get there faster than me. Keep your car doors locked."

"Okay," she said. I could almost picture her nodding, trying to be brave.

"I'm on my way," I repeated. "Hang up now."

The call went dead and I grabbed a shirt, not even bothering to button it before I was out the door and in my truck.

Miller was on scene when I arrived—not my first choice, but not the worst, either. He was intimidating and more than capable of handling himself.

He was also an ass who didn't like me very much, as I had gotten the job and title of detective he believed he deserved.

"Ford," he said, barely lifting his head in acknowledgment before raising his eyebrows. "Couldn't even bother to button your shirt?"

I glanced down, having completely forgotten. "Sorry," I muttered. "Where's Allison?"

"Inside. Giving a statement to Sanchez."

"Did you catch the guy?"

He shook his head and turned, spitting in disgust. "Nope. Back door was wide open though, and there are boot prints in the dirt back there. Looks like the guy spooked when she ran out and took off into the woods."

"Then why aren't you out there searching?" I demanded.

He raised his eyebrows again. "You know as well as I do that if someone wants to get lost, there's a hell of a lot of wilderness to do it. No way Sanchez and I are going to track someone down out there when he had a ten-minute head start."

Emerson could, I thought, but I kept it to myself. No need to give Miller even more of a reason to hate me. He already resented the fact that the sheriff and I regularly called on Emerson's tracking skills instead of Miller's, even though Miller considered himself one of the best trackers in the area.

"I'm going to go take a look out back," I said.

Miller stopped me, putting a hand on my chest. "Nope. The sheriff already told us you have a conflict of interest in this one." He gave me a sly smile, obviously loving the fact that he was in charge for once. "It's my investigation, and you're not going anywhere near it."

"It's *his* investigation," I retorted, unable to stop myself.

"Well, he's not here, is he? So I'm in charge."

I ground my teeth, refusing to take the bait. He'd be gone soon and I'd look around then. "Fine," I said. "I'm going to check on Allison."

"You'll wait until she's finished giving her statement." He was enjoying every minute of putting me in my place.

I crossed my arms and leaned back against my truck, fuming.

"Aren't you going to button your shirt?"

"Why? Is it bothering you? Turning you on, Miller?"

He sputtered. "You know I don't go for that."

"It's a joke, you moron." I rolled my eyes and fumed some more, waiting for Allison to finally come out.

It was all I could do not to rush over and grab Allison into my arms when she finally walked out of the house with Sanchez.

"Hey, Jackson," Sanchez said. "What are you doing out here?"

"I called him," Allison answered, locking eyes with me like I was the lifeline she had been looking for.

I cursed the fact that she had been alone when this had happened, that she had needed me but I hadn't been here. It was confirmation of what I had known all along. Allison deserved someone with normal work hours and a stable life. Even if it damn well broke my heart to think about losing my place in her life.

"Are you okay?" I asked, moving to her side.

"Yeah." It was clear from her face that she wasn't.

"Well, we're all wrapped up here," Miller announced. "Make sure your doors are locked, Dr. Bell, and call us if anything else happens."

She nodded, her mouth set in a firm line, as she wrapped her arms around herself like she needed the comfort.

And oh how I wanted to be the one comforting her.

We waited for Miller and Sanchez to pull out before going inside.

"How are you really?" I asked, following her through the door. I made sure it was locked behind us, even though there was barely a point. Whoever this was wasn't likely to come in with me here, and if he wanted to, he'd already proven locks wouldn't stop him. Still, the gesture made me feel better.

She shrugged, then sank into the couch, tears clouding her eyes. "I don't know. When it was just once, and the person was gone, and you were here...that was different. This was terrifying."

"I bet it was." I sat down on the other end of the couch, giving her space to talk.

"I'm tired, Jackson," she said, covering her face with her hands. When she let them fall to her lap, I saw exhaustion I'd never seen there before. "Tired of my patients hating me. Tired of putting up with Beverly. Tired of whoever this is making it to where I don't even feel safe in my home." She looked away, avoiding my eyes. "I don't know. Maybe Mama's right. Maybe I should just go back to Memphis."

"Is that what you want?" I asked carefully.

"I don't know what I want right now." Her voice was broken. Like everything had piled up and piled up and it was finally too much.

I sat silent, not trusting myself to say anything. I knew I couldn't be what she needed—what she deserved—but the thought of her moving away again? It killed me. It was the last thing I wanted.

"Jackson?"

"Yeah?"

"Are *you* okay? Greg said you had a tough case today."

My heart stopped in my chest. After everything that had happened, she was worried about me? It was a strange feeling. I was used to being the one checking on everyone else. "I don't know," I said, giving her the most honest answer I could. "It's hard to explain."

"That's okay. You can tell me anyway."

I turned toward her. "When you work this kind of job, you learn to compartmentalize, you know? But when it's a kid being abused... Well, it gets hard for me to do that."

"I imagine." She reached over and squeezed my hand.

"All I can do is show up as the person I wish I would have had back then," I said, swallowing over a painful lump in my throat. "Even if what I really want to do is tear the suspect to pieces."

"I wish someone would have shown up for you," she said softly.

I nodded, trying to squash down the old hurts. "You know people called, made reports. But everything was always dismissed because the investigators were too busy, too pulled in a million directions. Mom would cover for him, and Russell would talk his way out of it. Couldn't lose his errand boy—or his punching bag."

"What changed?" she asked, tilting her head. "Was it because it was your mother who reported him?"

The memories of it all brought a swell of emotion I tried to avoid. "Nah. Timing wise, I'm pretty sure it was her, but the report was anonymous. The difference this time was a sheriff's deputy who made it her mission to make sure Russell could never get his hands on me again. She left no stone unturned in her investigation. Pressed criminal charges against him. And even though he managed to weasel out of those, she showed up at every one of my court dates. I'd have gone straight back into his hands if not for her."

"Is that why you became a detective?" She looked at me like she was beginning to understand.

I nodded, slowly. "Yeah. One reason, anyway. I want to be that person for other people. The one who doesn't give up."

She reached out and placed her hand on my arm. "You're a good one. Rosemary Mountain is lucky to have you. That kid is lucky to have you. *I'm* lucky to have you."

I looked at her and knew we had to have a conversation I'd been hoping to avoid—a conversation that would slice my chest open and rip my heart out. But it had to happen. Because I couldn't deny my feelings or ignore how close we were getting. And if we kept getting closer, I was going to cross a line and lose her altogether.

"Allison," I said, looking down at my shoes. "I've told you how I feel about relationships."

"You have." Her voice was small.

"But I'm attracted to you," I said, confessing it like it was a mortal sin. "No, it's more than that. More than just attraction. I have feelings for you. Strong feelings. But today just showed me why I have the rules I have. You needed me—you called *me* instead of nine-one-one."

"And you answered," she said, a look of sadness crossing her face like she knew what was coming.

"I did," I confirmed, "but what if I hadn't? What if I had stayed at work even an hour later? It happens, you know. Sometimes I'm there all night. I work long, crazy hours. I can't be the person you depend on, no matter how much I want to be. You deserve more than that."

She leaned her head back, staring at the ceiling as she took a deep breath. "I have one request."

"What?"

"Stop worrying about what you think I need."

"But—"

Allison interrupted me. "I mean it, Jackson. It seems like all you do is worry about what everyone else needs from you. But I'm a big girl. Was I disappointed to not have dinner with you tonight? Yeah, I was, because I enjoy spending time with you. But I understand how important your job is. I'm a *doctor*. You think I'm available all the time? I know what it's like to be on call, to pull double shifts, all of it. And tonight, if you hadn't answered? I would have called nine-one-one. So you can stop worrying about me."

I stared at her. "I don't know how to stop worrying about you."

She gave me a little half smile. "So you can worry about me a little. But..."

"But what?"

This time she was the one to look like she had something life-changing to tell me. "Jackson, I have feelings for you, too. But is that really so bad? What if... What if we gave this a shot? A real shot. I think... I think we would be good together."

My heart nearly stopped. Allison Bell was offering me everything I had ever wanted. It was almost too much, like someone had presented me with a chest of jewels. For a split second, I wondered if it was possible. I saw a vision of a future together, and it was the most beautiful thing I'd ever seen.

But it was immediately clouded out by Russell's face. *My blood runs through your veins, boy, and don't you forget it. Don't matter what you do, or who you try to be. You're a Sharp. Blood don't lie.*

I knew I couldn't. "I can't. I'm sorry, Allison." More sorry than I could possibly say. "You're the only real friend I have who knew me back then. The only one who knows the whole me, past and present. Your friendship means everything to me. I won't risk it for anything." My voice got thick. "And I could never give you everything you want. Everything you deserve. Not with my job, or...or with Russell's blood running through me."

She looked at me with sadness. "Jackson, when are you going to stop selling yourself short?"

"You're the one selling yourself short if you think you want to be with me."

She shook her head, clearly angry at my words. "So that's it, then? We have feelings for each other, we're obviously compatible, we're best friends, but you're saying there's no chance of us making it work?"

"No chance," I said, keeping my voice firm, even though every part of me wanted to hope it was possible.

"Okay," she said in a voice that somehow seemed even more defeated than earlier. She slapped her hands down on her knees and leaned her head back, staring at the ceiling. "I'm really tired. I know it's early, but I feel like I'm crashing. I need to go to bed."

I nodded. "I'll stay here again tonight."

"You don't have to." It broke my heart because I knew how scared she was—and how much I had hurt her if she was willing to stay here alone despite her fear.

"I do. He might come back again. So either I'm staying here or you're coming to my apartment, but I have to warn you. My place isn't nearly as nice as yours."

She smirked. "Yours doesn't have someone breaking into it every night though."

"That's true. Would you rather come home with me?"

"Honestly?"

"Of course."

"Yeah," she said, glancing around the room. "Even with you here, I'm not sure I'm going to feel safe until they catch this guy. And I don't want you getting hurt, either."

"Then pack a bag. I'll wait."

CHAPTER TWENTY-ONE

Allison

I WENT UPSTAIRS AND BEGAN PACKING AN OVERNIGHT BAG, somehow hurting and feeling numb at the same time. This was all becoming a nightmare.

Jackson had drawn a line in the sand. He meant what he had said before. Friends only. And I was having a really, really hard time accepting that.

Hard because he was wrong. Not just about himself—though he was definitely wrong there—but about us, too. He didn't want to risk what we had, but he was risking it anyway by keeping our friendship platonic. If we never allowed ourselves to see what was between us, there would come a day when one of us fell for someone else. And the moment either of us began a relationship, the dynamic between us would change. It would have to. There was no way I could be in a relationship with another man and continue on the way I was with Jackson. It would be completely inappropriate. We would always be playing with fire.

There was an unknown expiration date on our friendship that would only be solved by promising each other forever. But that was a promise he had no intention of ever making.

Walking into Jackson's apartment felt like walking into a refuge from the rest of the world. The whole place felt like him—friendly, welcoming, and oddly familiar. I immediately felt the weight of the day fall off my shoulders as I stepped through the door, knowing that tonight I would be safe.

Jackson locked up behind me, then stood there awkwardly. "I'll just change the sheets on my bed. Then you can have it," he said.

"Don't be silly," I said, shaking my head at him. "I'll sleep on the couch."

"That doesn't feel right at all."

"I don't care," I said, feeling too tired to argue. "I'm not sleeping in your bed, Jackson."

Something in my tone must have indicated that I meant it, and I did. Sleeping in his bed, even without him there, felt like crossing a boundary that I couldn't come back from. If we could only ever be friends, I needed to put up some new walls between us in order to protect my own heart. Not to mention the fact that sleeping alone in his bed would be a cruel reminder that he didn't want me there with him.

"Alright," he said, defeated. "I'll grab you a pillow and some blankets."

"Thanks." I moved to the couch and sank into it, suddenly feeling even more tired than before.

Maybe coming here was a bad idea after all. I felt safe here. But I also felt the acute pain of a change in our relationship that neither of us had seen coming. Admitting our feelings had destroyed the ease between us, and I wasn't sure how to get it back.

I missed my best friend.

Jackson emerged minutes later, carrying a stack of blankets and a fresh pillow. "You sure you'll be okay out here?"

"I'll be fine."

"Okay." He handed me the linens, then turned to leave, but he paused in the doorway. "I feel like I let you down. That's the one thing I didn't want to do. I'm sorry, Allison."

My shoulders sagged with instant remorse. "You didn't let me down, Jackson. It's not your fault I developed feelings for you. We had a pact. I'm sorry I let *you* down."

"Think we can get back to being friends soon?"

"I hope so."

"Me too." He gave me a long look, then rapped his knuckles on the door frame and left me alone in his living room.

I sighed, feeling his absence in more ways than one. With nothing left to do or say, I slipped into the guest bathroom to change. Then I made up a bed on his couch and drifted into troubled sleep.

HOURS LATER, I JERKED AWAKE, STARTLED BY LOUD CRIES.

"No! Stop! Please don't hurt her."

It took me a moment to realize the yells were coming from Jackson. I rolled off the couch and ran toward his bedroom.

I threw open the door and flipped on the light. Jackson immediately sat up in bed. He was sweating, but he was alone. My body sagged with relief as I realized his screams had been from a nightmare.

I clutched my heart. "You scared me."

"I'm sorry." He ran a hand through his hair and ducked his head.

I crossed the room and sat beside him on the bed, squeezing his hand. "What happened?"

"Nothing." He looked away.

"Jackson." I repeated his name until he finally looked at me. Those eyes were full of grief—and humiliation. "It's okay," I said. "Everything's okay."

"I'm a grown-ass man—no, a grown-ass *law enforcement officer*—who has nightmares like a child. Nothing about that is okay."

I ran my hand over his face, wishing I could wash away all the years of hurt. "Don't even start with that. I know what you went through. Remember? I saw the way he beat you." I stroked his hair, patting him much in the same way I had when he was a kid, when I would find him hiding down by the creek. I spoke softly, like I had then, trying to ease the pain in the only way I knew how. "I saw, Jackson. You have nothing to be embarrassed about."

"I should be over this by now."

"Over trauma?" I gave a small laugh and shook my head. "That's not how it works. Your body remembers. And after working a child abuse case, it's completely understandable that you were triggered. There's nothing wrong with you. You just had a bad day."

"You have no idea." He covered his face with his hands and fell backward on the bed, groaning. "Allison, I need to tell you something. And you might not forgive me for it."

"What?"

He uncovered his face and looked at me. "I don't even know how to tell you this, but...I think Russell is the one breaking into your house."

"Russell?" The thought shocked—and terrified—me. I knew what that man could do.

Jackson nodded slowly.

"But why? Why me?"

He closed his eyes. When he spoke, his voice was low. "Because he knows what you mean to me. And he wants to use you to hurt me."

I stared at him, processing it all. If he was right, that was scary. Scarier even than an opioid-deprived patient breaking into my house. Russell Sharp was someone I didn't want to cross paths with, much less be targeted by.

"We found a cigarette butt in your backyard, the same kind he smokes," Jackson continued, his eyes still closed like he couldn't bear looking at me. "There was a boot print out back tonight. I checked when you were packing your bag. It looks to be the same size as his. And he's been threatening me. Following me. He knows we've been spending time together. He's seen us."

"No wonder you had a nightmare," I said weakly. "What are we going to do?"

"I don't think we can hang out anymore," Jackson said, his eyes still closed, his voice still low and full of pain. "It's not safe for you."

I kept staring at him—at this man who had lived through an unspeakable childhood and come out on the other side dedicated to keeping everyone else safe. This man who cared about me—probably more than he would admit—but wanted to walk away to keep me safe.

"Well, I'm here tonight," I said, making a decision. "So there's that. And I'm not going back to the couch. I'm sleeping in here with you."

"You shouldn't—" he started to say, but I cut him off.

"It's purely selfish on my part," I said. "I don't want to sleep in there, where I'd be the first thing Russell sees if he breaks down the door. I'm sleeping in here, where you can protect me." *And where I can protect you, too.*

Jackson might have been pushing me away, but I wasn't going anywhere—not when it was clear he needed me, whether he realized it or not.

He opened his eyes and looked at me, then gave a begrudging nod.

"It's settled, then." I climbed to the top of the bed and wiggled down underneath the covers. "Goodnight, Jackson."

"Goodnight, Allison."

He reached over and took my hand in his. It was the first time I could remember him reaching for me like that. Usually, it was the other way around. I was the one always reaching out, needing to comfort and show I was there. Jackson usually kept his hands to himself.

But he reached for me, and we fell asleep that way, hand in hand—and neither of us had any more nightmares that night.

Warm sunlight wrapped the room in a buttery glow when I woke the next morning, curled up in Jackson's arms. He was sound asleep with a little smile on his face. He looked so full of peace that I hated to wake him. But even though it was a Saturday and I knew neither of us had to work, we couldn't exactly stay in bed all day. Being in his bed was crossing a line. I couldn't regret it though, if it meant him getting a peaceful night's sleep.

It killed me that he was so haunted by the past. All these years later, Russell could still inflict pain without touching him at all. It wasn't fair. Worse, there was nothing I could do about it.

Jackson's words from the night before came back to me, stealing the smile from my face. He wanted to keep his distance so Russell would leave me alone and stop trying to hurt him through me. I understood that.

But I hated it.

Full of regret, I slipped out of his arms.

I padded into his kitchen, found the coffee pot, and started a strong pot to get us going for the day. We both had a lot to face, but there was no need to face it without coffee.

When Jackson came into the room, looking sleepy-eyed, with mussed-up hair and flannel pajama pants riding low on his waist, I didn't really want coffee anymore. I wanted something else entirely, something I wasn't allowed to have.

"Morning," I said, forcing a smile.

"Good morning." His eyes searched my face like he was looking for a sign that I was okay—that *we* were okay—after last night.

"I made coffee. Hope you don't mind."

"I could never mind that," he said, giving me a small smile. "Listen, about last night. I'm sorry. About the nightmare, I mean. Sorry you had to see that."

I reached over and squeezed his hand. "I'm glad I was here. And I hope you slept better after.

"I did," he said, appearing to choose his words carefully. "Allison, I—"

But he was cut off by his cell phone, which buzzed on the counter.

He looked at it and frowned. "It's Greg."

CHAPTER TWENTY-TWO

Jackson

ALLISON'S FACE TURNED WHITE AND SHE LEANED UP AGAINST the counter, nervously rubbing the coffee mug in her hands. I answered the phone and listened to what Greg had to say, keeping my responses brief.

My stomach was in knots by the time Greg finished catching me up to speed. I felt a thousand emotions at once—anger, fear, grief. Emptiness.

I closed my eyes and took a moment to try to wrap my mind around it all before turning to Allison. "They got him."

"Russell?"

"Yes."

"Thank God," she said. Her whole body sagged with relief..

I swallowed hard, still not fully believing the words I was about to speak. "He's dead."

"What?" She instantly straightened.

I gripped the counter, needing something to hold on to.

Allison grabbed my arm and led me to the couch, forcing me to sit. "You need water," she said. She went back to the kitchen and opened the cabinet doors until she found a cup. Then she filled it with water and came back, forcing it into my hands. "Drink."

I did as she'd said.

"What happened?" she asked, sitting beside me.

I felt sick now, knowing I had to tell her the whole story. "You know that empty lot just down from your house? The one they're clearing to be a new subdivision?"

"Yeah," she said, nodding. "I know what you're talking about."

"Last night, they got a call about an unresponsive man sitting in a truck on that lot. Went to do a welfare check and it was him. He was parked within easy walking distance from your place. And he was dead."

"Cause of death?"

"Officially, still to be determined."

"Unofficially?" Allison seemed to know we'd at least have an idea.

"Suspected accidental overdose. He apparently had lung cancer. I didn't know..." I trailed off, feeling so detached from my words. How was it possible to feel so much and so little at the same time? "He was on a lot of pain meds. Some legit scripts, some not. All that on top of his normal habit. We don't know yet if it was an overdose, the cancer, or something else that got him in the end."

"I'm sorry, Jackson," she said, rubbing my arm. Thinking only of me, when I was the one who should have been apologizing to her.

"There's more." More I hated to tell her.

"What is it?"

I blew out a breath, then told her the rest. No matter how it might change her feelings for me, she deserved to know the full truth. "He had a loaded gun in the vehicle. A photograph of me and you leaving the clinic together. And a note in the driver's seat with your address on it."

Her jaw dropped. "I don't even know what to say to that."

I clenched my jaw. "I'm sorry, Allison. I'm so sorry. It's all my fault he wanted to hurt you." I wanted to crawl into a hole forever, knowing that his darkness had come so close to touching her.

Fury flashed in her eyes as she stood. "Do not. Jackson, nothing that man did is your fault, do you understand?"

"But—"

"No buts. You are not him. You are not responsible for his actions. He wanted to hurt me because he was a hateful, miserable person who couldn't stand to see you happy. But that is not your fault, and I won't listen to you apologizing for it."

I just stared at her. Her angry outburst was so unlike her that it brought a smile to my face, something that had felt impossible moments before. "You know who you remind me of?"

"Who?"

"My mom. My adoptive mom, that is. She has your same passion. And she's always telling me I'm not responsible for Russell."

A smile teased at Allison's lips. "Smart woman," she said. "You should listen to her."

Knowing Russell was no longer a threat, I felt safe leaving Allison. I dropped her off at her house with a promise that I'd come back for dinner. She had insisted, and I thought I knew why—she wanted to make sure I wasn't going to pull away now that our friendship was no longer a danger to her.

It was still a danger to me, though. To my heart, anyway.

Even so, I promised her I would come back, then headed straight to the morgue. I wasn't needed for official identification, but I wanted to do it anyway. Needed to see it for myself.

I pulled up and saw Greg standing outside, waiting.

"Hey, Sheriff," I said, stepping out of my truck and heading his way.

"Jackson," he said, nodding.

"What are you doing here?"

"I knew this is where you'd come. And I sure as hell wasn't going to have you face it alone."

My throat tightened. "Thanks," I said, my voice oddly gruff. I reached out and shook his hand, unshed tears stinging my eyes.

"How are you holding up?" He put his hand on my shoulder.

"I don't know," I said weakly. "It's been a hell of a week."

"Doesn't feel right to say I'm sorry for your loss, but just know that I'm here for you. Whatever you need."

I nodded, unable to speak.

We headed inside and walked down the long hallway to where the bodies were kept. As a detective, I'd done this before. But it had never been personal.

When I saw Russell's body, I expected to feel relief, and it was there —but so was grief. Even after all these years, part of me had still hoped he would change. That he would actually have some small desire to be a decent member of society. To do the right thing for once. Even to patch things up with me and actually have a role in my life as something other than a villain. I'd always held on to this little bit of hope that some-where, deep inside him, there was some good left.

He had died without showing a bit of that goodness. In the end, he had been just as horrible as he had in the beginning. Maybe even worse.

The Sharp blood. It was poison.

"This isn't what I wanted," I said, staring at him. "Even after every-thing. I wanted—" My voice broke.

"I know," Greg said quietly, reaching out to put a hand on my shoulder. "I know."

TWO HOURS LATER, I FOUND MYSELF DOWN AT THE OLD creek, not entirely sure how I had gotten there. It was more habit than anything, an old childhood ritual that had lain dormant but apparently never died. Russell did something awful; I ran away to the creek. It's just how it was.

I picked up a stone, flipping it over in my hand and rubbing my thumb against the smooth surface before skipping it across the water. Five skips. Not bad at all.

"Bet I can still beat you." The voice came from behind me, startling and soothing me all at once.

"How'd you know I'd be here?" I asked, not even bothering to turn around.

Allison walked forward, her tennis shoes squeaking on the rocky bank, until she plopped down beside me. "I just knew. You okay?"

"Yeah." I picked up another rock. Flipped it. Rubbed it. Skipped it. Six skips this time.

"Nice," she said before picking up one of her own. She rubbed it in between her palms, then brought it to her lips for a kiss before letting it fly. Seven skips.

"Damn," I said. "You can still beat me."

"It's all in the kiss," she said, laughing.

"That's what you always said." I just shook my head.

She put her arm through mine and laid her head on my shoulder, bringing back a million memories. This place had been our refuge from the world, a private oasis where adults never seemed to bother us or spoil our fun.

"It's okay to have mixed feelings," she whispered, squeezing my arm.

"How did you know?"

"He was your dad," she said. "Trust me. I get it."

"Did you stay in touch with your dad after you and your mom left?" I had always wondered, but it was a topic we hadn't spoken about since her return.

She let out a deep, shaky sigh. "No. Not really. He fought for shared custody—briefly—but in the end, he chose alcohol instead. Ruined every chance the judge gave him. He never even showed up for visitation. Mama ended up with sole custody. He sent letters on my birthday for a few years. That was it."

"So you didn't see him before..."

"Before he died?"

"Right."

She shook her head, then laid it back on my shoulder. I reached up and stroked her hair as we shared our grief together.

"When he passed, Grandmother wrote to Mama and let her know. She told me casually, like she didn't expect it to affect me at all because I hadn't seen him in years. But it broke my heart, even though I rarely even thought of him anymore."

"Of course it did," I said. "He was your dad."

"Mixed feelings," she repeated.

"Yep."

"He chose alcohol, and in the end, it killed him. Your dad chose..." She trailed off, as if realizing she might offend me by stating the truth.

"He chose hate," I said, filling in the blank. "In the end, he always chose hate."

She snuggled into me, her voice impossibly small as she asked, "Do you ever wonder why they didn't choose us?"

"Every damn day."

WE SPENT THE AFTERNOON AT THE CREEK. WE SKIPPED rocks, walked along the bank, and waded ankle-deep in the warm water as the sun sank lower in the sky, rays of light cutting a path through the trees to sparkle on the dark surface. Neither of us spoke much. It was clear we were both deep in thought, reliving some of the best—and worst—moments of our lives. But we didn't have to talk much to get something out of it. We were together and that was enough.

When we finally decided to leave, Allison pulled her car beside mine. "Dinner?" she asked through the open window.

"You still want to hang out tonight, after I moped around feeling sorry for myself all afternoon?" I chuckled, even though I was genuinely asking. I knew I wasn't the best company right now.

"I do." She nodded. "I'm picking up takeout. I don't know about you, but I'm starved. Pizza?"

"Pizza sounds great," I said.

"And wine," she said, eyebrows raised. "Red probably. That goes with pizza, right?"

"Pizza *and* wine? What happened to setting an example of healthy eating?" I grinned, enjoying the ease that had somehow come back in our friendship, at least a little.

"We need comfort food tonight."

"Alright, well, you get the pizza and I'll pick up a bottle. Do you have a preference on type?"

She shrugged. "Not really. Something smooth and easy to drink. Not too dry, but not too sweet. You probably know more about them than I do."

"Got it."

. . .

AFTER A DAY OF GRIEVING TOGETHER, WE BOTH AVOIDED any talk of Russell or the past at Allison's that night. We shared a pizza and a bottle of pinot noir and swapped stories about crazy things that had happened in our jobs. It was a fun night, one where the ease between us seemed to return, even though there was an unspoken tension under the surface I was sure we both felt. Things had changed for so many reasons. But we both seemed determined to get back to normal somehow.

I was getting ready to head out for the night when the house practically shook.

"Was that thunder?" Allison asked, her eyes wide.

"Sounds like it," I said before my voice was nearly drowned out by the roar of heavy rain pounding the metal roof.

Allison got up and opened the front door. Then she stepped out on the porch and closed her eyes, filling her lungs with the scent of the rain falling on the forest. "It's beautiful," she said, her tone wistful.

"What's beautiful?" I asked, moving out onto the porch with her, even though I agreed completely. It almost didn't matter what her answer was. The sight of the rain was beautiful. The scent of it was incredible. And when her own scent—delicate and rich at the same time, like lilacs—combined with the familiar smell of a Tennessee rainstorm in the summer, I thought I could just about get drunk on the combo.

"This," she said, turning toward me and opening her eyes. There was an earnest look in them, a longing I recognized. "I had almost forgotten this."

"Almost forgotten what?" I moved toward her without realizing it, standing so close we nearly touched. There was a good two inches between our bodies, but I could almost feel her just the same.

She gave me a long look, one that was filled with a complicated mix of emotions I couldn't fully identify. "This. How the world works differently here. Life doesn't just continue on at the same fast pace, come rain or high water. A rainstorm like this, here, is almost magic. It can slow everything down. Stop life in its tracks. Force you to just experience it for once—to step outside onto your porch to listen to the rain and watch it dripping from the roof." She held out a cupped hand and let the water hit her palm, filling it, like she was collecting a precious gift.

"That's true," I said. "The weather dictates life here on the mountain, whether we like it or not."

"It's such a gift to slow down," she said quietly, still letting the raindrops bounce off the palm of her hand. She finally turned her hand upside down, letting the water inside fall to the earth with the rest, then turned back to me. Her face was still that mix of emotion, somehow full of trouble and peace at the same time.

"It is," I agreed, wishing time would slow down completely. I could stand out here with her listening to the rain for the rest of my life if the world would just let us.

"I had forgotten," she said again, almost in a whisper.

"Forgotten what?"

She looked up at me, and her expression finally changed, like she had somehow let go of the trouble that was clouding it and grabbed on to the peace with both hands. "I had almost forgotten what it feels like to be free."

I wasn't sure how it happened—whether she reached for me or I reached for her—but suddenly her head was on my chest and my arms wrapped tightly around her waist, holding her like I never wanted to let go.

It felt right. But it was wrong. We had already agreed to just be friends. Nothing could happen between us.

Without meaning to, I had broken our pact. I had fallen in love with my best friend.

Chapter Twenty-Three

Allison

With my eyes closed, I let my mind drift away, focusing only on the sound of the rain falling on the tin roof of the porch. For the first time in so very long, I felt completely at peace.

But as the realization slowly dawned that I was embarrassing myself, clinging to Jackson like he was mine, I slowly pulled away.

"Thanks," I said, too embarrassed to meet his eyes. "I guess I needed a hug with everything that's been going on. It's all been a lot, you know?"

"Anytime," he said in that rich voice of his, which was becoming almost as familiar as the one he'd had as a kid. It was surreal in a way, connecting this Jackson standing in front of me—a *man* in every sense of the word—with the little boy who had been my childhood best friend.

And suddenly, I felt restless, itchy, and desperate to do something—anything—other than stand on this porch with him. If we stayed here, I might throw myself into his arms again, and that would be breaking our pact.

Friends.

That's all we were and all we could be. He had made his position abundantly clear last night, and if I had hoped he would change his mind after Russell's death, our afternoon at the creek had made me realize he wouldn't. There was still too much pain there, too much blame, and too much worry that part of him came from that man.

Jackson needed a friend more than ever, and I needed to respect his boundaries and be that for him. But it was fine. It was just a hug. I had needed comfort after a cathartic day, and he had provided it, like any friend would.

"What's wrong?" His eyes narrowed as he searched my face.

"Nothing." I smiled brightly and turned my gaze away from him, looking again at the rain falling steadily on my gravel driveway. The low spots had already become dark puddles, and the sight of them brought back memories.

"Where'd you go?" Jackson asked softly. He reached out and rubbed my arm before dropping his hand again, shoving it into his pocket.

I moved my own hand up to the place where he had touched, trying somehow to keep the feeling there. "I was just remembering how, when we were kids, we'd run through the rain. It would be pouring cats and dogs and we'd both run outside into the yard, splashing in the puddles and catching raindrops on our tongues. Remember that? Mama would get so mad because I'd come back to the house wet and muddy, and she'd have to put me straight into a bath. Unless it was storming and she couldn't, in which case I'd have to sit on the kitchen floor until the lightning stopped." I laughed out loud. "We were silly, weren't we? Entertaining ourselves that way."

He grinned, his face relaxing again. "Entertainment options were slim, Allison. I'd say we did the best we could with what we had."

"It was fun," I admitted.

A devilish look came into his eyes. "Want to do it again?"

My jaw dropped, even as I felt the grin spread across my face. "We can't."

"Why not?"

"Because we're adults now. Adults don't splash in mud puddles and dance in the rain."

"Who says?" That devilish look grew, and I knew what was coming. But I didn't back away.

"It would be irresponsible," I said, pointing my finger at him and mimicking my mother's tone, even though I couldn't keep a straight face.

"Exactly. Didn't you just say something about remembering what it felt like to be free? This is freedom, Allison." And with the same mischievous look on his face I remembered so well from our childhoods, Jackson grabbed my hand and took off down the porch stairs, pulling me behind him.

I shrieked, ducking when the raindrops hit the top of my head. But then something inside me shifted. I lifted my head to the sky and invited the rain to hit my face. Jackson let go of my hand—breaking my heart a bit in the process—and I stuck out my arms and slowly turned in a circle, just like I had as a kid. The rain pelted me so hard I couldn't open my eyes, but it didn't matter. It felt like a gift, a baptism of freedom, as the water washed away what felt like years of stress and striving.

Here, none of it mattered. Here on the mountain, I was loved just for who I was.

I finally lowered my head and opened my eyes. I saw Jackson standing in the pouring rain, watching me. The look on his face was something I wanted to hold in my heart forever.

Then he was moving toward me, and before I knew what had happened, I was in his arms again. He pulled me close and held me tight as he dipped his lips to mine. They were cold from the rain, yet somehow perfect, and our mouths fit together as if we had been made for each other. My hands went to his face as I sank into the feeling of his lips on mine.

And suddenly I knew it was always meant to be this way. That no matter what we had said, what pact we had made, or any of the other reasons Jackson would come up with, it didn't matter. Our souls had been connected our entire lives, and here, in this moment, the world finally made sense. I was always being led back to him, and he was always being led back to me. Our bodies melded together in this one, perfect moment of clarity, this moment of knowing who I was and who he was and who we could be together.

Until he broke away.

"I'm sorry," he said, his voice hoarse. "I don't know what I was thinking. You just... Standing there... I'm sorry. I shouldn't have."

"It's okay," I said, moving toward him again—until I realized he genuinely regretted it. What had been a perfect moment of clarity for me was a moment of regret for him. So I stopped.

"No, it's not okay," he said. "We had an understanding, and I broke that. I'm sorry, Allison."

"Jackson," I said, looking up at him, wishing I could get the connection we had just shared back somehow. "I'm not upset at you. Not at all."

But it was clear by the look on his face that he was angry with himself. It was that look that made me step back yet again, away from the warmth of his embrace. I knew this was real, that it was more than just attraction. It was solid and true and something I'd never felt for anyone else. But something stopped me from telling him, because the last thing I wanted was for him to push me away. He had made it clear he still didn't trust himself. I knew if he thought he might hurt me, he would just stop coming around.

It felt like part of me would die if I lost him again.

"Friends practice kissing each other sometimes, right?" I teased, attempting to lighten the mood. "At least that's what Tommy Reynolds tried to tell me in third grade."

His face changed to surprise, which was exactly my intention. "He did not."

"He did," I said, laughing. "I told him no, though."

Jackson grinned. "Good. You were too good for him." A look of pain quickly flashed across his face, so quickly I almost missed it.

I knew what he was thinking. He thought I was too good for him, too. And my heart ached to tell him all the things he needed to know— that he wasn't his dad. That he was his own man, with a good heart. That he was strong, brave, and selfless. That, truth be told, he was probably too good for *me*.

But I knew if I said those things now, he wouldn't believe me. Even if he wanted to.

So I just kept things light.

"You're soaked," I said, laughing again.

"You are too," he said, grinning back at me.

"Come on in and get dry." I grabbed his arm and tugged him toward the house. "I'm afraid I don't have any clothes that will fit you, but you can borrow my robe if you want to throw your stuff in the dryer."

But he held back, stopping me. "I think I better go home," he said. "I'll just make sure you get inside safely. Then I'll head out."

"You don't have to."

"I do. It's getting late and I already interrupted your sleep last night. I'm not going to do it again." He kept his tone light, but I could tell he was still upset.

"Okay," I said, not wanting to push. "See you soon?"

"Yeah. And if you need anything, you know you can call me. Anytime."

"I know," I said.

"Alright then. Let's get you inside."

I turned away, disappointed as I walked up the stairs. He followed me to the door and waited for me to go in.

"I'm going to wait to hear you lock up," he said. His face was neutral, but he couldn't fool me.

I saw the old pain in his eyes, the lies he still believed. Raindrops ran from his hair down his face, reminding me of tears. I was tempted to smooth them away, wishing somehow it could wipe away all the hurt he hid so well from the rest of the world. But I kept my hands to myself.

"Goodnight," I said softly. "Thank you for taking care of me."

"Always," he said.

I swallowed the lump in my throat and closed the door between us. I stayed there, listening to his footsteps as he slowly walked away.

When his truck pulled out, I ran upstairs to get a towel to dry my hair. My clothes were so wet I had to peel them off of me before trading them for a dry pair of sweats. I had just changed when I heard a knock at my door.

He came back. I smiled, feeling hope bloom again. But when I opened my door, it wasn't him on my steps.

"What are you doing here?" I asked.

"Honey, I'm home," Mike quipped, pulling a giant bouquet of roses from behind his back.

"That's not funny," I said, shaking my head. "I didn't invite you to come."

"Come on," he said, dipping his head and giving me his most charming smile. "I drove all this way. The least you could do is let me in. I just want to talk, Allison. Hear me out. If you don't like what I have to say, then we part as friends and I'll never darken your doorstep again. But even if that's the case, don't I at least deserve some closure?"

My shoulders sagged. "Fine." I opened the door wider, making room for him to enter. "But I hope you booked a room at the motel, because you're not staying here tonight."

CHAPTER TWENTY-FOUR

Jackson

Alone in my bed, I spent a restless night haunted by nightmares of Russell. Knowing he was dead wasn't even enough to convince my brain I was safe.

I was starting to wonder if I would ever truly be free from him.

Sleep or no sleep, Sunday morning started bright and early with a call from my mom. "Morning, Jackson!" Her cheery voice rang through the phone, exactly the same as it did every week, bringing a small smile to my face.

"Morning, Mom."

"What's wrong?" Her tone changed instantly.

"Nothing. Everything's fine." I stifled a yawn. "I was asleep, that's all."

"Jackson"—I could practically hear her rolling her eyes on the other line—"I'm your mother. I can tell by your voice that everything is *not* fine. What's going on? Rough case?"

I forced myself out of bed and headed for the coffee pot, knowing we were in for a long conversation. "Russell's dead."

The other line was so quiet I thought I had lost her.

"Mom?"

"Sorry," she said. "I'm just processing that. How?"

"Looks like an overdose."

She was silent for a beat. "Will it offend you if I say that's kind of fitting?"

I snorted. "Nah."

"You know I have a hard time feeling compassion for him after the way he treated you," she said, her voice quiet. "But I also understand he was your father. I want you to know that you're allowed to feel however you feel about it. It's okay to be happy, sad, or both. This is complicated, and whatever you're feeling? It's okay with me."

I gripped the phone in my hand and closed my eyes, leaning back against the counter. "Thanks, Mom. I think I'm feeling a lot of different things honestly. Relief. Hurt. You're right. It's complicated."

"What do you need right now?"

I smiled, unable to help it. It was Mom's favorite question. She asked because she legitimately wanted to know, and if she could meet that need, she would. She was one of those rare people you could actually count on.

But the image that sprang to mind wasn't something she could give me. I needed Allison. And that was the one thing I couldn't have. Not in the way I wanted, anyway.

So I shifted my mind to more practical things. "I'm the only family Russell had left. I need to do some kind of burial for him or something. I don't know." I ran my hand through my hair, feeling exhausted from thinking about it. This was completely out of my scope of experience, and it wasn't something I was looking forward to at all.

"You're a good person, Jackson." Mom's voice was soft. "And you don't have to handle that alone. Dad and I will pack bags and drive up tonight. We'll help with the arrangements and stand with you."

"Thanks, Mom," I said, my voice feeling thick.

"I'll put together some sort of meal afterward," she said. "Just tell me how many people you think you might want to have there. Greg and the rest, I'm assuming?"

"Yeah," I said, letting out a breath, knowing Greg would be there for my sake—not Russell's. Truth was, I was probably the only one who would actually be there as any sort of griever. But I'd have people there to support me, and that meant something. "And Allison."

"Allison?" Mom's tone perked up. "Are we talking about Allison Bell?"

"Yeah," I said, grinning at the change in Mom's mood. "I'm surprised you remember her name."

"How could I forget the girl my son talked about nonstop as a kid?" She sounded amused. "I didn't know you guys were back in touch."

"She moved back a few weeks ago," I explained, feeling sudden guilt for not mentioning it to Mom sooner. I hadn't thought of myself as being deliberately evasive, but I hadn't really wanted to answer any questions.

"That's wonderful. I can't wait to meet her." Mom's voice was full of warmth. "What does she do?"

"She's a doctor now. Just took over Doc Rogers's old practice."

"That's great! Tell me everything."

So I did. Somehow, Mom knew exactly what I needed. I couldn't have Allison, but talking about her to someone who was interested turned out to be the next best thing. By the time we hung up the phone so Mom could pack up to drive in, I was feeling about a thousand times lighter than I had before.

Allison didn't text that morning, and I didn't reach out, either. I missed her more than I wanted to admit to myself, but some space was good. No matter how in love with her I was, nothing had changed. Not really. I was Russell Sharp's son, and I wasn't going to risk bringing that kind of darkness into Allison's world. She deserved better than that.

But I'll admit, when I walked into the coffee shop that afternoon and saw Allison sitting at a table with another man, I wanted to throw all my good intentions out the window.

She was listening intently as the man talked, so engrossed in what he was saying that she didn't even notice me walk in. I ground my teeth and walked up to the counter to order, trying to keep my eyes from wandering over to her table.

I was unsuccessful.

When I got my drink, I decided to say hi. That was what a friend would do, right? Of course it was. It had nothing to do with my inner caveman wanting to go over and stake my claim.

I put on my official Rosemary Mountain grin, the one that let people know I worked for them and was on their side. Then I walked over to their table with practiced nonchalance.

"Hey, Allison," I said when she looked up.

Relief flashed on her face. "Jackson! Hi! I've been wanting to check on you today. How are you?"

"I'm good," I said. "How about you? Who's your friend?"

The words almost came out with the casual tone I was going for.

This time, her eyes revealed irritation. "Jackson, meet Mike. Mike, this is my old friend Jackson."

Old friend. It was true. In fact, it's what I had insisted I wanted. But after that kiss last night, being referred to as an old friend felt like salt poured in a fresh cut.

"Nice to meet you," I said, sticking out my hand. I felt a sense of satisfaction when he shook mine with a noticeably less firm grip than my own.

"Nice to meet you, too," he said, though his eyes told a different story. I could read it all over his face. He was irritated as hell that I had interrupted whatever speech he was giving Allison.

But it was even more clear that she was grateful for it, and I was on her side, no matter what.

"Allison," I said, turning toward her, "my parents are driving in tonight. We're going to arrange a private burial for Russell, followed by a meal. Mom's pushing for Tuesday, and if anyone can get the arrangements together that quickly, it's her. It'd mean a lot if you came."

She reached over and squeezed my hand. "Of course I'll be there."

Mike frowned. "On a Tuesday? This short of notice? Won't you have patients?"

She gave him an annoyed look. "They can be rescheduled."

His eyebrows shot to the roof. "That seems unprofessional. What kind of clinic is this, anyway?"

Her jaw tightened as she took a deep breath, clearly trying to keep her temper under control. "Why do you care about my professional life, anyway? It's mine, not yours. And this is none of your business."

Score.

He frowned and put his hand over hers. "*You* are my business."

She delicately pulled her hand away. *Score number two.* "I can't wait to meet your parents," Allison said, turning back to me and ignoring Mike completely. "Please tell them thanks for the invitation. Shoot me a text with the details."

"I will," I promised.

Allison stood up to give me a quick hug before I left, scoring me yet another point. Mike's ears were practically steaming as he watched. I wasn't sure if Allison was even aware of the competition happening right under her nose, but if she was, she was making it clear that I was ahead.

But when I said goodbye and headed out the door, high from my win, a stab of guilt hit me. This was not how a friend acted. Mike was clearly a loser who didn't deserve her, and I felt zero guilt for knocking him down a peg or two. But I had no business competing with her potential boyfriends if I didn't plan on being one myself.

I was a man who lived by lines. Boundaries. Clear rules about right and wrong.

But with Allison, all my lines seemed to get swept away, and I found myself constantly losing perspective. Just another reason I needed to get some space. She brought out a side in me that reminded me entirely too much of Russell. He had been a man who lived in a world that was shaded with gray, only concerned with what he could get away with. Right and wrong didn't matter to him. Winning did.

Allison brought that out in me, just like Russell always said she would. No matter how much I loved her, I needed to stay away.

Chapter Twenty-Five

Allison

When my alarm clock went off Monday morning, I was even more exhausted than I had *before* the weekend. Mike had insisted on hanging around all day Sunday, and I'd hated every moment of it. When we had talked Saturday night, I had told him—again—it was really over and tried to give him the "closure" he'd said he needed by rehashing all my reasons as to why. After that, I couldn't imagine either of us had anything left to say. But even after I kicked him out and made him stay at a hotel, he showed back up Sunday morning, wanting to hang out "as friends."

His friendship was honestly the last thing I wanted at that point.

But having been raised by a Southern mama, I felt unable to say no. The rules of Southern hospitality were unbreakable. So I attempted to show him around town—and keep him out of my house as much as possible. Having him there, where Jackson and I had shared that kiss and so many other amazing moments, felt wrong. Like he tainted the memories somehow with his presence. But even when we wrapped up dinner Sunday evening and I tried to say goodbye, he followed me back to my house and hung around until late, despite my less-than-subtle attempts to get him to leave.

The man was infuriating. He seemed to think that if he just talked long enough, I would eventually agree I had overreacted and come back to Memphis—and him. It didn't matter that I didn't have a job there, he argued. He had scored a good position, even if it wasn't the one he wanted, and would be making enough to support me while I "figured things out."

He didn't seem to understand that I had already figured things out on my own. Despite everything that had gone down since I'd arrived, I actually liked it here. It was home. And now that I had reconnected with Jackson, I couldn't imagine what I had ever seen in Mike. Jackson was my new standard for what a man should be, and Mike would never measure up.

Although, my resolution to stay in Rosemary Mountain wavered when I got to the clinic and had to face Beverly again. She waltzed uninvited into my office as I was looking over my charts for the day.

"Heard you had an interesting weekend," she said as if it were a personal triumph. She plopped into the chair across from my desk, staring at me expectantly.

"Oh yeah? Which part?"

"The news is all over town. Russell Sharp? He could have killed you!" Her face practically lit up with glee.

And you would have likely danced on my grave.

"So I've been told," I said, continuing to stare at my charts like they were the most interesting thing in the world.

"I also heard you had a fancy boyfriend visiting from the city. The girls said he's a real sharp dresser and a big tipper."

"Not a boyfriend," I corrected, though I wasn't about to tell her he was an ex. "A colleague. We went to medical school together. And how do you know all this anyway?" I asked, finally looking up.

She rolled her eyes. "There are no secrets in Rosemary Mountain."

My eyebrows lifted. "Well, I'd say you're wrong about that. But apparently *I'm* not allowed to have secrets here."

"If you don't like it, you can always go back to the city," she suggested with a glint in her eye before getting up and walking out, apparently realizing I wasn't going to give her any more dirt. She popped her head back through the doorway for one final dig. "Rumor has it your boyfriend was begging you to come back to him. Might be the best move you can make, honey. Let's face it. You're never going to fit in here."

I refused to dignify that with an answer.

Instead, I picked my phone up to ask Jackson if he wanted to meet for dinner, But I stopped, realizing I shouldn't. His parents were in town. He'd be with them tonight, and if I messaged him, he'd feel obligated to invite me. I was dying to meet the people who had raised him, but the last thing I wanted was to infringe on their family time.

I didn't want to eat at a restaurant alone, I was tired of takeout, and I barely had anything at the house. But if I made a quick grocery trip, I could throw together a nice dinner and even have leftovers for a few days. Maybe pasta with mushrooms and veggies, or a quick curry. I could be in and out of the store in ten minutes, Then I could go home, throw on some sweats, and have a leisurely dinner to recharge.

My "quick" grocery run stretched into half an hour. Instead of being the town outcast, I was now a celebrity of sorts. Multiple people stopped to tell me they were glad I was safe, had been meaning to come establish care with me, and would be sure to make an appointment soon. Apparently, Russell had been even more hated than my own father, and by making himself my enemy, he had aligned me with the town. It wasn't how I had planned to win their acceptance, but I'd take it.

As I wheeled my cart to the checkout, I saw one of my current patients in line ahead of me: a pregnant woman who, from the looks of it, was grocery shopping in active labor.

"Trudy," I said, tapping her on the shoulder. "Are you feeling okay?"

She turned to me, her face pinched and white. "Oh, hi, Dr. Bell. Just false labor pains, I think."

I looked at her skeptically. "Are you sure?"

"Oh, sure, yeah. It's too early for anything else." She closed her eyes tightly, gripping the handle of her shopping cart as she breathed through a contraction.

"Right," I said, searching my mental files for her due date. I couldn't be sure without checking, but I thought she had told me the baby was due in September, which definitely made this too early.

However, my fears were confirmed when a sudden gush of water flowed from her skirt onto the floor.

"Oh, my," she said, her eyes wide as she looked down and saw what had happened.

"You're definitely in labor. We need to get you to the hospital," I said gently.

"No." She shook her head emphatically. "I'm going to check out my groceries. Then I'm going home and birthing this baby in my bed, the same way I've birthed all my babies."

"Trudy," I said, my stomach dropping, "You told me you're due in September, right? I don't want to scare you. But this is very concerning medically speaking. The baby isn't fully developed yet. It's crucial we get you to the hospital. I assure you they have the best training and equipment and it's the safest place for you *and* the baby. I'll drive you there myself."

"No," she repeated, grabbing my hand so hard I knew it would leave a bruise. She shook her head frantically. "If you want to help me, call Fiona. She'll know what to do."

"Fiona's a midwife. You need a doctor—and a hospital." I kept my tone firm, hoping to impress the seriousness of the matter on her.

She shook her head, closing her eyes as she braced against the pain of another contraction. "I'll be driving home. Then I'll call Fiona myself, since you refuse to be of any help to me. Thank you anyway." The woman actually pushed her shopping cart forward in the line and started unloading it on the register belt.

Everything warred within me, but I couldn't let her walk out to deliver that baby at home.

"Stop," I said, rushing to her side. I looked quickly at the carts, making some mental calculations, and pulled a wad of bills out of my purse to hand to the cashier. "Can you take care of these groceries? Bag up both our carts. I'll send someone to pick everything up. Keep the change."

"Um, sure," the guy said, taking my cash. His eyes lit up as he flipped through it and did his own mental math, realizing he was going to get a generous tip for his trouble. He straightened his posture and nodded. "Yes, ma'am. I'll take care of it."

"Thank you," I said, then turned my attention to Trudy. "I'll take you home. We'll call Fiona on the way, and I'll stay with you, okay? But listen. You have to promise that if Fiona says you need to go to the hospital, you'll go. If she says that's where you need to be, that means it's serious, right?"

She hesitated for just a moment, then nodded. "If Fiona says to go, I'll go. But only her."

"Okay." I breathed a sigh of relief. Fiona would surely listen to reason and could manage the situation. In the meantime, I would at least be there to monitor.

I helped Trudy to my car. The walk was excruciatingly slow, but we finally made it. She choked out directions to her house, and I put on my flashers and began speeding that direction, calling Fiona on the way.

"Hello?" she answered, her voice filling the car through my speakers.

"Fiona? It's Allison—" I began, but Trudy cut me off.

"Fiona, it's time," she said, breathing heavily. "How quick can you get to my house?"

"Trudy? Is that you?" Fiona asked sharply.

"It's me. The baby's decided to make his appearance early," she said, reaching over to squeeze my hand as another contraction hit.

There was a brief pause before Fiona spoke. "I'm on my way," she said, her voice somehow soothing even me. "You're lucky I took it to mind to take a trip to the library today. I'll be at your house in less than five minutes. How far apart are the contractions?"

"About four minutes," I answered.

"Oh my," Fiona said. "Lucky indeed. Hang tight now." She ended the call, seemingly in as much of a hurry as I was.

"It'll be alright now," Trudy said, patting my hand as if it were her job to comfort me instead of the other way around. "You'll see. Fiona's the best there is. I'll be in good hands with her by my side."

But Fiona could be the best midwife in the country and it wouldn't matter. The baby was viable, but it was way too early to be taking a chance with a home birth. I could only pray Fiona would insist on taking her to the hospital. Otherwise, I was going to make two people very unhappy when I called an ambulance. Or perhaps asked a certain deputy to haul her to the hospital himself.

CHAPTER TWENTY-SIX

Jackson

I was packing up to head out from work when my cell phone rang. *Allison.* My heart accelerated. Last time she had called, it was because Russell was in her house. I hoped this time it was good news and not something else going wrong in her life.

"What's up?" I answered, grabbing my gear and heading out to my truck with a quick wave goodbye to my coworkers.

"I'm so sorry to bother you," she said, speaking quickly—and based on the tone of her voice, something was definitely wrong. "But I really need a favor. Are you busy right now?"

"You're never a bother," I said. "And I'm just walking out from work. What do you need?"

"Could you swing by Bob's Market and pick up two grocery orders for me? They're already paid for and bagged, ready to go. One is mine. One is Trudy Hamilton's. She went into labor at the store. I'm driving her home."

"To Trudy's house, you mean?"

"Yes." Allison's voice was pinched, like she didn't approve. "Fiona's her midwife."

"Got it." I opened the truck door and tossed my stuff onto the passenger's seat. "I know where she lives. I'll grab everything and be right there."

"Thanks, Jackson."

"Anytime, Allison. Anytime."

Chapter Twenty-Seven

Allison

Fiona's steel-blue truck stopped in front of Trudy's house just as I pulled into the driveway. The spry woman hopped out of the cab, moving like someone half her age. She gave a little wave, then pulled a bag from the back and headed up the driveway, catching up to us before we had even made it in the door.

Trudy visibly relaxed in Fiona's presence. Relief flooded her features, and she finally let go of the death grip she had on my hand. "Oh, Fiona," she said, her shoulders sagging. "I'm so glad you're here."

"There, there," Fiona soothed, patting her gently and taking over as emotional support while I fumbled with the keys Trudy had shoved into my hand.

I got the door open and ushered her inside, helping her into the bedroom, where Fiona immediately began setting up equipment. I walked out and paced the living room, trying to decide what to do next. This was not okay. This was not a situation for a midwife. Truthfully, I had expected Fiona to tell the woman to go to the hospital when we called. Surely she knew how dangerous this situation was for the baby. We needed NICU and a full support team. It was the only chance the infant had.

I shook my head and clenched my fists, wishing I would have driven Trudy straight to the hospital no matter what she'd said. But I had told her I would take her home, and after saying that, I couldn't bring myself to go against it. Something had to be done though, before this baby was born without a fighting chance.

With my mind made up, I took a deep breath, braced my shoulders, and headed toward the bedroom to take over.

Fiona came out as I did with a warning look on her face.

"Dr. Bell," she said quietly, leading me away from the door. "You're wound up tighter than a long-tailed cat in a room full of rocking chairs. Surely I don't have to tell you that's not helpful for Trudy."

"Fiona," I said, meeting her eyes. "We have to go to a hospital. You understand that, right?"

Fiona looked up sharply. "A hospital? No, I don't think that's needed right now. In fact, that would be the worst thing in the world."

I forced myself to take a deep breath before responding, hoping it gave me at least a little bit of grace—though I was losing patience. "I understand you're renowned as a midwife, but unless you know something I don't, you're not equipped to be a neonatal intensive care unit," I said, unable to keep the sarcasm out of my voice.

Fiona's face blanked. "NICU? Why in the world would you be thinking we need NICU? You haven't even seen the babe yet."

"Because," I said, gritting my teeth, "I don't have to see the baby to know. NICU is necessary one hundred percent of the time for a baby who *hasn't even fully formed his lungs yet.*"

Fiona stared at me with confusion on her face before letting out a breath. "Oh, I think I understand," she said, shaking her head. "Trudy told you she was due on September seventeenth, didn't she?"

"Yes, that's right."

She waved a hand at me and headed toward the kitchen. "That's just wishful thinking on her part." She looked back at me over her shoulder with a faint look of amusement on her face. "Didn't you realize she's far beyond that?"

"What do you mean?" I sputtered, still standing in place.

"She's thirty-seven weeks, dear."

"What?" I was utterly confused. "Are you sure?"

Fiona nodded, fighting back a smile. "She came to me at six weeks and I've followed her the whole time. All the dates are logged in my notebook, if you need reassurance. Though I'm surprised an *educated* doctor like yourself didn't notice the signs of late pregnancy or how her belly had already dropped." She tried to keep her face straight, but she couldn't hide her amusement. She was right, I was wrong, and it tickled her to death.

I paused and took a breath, thinking the situation over with different eyes. She wasn't wrong. Trudy was a bit swollen and carrying quite low, though it wasn't as if that were an exact indicator. She wasn't nearly as large as I would have expected for being full term with a fifth baby, but I knew that some women were just blessed that way. When I had seen her, she was at sick call for a head cold—not a prenatal visit. I had asked her due date and accepted it as the gospel truth without thinking much about it. When I'd asked the date of her last period, she'd waved me off, saying she couldn't possibly remember at this point. Even so, Fiona was right. I should have realized something was off.

"Why would she tell me she was due on September seventeenth?" I asked, still confused.

"Because September seventeen is the feast day for St. Hildegard." Fiona chuckled. "She asked the saint for help conceiving. She argued with me the entire pregnancy that her baby would be born on the good saint's feast day."

"I see," I said as I breathed out some of the tension I had been carrying. This wasn't the emergency I'd thought it was. I was grateful but also annoyed with myself.

Fiona came back and patted my arm, her amused expression replaced by one of sympathy. "You may be one of our own, but you're also new to town, so you don't know Trudy. She's what you might call a bit stubborn and more than a wee bit superstitious. You'll have to learn to take what she says with a grain of salt."

"Apparently," I replied, shaking my head. How could I not have realized she was full term? "I feel like the most oblivious doctor in the world."

"Don't be so hard on yourself," Fiona said with kindness in her voice. "And don't be so hard on her, either. She's had a rough time of it lately. Within the past three years, she's lost her mother, her father, and her sister—all in hospitals, you see. Her sister died last year, not too long after giving birth, while they were all still at the hospital celebrating the new baby. Preeclampsia followed by a stroke."

"That's terrible," I said, my annoyance gone as a wave of empathy rolled through me. "It's so frustrating that, even with all our medical advances, tragedies like that still happen."

"Yep," Fiona said, nodding. "Very sad situation. Trudy can't set foot in a hospital now without having a panic attack. It's too tainted with death for her. The best place for her is here at home, where we can get her to calm down a bit. And you see, it's not necessary after all, at least as far as we know right now. She's a bit dramatic about labor, but I think we're doing just fine."

"Okay," I said, nodding. It hit me that, despite all of my training, I still had a lot to learn about how to work with people in Rosemary Mountain. I hesitated, then swallowed my pride and asked, "Fiona, do you mind if I stay? I don't want to take over or get in your way, but I'd like to help if I can. I'd like to, well, learn from you. There's a lot I've forgotten about working with people instead of working for a system."

Fiona beamed. "As long as it's fine with Trudy, it's fine with me. Besides, I wouldn't mind the extra set of hands," she admitted. "I'm not as young as I once was."

"Thank you." I started to ask her a question, but we were interrupted by a cry. We ran back to the bedroom, where Trudy was gripping the sheets, her face white as she worked through a contraction.

"Fiona!" she said when she could finally speak. "I need the ax!"

Fiona nodded solemnly. "I'll get it." She dashed off before I could ask.

I moved to Trudy's side and attempted to soothe her. Fiona returned quickly, carrying a giant wood ax on her shoulder. I felt all the blood drain from my face as she moved toward the woman in the bed.

"What—" My jaw dropped. I didn't even know what to ask.

Fiona showed her the ax, then crouched down and shoved it under the bed.

Trudy took a deep breath and smiled. "Thank you, Fiona," she said, reaching out to squeeze the woman's hand. "That's better."

"Of course, dear. I'm going to get the rest of my supplies, okay? Won't be much longer now. You called me in the nick of time for this one." Fiona tenderly stroked the woman's hair away from her face.

Trudy smiled and nodded, looking peaceful even as another contraction began.

I followed Fiona out of the room. "What just happened?" I sputtered. "What in the world?"

"The ax," Fiona explained. "It's an old Appalachian tradition. It's said to cut the pain."

My jaw dropped. Again. "But that doesn't work."

Fiona's face crinkled in amusement. "Seems to, doesn't it?" she said, pointing to the bedroom where Trudy was no longer screaming in agony.

"But that's ridiculous. It's an ax."

"I think you might prefer to think of it as a placebo effect," Fiona said with a wink. "Sometimes, if you believe something works, it will. Now, come on. Help me carry in the rest of my things. It's time to get serious."

The woman marched out of the house on a mission, and I followed her, my jaw trailing somewhere behind me on the floor.

TIME BLURRED THEN SEEMED TO STAND STILL ALTOGETHER while I assisted Fiona. It was a completely different experience than the hospital births I had attended, and while part of me still longed for the support staff, monitoring equipment, and sterile environment of a hospital—and the knowledge that NICU was right around the corner— I had to admit that this felt different in a good way. Fiona was as cool as a cucumber, taking everything that came with practiced wisdom, as if she had done this a thousand times before—which she likely had. She was probably more experienced than any doctor in labor and delivery at our little hospital.

Trudy had calmed significantly with Fiona's presence and with the ax—a placebo effect I still wanted to shake my head at but couldn't deny. The room felt peaceful, filled with sacred expectation, when she finally pushed her baby into our world.

A healthy nine-pound baby with a head full of black hair and a cry that spoke of lungs as fully developed as I could have possibly hoped for.

"He's beautiful," I gasped, already half in love, as Fiona placed him gently on his mother's bare chest.

"Every baby is," Fiona said, laughing. "But he's a handsome one, alright. That hair! And look at that smile. It's a good sign, you know. A smiling newborn means he has angels watching over him."

"That he does," Trudy said, a blissful look of happiness settling on her as she stroked the sweet babe's cheek. He did indeed appear to be smiling, though I knew it was just a reflex smile and not a real one. But this time, I was wise enough not to ruin the moment.

"What are you going to name him?" I asked.

"I think I'll name him Gabriel," she replied, still gazing with love and adoration at this child she had just birthed. "If his daddy approves, that is."

"Did I hear my name?" A disheveled man ran into the room. "I'm sorry it took me so long to get here. Did I miss it all?" His eyes lit up when he spied the baby on his wife's chest, and he rushed over to get his first real look.

Trudy laughed. "You did. Once he decided he was coming, he came quickly."

"He's perfect," the man said, his voice thick with pride. "Has he got all ten fingers and all ten toes?"

Fiona laughed. "He does. I counted 'em twice. We'll give you two a minute, then be back to deal with the rest." She motioned for me to follow her out of the room.

"That was wonderful," I whispered as we closed the bedroom door behind us, giving the couple a moment of privacy with their newborn son. I felt almost high from the experience—and from the utter relief that Fiona was right and NICU wasn't needed after all.

"It always is." Fiona grinned. "Never gets old. Makes all the hard work worth it."

"You're very good at what you do," I said.

"I am," she agreed with a twinkle in her eye.

I wanted to hug her and ask her a million questions, but all my attention shifted when I caught sight of Jackson.

CHAPTER TWENTY-EIGHT

Jackson

I HAD BEEN PACING THE LIVING ROOM FOR WHAT FELT LIKE hours, feeling nearly as nervous as I imagined I would if someone was having *my* baby in there. Just dropping off groceries didn't feel like enough. I had unpacked Trudy's and put Allison's in a cooler in my truck with a fresh bag of ice. Then I had waited. And waited. And waited some more.

When Allison and Fiona emerged from the bedroom, flushed with joy as they congratulated each other on their good work, all I could think was that Allison had never looked more beautiful.

Then she looked at me and her whole face lit up, and somehow she leveled that beauty up even more.

"I forgot all about the groceries," she said, laughing. "I'll help you carry them in."

"No need. They're all put away. Yours are in a cooler waiting on you."

"Thank you," she said, tilting her face and giving me a smile. Her eyes radiated happiness. "That was amazing."

"Miracle of life, huh?" I asked, unable to hold back a grin of my own.

"It really was. I thought I wanted to go home and crash in front of the TV tonight, but this was so much better."

"Don't worry," Fiona said, interjecting herself into the conversation from where she was starting to scrub things in the kitchen sink. "You'll get home and crash in front of the TV anyway. Unless you have better things to do." She winked at Allison, then gave me a meaningful look.

I felt my face turn red.

Allison took a tiny step backward. "Oh, Jackson," she said, her mood instantly shifting. "Your parents are in town. I completely forgot. I've taken you away from them for entirely too long."

"It's okay," I said. "I told them I was going to hang around until I made sure things were okay here. Mom's cooking dinner, and I'll head over in a few minutes, but I couldn't bring myself to leave until I knew everything was alright."

"Give me your keys and I'll go move everything to my car," Allison said.

"I'll do it—" I started to protest, but she interrupted me.

"No, let me do it—please." She laughed. "I need an outlet for all this energy bubbling up inside me right now. I should be exhausted, but I feel like I could run a marathon."

"Alright." I smiled and tossed her my truck keys.

She practically danced out the door, still vibrating from the joy of what she had just witnessed.

"There are better ways than that to burn off excess energy," Fiona called out, turning around to wink at me again. "You should take that girl home, Jackson."

"We're just friends," I said, joining her in the kitchen. I leaned against the counter and watched as she went to work scrubbing dishes in the sink.

"Right, and I'm Mother Teresa," she muttered under her breath.

"You practically are."

She looked up and grinned. Then her face went serious as she peered at me with her sharp blue eyes. It was a look I was familiar with, though I wasn't often on the receiving end of it. Usually, Daphne was the one about to get questioned. I swore Fiona should have joined the sheriff's office and worked for us as an interrogator.

"Now, Jackson," she said, pointing her finger at me. "It's clear as day you've got something troubling you."

"Well, I don't know if you heard, but Russell just died. So there's that."

"Yeah, I heard," she said, nodding. "But that's not it. Come on, now." She rinsed the soap bubbles off her hands and turned toward the stove. "Pull up a chair," she said, pointing to the chairs surrounding the little kitchen table. "I'm going to put on the teakettle."

And even though I was used to being the one giving the orders, I did.

"I'm going to make some tea and we're going to have us a little talk before you go. Okay?"

"Yes, ma'am," I muttered.

The woman had cast a spell over me, and all I could do was obey her. I realized I should have been taking notes, seeing if I could mimic her natural authority when I interviewed suspects. How a short little woman in her seventies could command everyone around her was beyond me. But she did it. I had even seen the sheriff himself jump to attention when she walked in the room.

"Now," she said, having lit the burner on the stove and placed the teakettle on top. She sat across from me and leaned forward, propping her chin on her fist. "Tell old Fiona what's troubling you."

I groaned and scrubbed my hands over my face. "I hate that I come from him." I muttered it under my breath, but she still heard.

"Not much you can do about that," she said drily. "We don't get much of a choice in the matter, now do we? That sweet baby we just delivered didn't get a choice over his parents, either. Now, as it turns out, he got pretty lucky. You didn't. But you've made a good life for yourself anyway, haven't you?"

I nodded reluctantly. "Yes, but even with him gone, he's still part of me. I'm his son. People in town know where I came from."

"So what?" She shrugged like it didn't matter at all. "It's not like they don't love you anyway. You're a hero, son. Beloved by the whole town. And that didn't happen until *after* you came clean about who you are and where you came from. The only one who seems to care anymore is you."

I dropped my head. "I work so hard to be different than him. But I'm still in his shadow. You don't think everyone's opinion of me would change in a heartbeat if I slipped up even once? Let's say I lost my cool on an arrest, got too physical with a suspect. Everyone in town would be whispering about how Russell's son finally showed his true colors."

She peered at me. "Maybe. But seeing as you're not the type to do something like that, why are we even worried about it? I don't think you're telling me everything. Come on. You can open up to old Fiona. You're practically family, son."

A bitter longing hit my heart. Practically family, yes, thanks to the sheriff and how his little created family had embraced me. But I'd never fit in. Not truly.

After all, I came from Russell Sharp.

"My life used to be split into two parts," I said, trying to explain. "First, there was my life as Jackson Sharp. Pitiful little Jackson, the kid Russell liked to beat up on. Then I got a new life as Jackson Ford. Fresh start, like I'd won the lottery. A chance to create my own future instead of being doomed to the one Russell planned for me. But now, the past and the present are all getting jumbled together. I don't know, Fiona." I broke off as Allison walked back in.

Fiona immediately transformed, slumping and looking terribly exhausted. "Oh, dear, I'm glad you're back. I'm afraid I'm plumb worn out. Jackson's getting some tea for me, but would you go tend to Trudy? I think I need to rest a few minutes before I head back in there to deal with the afterbirth." She held a fluttering hand to her head.

Allison's face grew concerned. "Of course. Jackson, holler at me if you need anything." She moved out of Fiona's sight and mouthed, "She looks awful," to me, shaking her head.

I just nodded, keeping my face serious even though I was fighting back a grin. I had seen Fiona's elderly woman act before. She could be extremely manipulative when she needed to be.

When Allison disappeared down the hallway, Fiona sat back up. "Now, where were we?"

I just shook my head. But the humor had me feeling lighter—and somehow able to open up more. "Sometimes I think I must be as broken as he is," I confessed. "Moving back here was a terrible idea, you know? I should have kept the two parts of my life completely separate. Should have stayed in Nashville and never set foot in this town again. You know I had been free of nightmares for years until I moved back here?"

She cocked her head. "So why did you come back?"

I shrugged and attempted to appear lighthearted. "I guess I never stopped missing the mountain. Despite everything, it felt like home."

She nodded. "I know what you mean. But there's more to it than that. I think you were pulled back because this is where you're supposed to be. Your fate is here."

I stared at her a moment, then confessed the thing I'd never told another soul. "Russell always said the Sharp blood would awaken in me, and sometimes... Sometimes I wonder if that's why I really came back. Like it was inevitable, and I knew it, and I was trying to get away from my parents so they wouldn't see me turn into him."

She flattened her lips in disapproval. "Russell said a lot of things. Doesn't make them true."

"It feels true," I said. It did. It felt like a curse that had been spoken over me, one I could never break.

She leaned forward and put her hand over mine. "You can't change where you came from. But you can change your future. You get to decide, Jackson. Despite all the good you've done, you're still walking around thinking of yourself as Russell Sharp's kid. Of all the ways you could think about yourself, why would you choose that one?"

"Because it's true," I said, confused. "Biologically speaking, he's my father."

She waved a hand of dismissal. "Biologically speaking, Allison is Brent's daughter, but the biggest difference between you and her is that she doesn't walk around thinking of herself that way. Can I give you a piece of advice, son?"

"Sure," I said, knowing she would give it no matter what I said anyway.

"When you bury Russell tomorrow, why don't you let that story you've been telling yourself die too?"

"What do you mean?"

"Stop telling yourself the story that you're Russell Sharp's son. And decide who you actually want to be."

"I'll try," I said. It was the most honest answer I could give her.

She patted my knee. "That's all I ask. And about those nightmares. I'll bring you some tea tomorrow. A blend of herbs to encourage sleep and calm the nervous system. Something to remind your body that you're safe now."

Was I, though? Because even though we'd be putting Russell in the ground tomorrow, I didn't feel safe. In fact, something nagged at me, like there was something I hadn't put together quite yet. A piece of the puzzle I was missing.

Maybe it was paranoia, but I didn't feel safe at all.

Chapter Twenty-Nine

Allison

MUCH TO MY DISAPPOINTMENT, JACKSON LEFT BEFORE I could say goodbye. Shortly after asking me to take over, Fiona came back into the bedroom looking as refreshed and energetic as ever. I slipped out, planning to talk to Jackson, but he was gone.

After there was truly nothing left to be done and even Fiona was getting ready to leave, I reluctantly packed myself up and headed toward home. A car pulled out of Trudy's neighborhood behind me and followed as I wound my way through town, heading toward the highway. My nerves prickled with fear. I stopped using my blinker and sped up, trying to put some space between us. The car sped up too, keeping pace.

When I got to the lonely road where I lived, I contemplated driving straight past my house and taking the loop back to Jackson's apartment. But then I rolled my eyes, realizing what my brain was probably doing. I missed Jackson, so it was probably just inventing an excuse to see him again. Russell was dead. There wasn't a threat anymore. I was safe, and it was just a coincidence that someone was taking the same route as I was.

When I turned into my driveway and the other car kept going on the main road, I breathed a sigh of relief and shook my head, annoyed at how very silly I had become.

TUESDAY MORNING BROUGHT GRAY SKIES AND THE THREAT of rain. It felt fitting for a day when Jackson would be putting his father to rest. With the exhaustion of yesterday finally setting in, I had to force myself out of bed. All I really wanted to do was pull the covers over my head and sleep. But I had only canceled my afternoon patients for the funeral. Everyone expected me at the clinic for the morning slots.

For about three minutes, I debated about calling in sick. But I knew if I did and Beverly found out I went to the funeral, I would never live it down. She'd make sure every patient I had knew I had lied. So I finally groaned, threw the covers off, and rolled out of bed. After a much needed cup of coffee, I admitted to myself it was good that I was staying on routine—for my own sake as much as my patients.

Right now, I needed to feel like things were as normal as possible. With everything that had happened, it felt like things had changed between me and Jackson. He was putting distance there after all. I could feel it. It felt like something was missing in my life without our normal routine.

I shook my head as I turned the shower on to get the water heating up. I didn't miss our routine. I missed *him*. I missed my best friend. And it killed me that I wasn't sure I was going to ever fully get him back.

I went to my dresser to grab fresh underwear, but I paused when I opened the drawer. Something was off. I wasn't sure what at first, but I quickly realized what the problem was. I organized my underwear drawer by type. But today, some of the pieces were in the wrong sections. One of my strapless bras was stuck in with my sports bras. And unless I was mistaken, my panty section looked...sparse. I could almost swear some of it was missing.

Had Mike gone through my underwear drawer while he was here?

The thought made me shudder. He was absolutely gross, and I was so glad he had left town.

I closed the drawer, hit the shower, and tried to put all of it out of my mind. There was no reason to worry.

I almost believed it by the time I walked out the door to head to work.

WHEN I GOT TO THE CLINIC, BEVERLY WAS WAITING FOR ME outside my office. "Morning," I said, raising my thermos of coffee to her.

"Good morning, Dr. Bell," she said in the most respectful tone I'd ever heard come out of her mouth. "Can I talk to you for a minute?"

"Sure," I said as I unlocked my office door and motioned for her to go on in. "Have a seat. What's up?"

She sat and fiddled with her fingers, looking down at the ground. "Well, this isn't easy for me, but I guess I'd like to apologize to you."

I blinked rapidly, wondering if I had heard her correctly. "You'd like to...apologize?"

"Yes." She looked up with genuine remorse on her face. "Trudy Hamilton is my best friend. She called me last night and told me what you did for her. How you drove her home in your own car, even though she was a mess, and stayed there with her. How, even though you're a doctor and Fiona isn't, you let Fiona run the show and followed her orders."

"Fiona knows a lot more than I do about delivering babies. It made sense to let her take charge."

"Yeah, but"—she swallowed hard—"I think what I'm trying to say is that... Maybe I was wrong about you."

"Thank you for saying that," I said softly. "Beverly, I'd like for us to have a good working relationship. I'm here for at least two years. We might as well get along, right?"

"Right." She nodded. She hesitated, then spoke again. "I'm sorry if I misjudged you. I just thought that, since you were from the city, you'd think you were better than all of us. And you were this pretty little blonde thing looking like you'd stepped out of a fashion magazine and not really having any *experience,* and well, we all knew you'd, you know, 'pulled strings to get the job,' and—"

"Whoa," I said, holding a hand up. "I did *not* pull strings to get this job. I'm not even sure where you heard that."

"Oh," she said, blushing. "Well, maybe assumptions were made. And then when I saw you, I thought the rumor must be true, that you really *were* the kind of woman who'd sleep with someone just to climb the ladder, but..."

I was completely taken aback. "Actually," I said, "I'm here because I *wouldn't* do that."

"What?" She gave me a confused look.

I put my elbows on the desk and rubbed my temples, suddenly feeling even more tired than before. "Beverly, I was offered a much more prestigious job back in Memphis, making twice what I'm getting paid here, I might add. But when I went to my final interview, I found out that the offer was contingent upon me sleeping with the department head. I said no, and he said I'd never work there and threatened to black-list me in Memphis. *That's* why I had to uproot my life and take a job somewhere else. Because I'm *not* that kind of woman."

Beverly stared at me in shock. "Really?"

"Really."

She swallowed hard, tugging at the collar of her shirt like it was making her uncomfortable. "I guess that rumor really got twisted around, although I'm sure you can understand why."

"Not really."

"Well, everyone knows about your mama—" Beverly started, but she cut off when she saw my face. She took a deep breath and shook her head. "It doesn't matter. I'm genuinely sorry, Dr. Bell. I misjudged you in more ways than one."

"Wait," I said. "What do you mean everyone knows about my mama?" A wave of nausea rolled over me. There had been little comments about my mother, but I hadn't paid them too much attention—until now. I had a sinking feeling that I was about to find out the real reason people had shunned me when I first arrived in town.

Beverly just stared at me like she was afraid to speak. "You mean, you don't know?"

I shook my head.

"Dr. Bell, I don't..." She trailed off like she didn't know how to tell me.

"What is it? What does everyone but me seem to know about my family?"

She shifted nervously in her seat. "You're aware that your daddy liked to play cards, right?"

I nodded. "Yes. It's one of the reasons we left him."

"Well, your daddy didn't always have the money to pay his debts," she said, biting her lip.

"Right. Mama had to work long hours to make up for it all."

Beverly nodded slowly. "Your mama 'worked' to pay off his debts." She stared at me, like I still wasn't understanding.

But then I did. I felt the color drain from my face. "Beverly," I said, my voice trembling. "Are you suggesting my mother was a prostitute?" It couldn't be true. Could it? I flashed back to my childhood memories, remembering her sadness as she'd get dressed up and leave for work long after everyone else was home for the night. I wanted to throw up.

"Not a prostitute," Beverly said, holding her hands up in defense. "Not exactly, anyway. But it was common knowledge that if your daddy owed more than he could pay, he'd, well, offer something he could give."

My stomach clenched as the nausea threatened to win. "You mean..." I couldn't even voice it.

She just nodded.

"I need a minute alone. Please." I had a patient scheduled first thing, and I had to somehow pull myself together so I could do my job.

She nodded. "I'm sorry, Dr. Bell. I didn't realize you never knew. Everyone else did." She looked like she was going to be sick too. She got up and slowly walked to the door. "For what it's worth, I'm glad your mama left. And I'm sorry for what she went through."

She slipped out and left me alone in my attempt to process a million memories through new information.

"ALRIGHT, BEVERLY, I'M HEADING OUT," I CALLED THAT afternoon as I locked up my office after finishing my last patient's chart.

She appeared around the corner, still looking timid after our earlier conversation. "I heard about the funeral. Give Jackson my condolences. I imagine this is a strange time for him."

"It is," I agreed, surprised by her perception—and how she really did seem to know every little thing happening in Rosemary Mountain.

She had known secrets about my own family that I had been blind to my entire life. If we were allies, I could actually use her, as I was quickly learning that patients here weren't always completely honest about their activities.

I gave her a small smile, trying to let her know there were no hard feelings despite what she had revealed, and turned to leave. It was amazing how much easier the day had gone now that we weren't at war with each other. My patients had been friendlier as well. I'd even convinced one man to try a different path than the opioids he had come in requesting. It gave me hope that I might be able to make a difference here after all, instead of just surviving the next two years.

I PULLED MY CAR UP TO THE GRAVESITE, WHERE JACKSON AND his parents were already gathered with Greg, Janet, and Fiona. Daphne and Emerson pulled in behind me, and back beyond them, I saw Cole's flashy car turning into the cemetery. It would be just us and the preacher today, a short, awkward service for a man who wouldn't really be missed by anyone.

I stepped out of the car, feeling chilled under the stark sky despite the summer heat. Graveyards had always freaked me out, and it felt even worse being here today. I couldn't pretend to grieve a man who'd literally planned to kill me. But I could be here for Jackson and support him.

I went straight to him, wishing I could erase the ghosts in his eyes. There was so much pain there, layered with guilt and embarrassment. All three things I hated for him to feel.

He looked down at me, piercing my very soul with those blue eyes of his. "Thank you for coming," he said quietly. "I didn't know if you would."

"Of course I came," I said. "I wouldn't want you to face this alone."

He tried to smile but failed. "I know this has to be weird for you, considering."

I gave him a brave smile. "Yes, but it's not exactly the weirdest thing we've ever done in a graveyard together."

He gave me a strange look, then laughed out loud. "I had forgotten all about that."

"What had you forgotten about?" asked the woman who had to be his mom. "I'm Jenna, by the way," she said, sticking a hand out for me to shake. Her smile was warm, and I instantly liked her.

"I'm Allison. You must be Jackson's mom."

"I am," she said, smiling. "But I still want to hear the graveyard story, since it made my son laugh on a day when I haven't even been able to get him to smile."

I looked at Jackson, who was grinning despite obvious embarrassment. "You tell it."

"Well," he said, flushing furiously. "Some of the older boys at school had told me that if you peed in a mason jar and buried it in a graveyard on the night of the full moon, then waited six weeks and dug it up again, it would have turned to liquid gold."

"But only if you buried it by the north-facing roots of an oak tree," I reminded him.

"That's right," he laughed, "I had forgotten that part. Anyway, I was pretty determined to score enough money to run away, and that seemed like a surefire way to do it. Allison stole a mason jar from her mama and gave it to me. I, um, filled it. Then we snuck away the night of the full moon to bury it."

Jenna closed her eyes and shook her head, even as a small smile played at her lips. "Did you ever go back and dig it up?"

He nodded. "Yep. Six weeks later exactly. We dug it up only to find that those boys were hiding behind the bushes, watching. They hooped and hollered and never let me live it down."

Greg had been listening with a look of amusement on his face. "Any of those boys still around here?"

Jackson looked right at him. "Oh yeah. In fact, I work with one of them every single day."

"Which one?" Greg asked, obviously surprised.

"Miller."

"You're kidding." This time, Greg was the one laughing out loud. "I should have known."

Janet stepped over. "The minister just pulled up," she said, motioning subtly with her head. "Perhaps we should all pretend to be a little more sober."

"Whatever for?" Fiona demanded, throwing her hands into the air. "It's not our fault Russell lived his life in such a way that there's not a sad person here today. If we can find a little laughter, I say all the better for us."

But I looked up at Jackson and saw the wave of grief pass over him. "Janet's right," I said, slipping my hand in his.

He squeezed tight and didn't let go.

Chapter Thirty

Jackson

I STOOD STIFF DURING THE SHORT SERVICE—A SERVICE THAT had to have been the strangest I had ever attended. I was often invited to funerals, as it was a small town and I knew pretty much everyone. But this was the first one I'd ever been to where every single eye was dry.

My own heart was heavy with grief, but it wasn't exactly because Russell was dead. Truth was, my life would be easier moving forward. At least I hoped it would. It was a kind of closure on the past, and if nothing else, I knew I wouldn't have to sleep with one eye open anymore. And there was intense relief that he couldn't hurt Allison.

But grief was there too, for what was and what never would be. A numb sadness that I hadn't been able to convince him to turn his life around. That I hadn't been worth fighting for. That I hadn't been enough—period.

Like she could somehow read my thoughts, Allison squeezed my hand. When the minister finally finished his awkward sermon, I turned to Allison and buried my head on her shoulder, sinking into her embrace. I wanted to cry—what kind of son couldn't shed a single tear for his own father? But I couldn't.

There just weren't any tears left for him.

I walked away from the grave without looking back.

GREG AND JANET HAD OFFERED THEIR HOME FOR DINNER after, even though Mom had insisted on taking care of the meal. Food was her love language, and based on the spread she had set out, she was intent on showing me all the love she possibly could.

"Did you stay up all night baking?" I asked, surveying the counters in wonder.

"Just about." She reached up and hugged me. "You doing okay?"

"Yeah." I looked down at this sweet woman who had taken me in, raised me, and loved me like I was her own. My heart swelled with gratitude for the million different ways she had been different than Russell. "Thanks, Mom. For everything."

She got teary-eyed but tried to hide it. "Well, of course," she sniffed. "Now, go eat. You need to put some meat on those bones. And I need to stop your dad from arguing with Greg."

"Arguing?" I asked, flicking my gaze toward the window. The two men were engaged in an animated conversation.

Mom rolled her eyes. "Something about sports. *I* don't know." She lifted her hands helplessly and walked outside to break up the discussion just as Allison walked through the door.

"Hey," I said. I had to clamp my mouth shut to stop myself from saying everything I wanted to say the minute I saw her—that she looked beautiful. That I couldn't stop thinking about her. That keeping my distance was killing me. That having her by my side was the only thing that really mattered to me anymore.

But I didn't. Not with Russell's words still playing in my head on repeat.

"Hey yourself." She glanced around the room, realizing we were alone. "Where is everyone?"

I nodded toward the deck. "Outside, setting up the table to eat.

Mom insisted we needed fresh air and sunshine, even though the sun's nowhere to be seen today."

"Maybe it will come out soon," Allison said.

"Maybe." I looked at her and for the first time today realized that I wasn't the only one shaken up. "What's wrong?"

She shook her head. "Nothing."

But I could see the hesitation in her eyes. "Allison. You don't have to lie to me."

She crossed her arms, rubbing herself for warmth—a move that I had learned was automatic when she felt scared. "It's been a rough day."

"What happened?"

She glanced outside to make sure no one could hear. "Beverly dropped a bombshell on me and I've been a mess ever since. She told me"—she dropped her voice to a whisper—"that Mama had to pay off Dad's gambling debts."

"What do you mean?"

Her face turned bright red. "I mean, she insinuated—no, flat-out said—that Daddy *traded* Mama to men when he lost big and couldn't pay. That all those nights she would dress up and leave to work late, she was basically prostituting herself out." Tears swam in Allison's eyes.

I opened my mouth to say that couldn't be true but stopped. Truth was, Beverly's story fit and answered a lot of questions about the past.

"Allison, what happened the night you moved away?"

She stared at me blankly for a moment before answering. "Mama woke me up. Told me we had to go. She started throwing all my clothes into a garbage bag before I realized what was happening."

"Brent had a poker game that night, didn't he? You told me your parents had fought about it before you came down to the creek."

She nodded slowly, catching up to my thoughts. "That's right." She raised her hands to her face and let out a long sigh, shaking her head. "She was always begging him to stop gambling. Now I understand."

"I'm so sorry," I said, pulling her into a hug. I held her in my arms, thinking over a million moments from my childhood that made sense now.

How Russell would make snide remarks about how he wished *he* could get in on Brent's poker games. But to play at those games, you had to have money or something better to bet. He'd sneer at my mother and tell her she'd be more valuable to him if she took better care of herself.

As much as I hated to admit it, Beverly's story added up. And I couldn't blame Allison's mom for leaving, no matter how much it had ripped me apart.

"Are you okay?" I asked, stroking a hand down her silky hair.

She sniffed. "Yeah. Look at me." She pulled back and shook her head, giving me a rueful smile. "You're supposed to be the one grieving today, not me."

"I guess we both have some things to bury from the past."

"Yeah. I guess so."

"Have you talked to your mom about any of this yet?"

She shook her head. "No. I'm not ready. I don't even know what to say. She never told me any of this, so I imagine she's pretty ashamed." Tears welled up in her eyes again. "And I'm so angry at her."

"That may not be fair," I said, shaking my head. "We don't know the whole story, but my gut says she was a victim, not a willing participant. At least not a fully willing one. Otherwise, why would she have left?"

"I'm not angry about that," Allison explained. "I'm angry because, after everything she went through, she still wants me to get back together with Mike—a man who practically asked me to do the same exact thing for a job. If she knew what it was like to be with someone who..." She clamped her mouth shut as Mom walked in the back door.

"Whew," Mom said brightly, glancing at each of us in turn but apparently choosing to pretend she hadn't just walked in on what was obviously an emotional conversation. "I think I got things sorted out. But your father needs to talk to you." She motioned for me to go outside.

The last thing I wanted to do was leave Allison's side, but Mom opened the door and didn't give me much of a choice. I glanced at Allison, who waved me on, letting me know we could talk later. I gave her a small smile before I headed out, hoping she would be okay.

After all, I was leaving her with an interrogator who was second only to Fiona—and who clearly had just orchestrated a private conversation.

CHAPTER THIRTY-ONE

Allison

Jenna gave me a warm smile. "Allison, I'm so glad you made it."

"Thank you for inviting me," I said automatically.

"Of course," she said. "Now, I don't want to pry into anything that isn't my business, but you've clearly been crying and I know it can't be over Russell. Is everything okay between you and Jackson?"

"Um, yes," I stammered. "I mean. We're just friends."

"Hmmm," she said, giving me a knowing smile. "So that wasn't a breakup I just walked in on? Sorry to be so forward." She lifted a tray and offered me a cookie. "I suppose I can't help myself."

It was such a motherly thing to do that I couldn't help but smile. "That's okay. I don't mind you being forward. But to answer your question, I'd had a rough morning at the clinic and was telling Jackson about it. That's all." I took a bite of the cookie and jerked my head back in surprise. "Wow, that's delicious. Like really, really delicious."

"I like to bake, and I tend to think chocolate makes everything better," she said, shrugging.

"Same." I adored her already.

"You know," she said, giving me a long look before taking a cookie for herself. "I've wanted to meet you for a very long time."

"Me?" I asked, surprised. "Why?"

She turned her gaze toward the big windows off the kitchen, where we could see Jackson and his dad having a quiet discussion away from the rest of the group. "When Jackson first came to us, he was closed off. Wouldn't talk to us at all, other than 'yes, sir' or 'no, ma'am.' He was respectful, quiet, and probably scared out of his mind. Not that I blame him. Foster care has to be a terrifying experience for children."

"Better than where he had been, obviously," I pointed out.

She nodded. "Yes. But kids don't always know that at first. The devil you know is never as scary as the devil you don't. Besides, foster care seems like a crapshoot to me. There are too many horror stories about awful homes where children are neglected and abused just as badly, if not worse, than they were before."

"That's true," I admitted.

"Jackson was cautious when he met us, and rightfully so. Part of being a foster parent is proving that you'll be a safe, trustworthy person. That takes a lot of time."

"I'd never thought about that."

She nodded. "For weeks, no matter what we did, it felt like he was walking around on eggshells, just trying not to be noticed. He didn't have any interest in an actual relationship with us at that point. He was biding time. He'd come home from school and I'd ask how his day was and get a quick, 'Fine, thank you,' with a timid smile before he disappeared into his bedroom to do homework. I'll never forget the day it all changed."

"What happened then?" I asked, entranced by the story. It was hard for me to imagine a version of Jackson where he was timid and quiet. This was a chapter of his life I had completely missed, and I was fascinated by it, even as my heart ached over the way life had chewed him up and spit him out.

Her eyes grew misty. "He had been living with us for a few weeks and was starting to relax a little," she said, smiling as she looked back out at him. "One day, he didn't disappear into his room when he came home from school. I was baking cookies—this same recipe, actually. It was a deliberate bribe, an attempt to entice him to hang around in the kitchen until they were done. It worked." She gave a gentle laugh. "Food always does with that one. Anyway, he sat down at the bar and watched me fold the chocolate chips into the dough. This time, I decided to try asking about something other than school."

"What did you ask him?"

"I told him I'd like to get to know him better. I said, 'Jackson, I'd love to know something that makes you happy. Something that makes you feel better when you're down.' I'll admit, I was expecting an answer like pizza or maybe a favorite TV show. I thought if he shared something with me that we could recreate, we would make it part of his life with us."

"That was sweet of you," I said, feeling a swell of gratitude for this woman who had cared enough about my childhood friend to want to make him feel more comfortable.

She just smiled. "He sat there thinking for a moment. Then his whole face changed. He gave me the first real smile I'd had from him, along with his answer. And you know what that answer was?"

"What?"

"You."

"Me?" Her statement caught me completely off guard.

She nodded. "You. He told me about his best friend, Allison, and how you two would slip off after school and play down at the creek. He told me no matter how bad the day had been, you made him feel like everything was going to be okay. It was the first real thing he had ever told me about himself."

Tears stung my eyes. "He meant a lot to me, too. Still does," I said, struggling to get the words out over the lump in my throat. I felt wave after wave of conflicting emotions. It was so hard to imagine Jackson living through everything he had, and I was so grateful to have been a source of comfort to him the way he'd been to me. But it also felt like I had abandoned him during the hardest period of all, and even though I hadn't had a choice in the matter, I hated it.

Jenna reached over and squeezed my hand. "I called his social worker the next day and asked if we could get you two back in touch," she said. "I even offered to drive here once a month so he could see you. It was clear your friendship had been a lifeline for him, and I didn't want him to lose it. But she did a little digging and said you had moved away too, and she didn't know where you were."

I nodded. "Yeah. Not long before Jackson went into foster care, my mother decided to move away. She wanted a fresh start and let me know visits were out of the question. I sent Jackson a letter but never heard back. He told me he never got it. I didn't know what had happened."

Her smile was empathetic. "You lost each other. But you've found each other now. And I hope I'm not crossing the line when I say I hope you'll have each other forever."

I was left speechless at her words.

Chapter Thirty-Two

Jackson

"Am I in trouble?" I joked as I approached Dad, repeating the phrase I had asked a million times as a kid, always needlessly worried that the good life I'd been given was going to get ripped out from underneath me if I made a mistake.

Dad stuck his hands inside his pockets, his face wrinkling up in that familiar smile. He was getting older now, with more lines on his face and white in his hair than the last time I'd seen him. Yet he was still young at heart, the same man who'd taken me in and taught me how to smile again.

"Oh, huge trouble," he said, joking back. He glanced through the windows, where we could see Mom offering Allison a cookie. He looked back at me and winked. "At least, I think your heart's in trouble. But I reckon she'll take good care of it."

I stilled beside him. "It can't be like that," I said.

He leaned back against the deck railing, shuffling change in his pocket. "Your mom said you'd say that. Care to tell me why not?"

I braced myself, leaning back beside him, thinking back to all the dad talks we'd had before. He had always been more of a goofball, the kind of guy who liked to chuck the ball around the yard with you or have water gun fights in the summer. Mom was usually the one who did most of the heart-to-hearts. But occasionally, she'd send him in for a "dad talk," just like this one. And though they were few and far between, I'd cherished every one of them.

He, more than anyone else, was the one I'd been able to talk to about growing up with Russell. I'd told him things I'd never told another soul—probably because those talks *were* so rare and I'd known there was a safety in his easygoing nature, that he'd never turn into one of those parents who wanted to rehash the hard stuff all the time. Like me, he'd rather leave some things unsaid and find joy in the present. It made him the easiest person to talk to when it really counted.

"You know about Russell," I said.

"What about him?"

It hurt to say it, even now. "Like it or not, I come from him. I have the Sharp blood."

Dad laughed out loud, shocking me. "Son, based on what I know about Russell, I'd say you couldn't be further from him as a person."

I shook my head. "That's only because I keep a tight control on myself. I choose to be different, I choose to laugh and grin and help people out. But..." I swallowed hard, feeling ashamed to say it—even to him. "I know where I come from. I know there's a monster living inside me. Sometimes I feel it, threatening to break through."

He turned toward me, taking on a serious look. "What do you mean?"

I couldn't meet his eyes, so I looked at the mountain instead. It took me a minute to even get the words out, and when I did, they felt like gravel in my throat. "Like when I'm tempted to cross the line on a case. When the thought crosses my mind that planting evidence would make things so much easier. Or when I go pick up a child abuser and can't help but think I'd really love to get a few punches in on him and pretend it was justified."

He didn't say anything

"I picked up a guy a few weeks ago, and I swear." I shook my head.

"After seeing his girlfriend in the hospital, half of me hoped he'd make a move on me. Do something—anything—where I could give him a taste of his own medicine."

"Okay. So you're tempted to cross the line sometimes. But have you ever actually done it?"

I thought it over. "Not those specific things, no. But I did cross a line once," I admitted. "Sort of, anyway."

"How so?"

I glanced over and saw curiosity on his face, not judgment. "I was stuck on a homicide investigation, and I arranged an opportunity for Daphne to be alone in a room with some evidence. I knew if she looked at it, she might get some insight I couldn't. I wanted to make her an official consultant but knew Greg wouldn't like it, so I did it unofficially instead. At best, it was a gray area."

Dad put a hand on my shoulder and looked at me solemnly. "My goodness. You're lucky you aren't in Rikers, being such a hardened criminal and all."

I cracked up, despite the heaviness in my heart.

"Son," he continued, "occasionally being tempted to do the wrong thing has nothing to do with being Russell's son. It's just part of being human. We're *all* tempted to take shortcuts or cross the line sometimes. Remember when you used to wake up screaming with nightmares? I tell you what, if I'd met Russell in a dark alley during those years, I'd probably be in jail right now."

"Really?" It was hard to believe. This was the man who would pull over on the side of the road to help a turtle cross so it wouldn't get injured.

"You bet your ass I would have. Used to daydream about it."

For some reason, that made me feel a whole lot better. "I've always felt like I had to work so hard to not be like him," I confessed. "And that I had to always be the happy, cheerful, smiling one. Like if I allowed myself to be angry, that part of me might grow and unleash into something awful."

Dad just rolled his eyes. "You're not Bruce Banner, son. I think we'll all be okay if you get angry sometimes."

"Maybe," I said, though I wasn't fully convinced.

"Look, it's clear as day you're head-over-heels in love with that woman in there. And I'd say it's pretty clear she's in love with you too. So if you're holding yourself back from a relationship with her because you're worried you're going to turn into Russell, I'd say you need to give yourself more credit than that."

I swallowed hard. "I've never let a woman get close. Russell always said my mother was the one who brought out the Sharp blood in him. He was sure it would be a woman to do it to me too. So I never risked it."

"But now part of you wants to risk it, don't you?"

"Yeah," I admitted. "But I don't want to hurt her."

"You will," Dad said, shrugging. He held a hand up when he saw my face. "I don't mean physically. You don't have that in you, no matter who your sperm donor was. But in relationships, we hurt people sometimes. It's just part of it. You think I've never hurt your mother? I have. I love that woman with all my heart, and yet I've hurt her and she's hurt me, because we're two human people who screw up sometimes."

He put his hand on my shoulder again. "You're a good man, Jackson. I'm proud of you, and I'll be proud of you, no matter what you decide about Allison. But I'm here to tell you that, sometimes, love is worth the risk."

"Is that what Mom sent you to tell me?" I asked, grinning.

"Actually, I think her exact words were that she's offended you're giving Russell so much credit for who you are when she's the one who went to the trouble to raise you." He winked at me.

"She said that, huh?"

"Nah. But I am. Don't forget, you may have come from Russell, but you've got me and your mom in you too." He glanced through the window to where Mom was pulling yet another dessert out of the oven. Like she could sense him looking, she turned around and blew him a kiss. He just grinned. "I'd like to think that gives you a leg up on everyone else, especially in the relationship department."

"You may be right," I said, turning my eyes from Mom to Allison, who was filling glasses with sweet tea. Just like Mom had with Dad, she lifted her head to look at me, giving me a little smile.

"Just think about it," Dad said.

"I will."

CHAPTER THIRTY-THREE

Allison

IN THE DAYS FOLLOWING RUSSELL'S FUNERAL, LIFE returned to normal. Jackson's parents went home to Nashville, and we settled back into our routine of texting throughout the day and eating dinner together every night.

The ease of our friendship had returned, but sometimes I'd catch him looking at me and wonder if he was rethinking our pact. Things remained completely platonic, but his touches lingered longer than they had before—his hand on the small of my back when he'd open the door for me, the way our fingers would brush when I passed him something at dinner. Our goodnight hugs had grown a little longer each night, and when he'd wrap his arms around me, it felt like he never wanted to let go. He'd look into my eyes with so much feeling that he seemed to be saying what he was terrified to speak aloud.

Somehow he made me feel deeply loved without ever actually saying it. It felt like we were characters in a Jane Austen story, expressing our devotion through finger grazes and longing looks. My inner romantic had awakened, and this unspoken courtship was making me fall head-over-heels in love with him.

And when Beverly bustled into my office Friday afternoon carrying a bouquet of roses, I thought my heart might burst.

"Looks like someone has a secret admirer," she said, her eyebrows shooting to the roof as she placed them on my desk. "Or maybe not so secret…"

I picked the card up and smiled. Jackson had left his name off of it, signing it only "devotedly yours." It was almost funny that someone who had such confidence at work could be so timid when it came to this.

"Do you know who they're from?" Beverly pressed again, always looking for the newest tidbit of gossip.

"A friend," I said simply. I wasn't ready for her, or anyone else for that matter, to know about what was developing between me and Jackson—especially when we hadn't even spoken it ourselves.

She looked annoyed. "I meant to tell you I got those meetings you requested scheduled this morning. They're all added to your calendar. You have two drug reps coming next week to talk to you about options for your new program, and Dr. Johnson is scheduled to meet with you Monday."

"Thank you, Beverly," I said, barely hearing her. I was too busy burying my face in the roses, daydreaming about what it would be like when Jackson finally kissed me again.

She cleared her throat. "I also ordered the supplies you requested."

"Great work," I said, still barely paying her any attention.

"Do you need anything else?" The irritation in her voice made me look up.

"No, I'm good," I replied, giving her a warm smile. "Thank you. Enjoy your weekend."

"You too," she said, a strange look on her face. She turned on her heels and walked out.

I sighed, realizing my romantic raptures had put a fresh fracture in my relationship with Beverly. It seemed to be two steps forward, one step back with her. Part of me still wished I had someone easier to manage working for me. Someone who didn't take things so personally, who didn't have to be handled with kid gloves.

On the other hand, my schedule had been almost completely full ever since I had taken care of Trudy. I knew that was largely due to Beverly's influence. She clearly had the power to help me turn this clinic around, and if I wanted to stay here, that's exactly what I had to do.

I'd have to find a way to bridge the gap again—without divulging anything about Jackson. That secret was still mine.

WHEN 4:15 HIT, I DECIDED TO TRY A MORALE-BOOSTING tactic. I went up to the front and addressed Danny and Beverly both.

"Exceptional work, guys," I said, even though I only meant it when it came to Beverly. Danny was still showing up late, screwing up basic vitals, and being generally lazy. We'd have to address it sooner rather than later, but not today. Today was for building the team. "We're finished with patients, so I vote we close up early and have a team meeting at O'Malley's. We need to discuss the new program, and I thought we could do it there instead of here. I promise to wrap up by five so you aren't stuck working late, and you can have a drink on me. Deal?"

Beverly looked from me to Danny then back again. The expression on her face said she clearly disapproved of my plan. But Danny was beaming. So she reluctantly gave a little nod.

"Great! I'll meet you there in ten minutes."

WHEN I ARRIVED AT O'MALLEY'S, DANNY WAS ALREADY IN A booth with a pint in front of him, but Beverly was nowhere to be found. I slid in across from him and pulled out my meeting notes.

"I saw you got flowers today," he said, giving me his weird little grin. "Did you like them?"

"I did," I said, glancing at my watch. "Hey, where's Beverly? It's not like her to be late."

He shrugged. "You know how she is. She's got to make sure everything's perfect before she leaves."

I hesitated, then decided maybe it was time to have our talk after all. "Yes. That's one reason why she's so good at her job."

He stared at me blankly, like he didn't understand what I was getting at.

"Danny, I've noticed a lot of your assessment information is incorrect. What do you think is going on with that?"

He blushed furiously. "What do you mean?"

"I mean, half the time the blood pressure information isn't even in there. Medication lists aren't being updated. The rooms aren't getting cleaned properly in between patients. Basic things that fall under your purview simply aren't being done. "

His blush turned to a glare. "If you don't like the way I'm doing my job, then maybe you need to find someone else to do it."

"Maybe I do," I said calmly. "But I know you have a long history at that clinic, and I'd like to make this work. I should have talked to you in the beginning about how I prefer for things to be done, and I apologize for not doing so. If you need to brush up on any skills or need any assistance, we can make that happen."

He picked up his drink and downed it. Then he stood up and walked off without saying a word.

After a tense meeting with Beverly, who still hadn't forgiven me for not dishing to her in my office, I dismissed her and waited for Jackson to arrive for dinner.

The moment he walked in, I felt half the tension I'd been carrying melt away.

"Hey," he said, flashing me the grin I loved so much as he slid in the booth across from me. "You look like you've had a long day."

"You have no idea," I groaned. "And my attempts at building team morale this afternoon were a complete failure."

"Hmmm. You know what you need?"

"A new staff?"

He laughed. "Nah. To blow off some steam. You free tomorrow?"

"I am. What do you have in mind?"

He grinned. "Just trust me."

. . .

SATURDAY MORNING CAME AND I DISCOVERED THAT JACKSON and I had entirely different ideas about what it looked like to blow off steam. What was pure fun for him had my body tensing in fear.

"Come on!" Sunlight glinted through the trees as Jackson raced barefoot down the path, motioning for me to catch up.

I bit my lip, hanging back. I knew exactly where this path led—and I didn't like it. "I don't know if this is a good idea," I called out, pausing.

"The Allison Bell I knew wasn't a chicken," he answered, grinning as he stopped on the path, waiting for me.

"The Allison Bell you knew hadn't done ER rotations yet."

He threw his head back and laughed. "Come on. I'll catch you." With that, he chucked off his shirt and jeans—making my mouth go dry at the sight. Then he gave me a salute and took off running.

Before I could holler out for him to stop, he had jumped. I ran to the edge, but he had already disappeared into the water below.

My heart nearly stopped. But in a split second, he emerged, his blond hair bobbing in the water.

"I told you it's fine," he called out. "The water's thirty feet deep here. No rocks. And it's only a fifteen-foot jump, despite what it looks like. Kids dive off this all summer long, every summer, and we haven't had a single injury. Go feet first and you'll be fine."

"I still don't know," I yelled down.

"I wouldn't let you do it if it were dangerous," he yelled back.

The truth of his words struck me. Jackson had never led me wrong, not once. Even as kids, he had always looked out for me. He would never coax me into doing something if he believed there was any danger to me.

Didn't change the fact that I knew it was potentially dangerous anyway. But part of me wanted to feel as carefree as he did, if just for a moment.

"Okay," I called out, still hesitant—but determined to try. "Just a second."

I stepped away from the edge and let out a breath. I pulled my sundress off, feeling ridiculously exposed in my bra and panties. It was hard to believe I was the same girl who'd once skinny dipped with my friends without thinking a thing about it. Not today. I thanked my lucky stars I had chosen a thick navy-blue matching set that didn't show anything more than a bikini.

But I was going to do this. Maybe not with the enthusiasm and running leap Jackson had, but I was going to do it. Unlike him, I knew that serious—even fatal—injuries could happen from diving short distances. But I also knew those typically happened because someone attempted a trick and hit the water wrong or dove into an area that was too shallow or had obstacles. I wouldn't dive or do tricks. I would jump feet first and keep myself straight. Plus, Jackson was waiting at the bottom.

It was only fifteen feet. But it felt like an enormous leap of faith.

I walked back to the edge and looked down at him, focusing on his easy grin as he treaded water, waiting on me. I took a deep breath, closed my eyes.

And jumped.

For an exhilarating second I was flying. Surrounded by warm sunshine, the world was bright, even with my eyes closed. Then my feet broke the water and the world turned dark as I plunged into the lake. My body took over and I swam up, my head breaking the surface in less time than it had taken to sink into it.

I emerged and took a breath, wiping the water from my eyes.

"Well?" Jackson asked, swimming over to me.

"It was amazing," I said, grinning back at him.

His eyes met mine and time seemed to stop. The sunlight danced on the water like diamonds sparkling on the surface. My heart pounded from the thrill of what I had just done—and from the thrill of being here with him. Alone, in a sparkling paradise.

I knew what was happening. My brain was currently enjoying a cocktail of dopamine, adrenaline, and endorphins. The safe thing to do was wait until the chemicals passed before making any moves that might change anything.

But I didn't feel like doing the safe thing anymore.

I floated toward him until our faces were mere inches apart.

"Allison," he said in a way that sounded like a warning.

But I pushed forward and covered his mouth with mine.

He froze for an instant. Then his hands were on my hips, pulling me to him. I wrapped my arms around his neck and my legs around his waist, and we floated together in the sunlight, kissing—exploring—as diamonds of light glimmered all around us. It was magic. I parted my lips slightly, begging for more, and he took it, teasing me with his tongue as he deepened the kiss.

"Allison," he repeated, his voice ragged as he finally pulled away. "We shouldn't. It's a bad idea. You know why."

"I wouldn't let you do it if it were dangerous," I whispered, repeating his words from earlier. "Jackson. I jumped. I took a leap of faith. And now I'm taking another one."

"What do you mean?"

"I choose you."

"What?" He looked at me like he couldn't comprehend what I was saying.

"I choose you." I gripped his face in my hands, needing him to hear me. "I choose all of it. All of you. I don't care about your past. I don't care who your father is. I choose *you*."

My heart pounded in my chest, no longer from the adrenaline of the jump. I was laying it out on the line here. Putting all my cards on the table—and just hoping. "I believe in you. I believe in *us*, Jackson. We aren't our parents. They both screwed things up, but we aren't them. We have a lot to learn, but we can do it together. All I need to know is if you choose me, too."

The look he gave me was so full of feeling, somehow so broken and restored at the same time. It was full of love and hope—but also fear and grief. For a moment, I thought the fear was going to win and he was going to say no. My heart began to sink.

But then he grabbed me tighter and buried his face in the crook of my neck. "I choose you, too," he said, his voice thick with emotion. "I always have. Since the day I met you, there's never been anyone else I could ever feel this way about. You know that. I'm terrified that I'm going to mess this up, but I can't imagine ever losing you again. Can't imagine living a single day of my life without you."

"Then we're in this," I said, "no matter what."

He pulled his head back, searching my eyes, and nodded. "No matter what."

He kissed me again, this time joyous as we both celebrated what we already knew. It was me and him against the world. It always had been, and it always would be. Because there could never be another for me, either.

CHAPTER THIRTY-FOUR

Jackson

I was in heaven. There was no other explanation.

But as the woman next to me rolled over, snuggling in even closer, all I could think was, if this was heaven, I was fine with dying. Because this had been the best damn afternoon of my life.

Allison and I had swam for what felt like hours, exploring the lake even as we explored each other, eventually shedding what remained of our clothes and enjoying a first time together that I'd never forget in my whole life.

Then we left the water, grabbed a blanket from my truck, and did it all over again on land.

Now we were cuddled up on that blanket, letting the sun warm us as we napped the day away. It was paradise, and I never wanted to leave.

"By the way, I forgot to tell you thank you for the flowers," Allison murmured beside me.

"What flowers?" I traced a finger down her arm, marveling that we were here and this was real. All my dreams had come true, wrapped up in one beautiful soul that had chosen me.

"The roses." She sat up on her elbows, leaning over and kissing me softly, her damp hair brushing the side of my face. "They were beautiful."

I frowned. "What are you talking about? I didn't send you roses."

She gave me a blank look. "At the clinic. Yesterday. A bouquet of roses with a card..." She trailed off, turning pale. "Those weren't from you?"

"Not me. Though you can be sure I'll send you the next set. What did the card say?"

"'Devotedly yours.'" She looked confused and slightly worried.

I frowned again. "That's weird. Mike, you think?"

"Probably." She shivered.

I pulled her into my arms again. "You're cold. Maybe we should head back."

But she was silent.

"What is it, sunshine?" I could almost feel her smile, even though I couldn't see it.

"Sunshine," she repeated. "I like that."

"It's how I've always thought of you. Like you were the sunshine in my life."

She sighed. "That's sweet. And the last thing I want to do is ruin today by dragging any nastiness into it."

My muscles tensed. "What nastiness?"

She covered her face with a hand. "I didn't tell you this, but the day of Russell's funeral, I noticed that Mike had gone through my underwear drawer while he was at my house."

A fierce protectiveness rose up in me. "What the hell? That's creepy."

"I know. I made him stay at a hotel and never even invited him upstairs, but he must have poked around while I was taking a call or something."

I held her tighter. "You're too nice. You should have slammed the door in his face. After all, you'd already told him you didn't want to talk to him. For him to show up and demand your time after that was out of line."

She sighed again. "I know. I hate confrontation. I'm too weak for it."

"You're not weak. You're one of the strongest women I know." I kissed her on the forehead. "And you're mine. So you don't have to fight any battles alone anymore. Now should we get you home and warm you up?"

She traced a finger down my chest. "Why would we do that when you can warm me up again right here?"

ANOTHER HOUR PASSED BEFORE WE MANAGED TO GET BACK TO my truck. We drove straight to Allison's with a plan to clean up and then go to dinner. But when we turned into her driveway and saw two county vehicles there, we exchanged looks, knowing our plans were about to change.

She grabbed my hand. "What do you think happened?"

"I don't know, but we're about to find out."

I was as relieved to see Greg standing on Allison's porch as I was irritated to see Miller with him. As soon as we got out of my truck, I took her hand in mine and we headed up together. I didn't miss the look the men exchanged at the sight of it.

Greg held a hand up and stopped us from coming up the porch. "I tried calling you both but couldn't get an answer. We were starting to get worried."

"Sorry," I explained, with a stab of guilt. "We were at the lake. Left our cell phones in the truck."

His face was grim. "I had an update on Russell. When I couldn't get you on the phone, I drove to your apartment. Came here next when you weren't there. The front door was open. Someone left a message." He glanced at Allison. "You sure you want to see this?"

"We're sure."

He nodded and moved to the side. "Looks like we've got a stalking situation going on here."

We walked up the steps into the house. Allison's face turned to shock when she saw the ugly display in her entryway. Pictures of us, from just hours before, making out in the lake. Her roses, chopped to pieces. Torn lace. And a note.

Greg picked up the letter with his gloved hand, holding it out for us to see.

You've been naughty, Allison. You belong to me, and you always have. You'll regret it if you ever let that man put his hands on you again.

"MIKE," ALLISON SAID, SHAKING HER HEAD. "IT HAS TO BE. But I didn't—I don't—" She looked like she was going to be sick.

I put my arm around her, practically holding her up for support. "She needs to sit down," I said in a tone that didn't leave it up for discussion.

Greg nodded, gesturing toward the living room. He and Miller followed with dark expressions on their faces.

"Tell me more about this Mike," Greg said, taking the seat across from the couch where Allison had sunk down the minute we got inside.

"He's my ex," she said. "He cheated on me and I broke up with him right before I moved here. He wants me back. He's sent flowers and called my mom and even showed up here last weekend." She shook her head. "I don't understand. He's always been a little different. But I didn't know this side of him. When we were together, he didn't seem to care what I did. Now that we're not, he's become obsessive."

"You've met him, right?" Greg asked, directing the question to me.

"I have."

"Your thoughts?"

I glanced at Allison, not wanting to hurt her by saying too much. "I'm not a fan. He's territorial. Sleazy. It was clear when I met him that he was possessive over her, even though they weren't together."

"You think he's behind this? Were we wrong about Russell?"

"I don't know," I said slowly. "Mike's been harassing her for sure..."

"But?"

I shook my head. "Russell was a slam dunk for the previous break-ins. But he has no connection with Mike. Plus, Allison, Mike was fine with you sleeping with Dr. Barkley to get that job, right?"

"Right," she confirmed, realization dawning on her face.

"So he's harassing you and wants you back, but he also has a history of pretty loose boundaries. Hard to believe he'd fly off the handle about us kissing. Unless something's changed." I mulled it over. "A switch that drastic would require a trigger of some sort. If that's true, we need to find out what that is. And it still doesn't explain Russell's involvement."

Greg tapped his pen, setting his mouth in a firm line. "Hold up. Before we go down that path, what's the story with this Dr. Barkley?"

Allison explained, blushing as she recounted what had happened with him. Greg took careful notes, taking down the whole story, then exchanged glances with Miller again as they stood up to leave.

"What are you thinking?" I asked, even knowing he wouldn't answer. It was killing me to be on the outside on this one. Everything in me needed to be bouncing ideas off of Greg, working together the way we normally did. Trusting Allison's safety to someone else—even the man I'd trust with my own life—was the hardest thing I'd ever done.

"I think you two should stay with me and Janet tonight," Greg said, giving me a pointed look. "Allison's a target, but you are too now."

This time, Allison and I were the ones exchanging looks. "Okay. Thanks," I finally said.

"Good. 'Cause I don't want you staying here or even in Jackson's apartment," Greg said flatly. "This guy has eyes on you, and he could be dangerous. Get what you need. Miller and I will be outside waiting."

WHILE ALLISON WENT UPSTAIRS TO PACK SOME FRESH clothes, I stepped out to talk to Greg and Miller. But they went quiet the moment I joined them. It burned like acid, even though I knew they were completely in the right. This wasn't my case. It couldn't be.

But I also couldn't stay away.

"What are we thinking?" I asked.

Greg gave me a look of empathy this time. He, too, had once been on the outside of a case involving the woman he loved. He knew what it was like.

"I don't know what to think," he confessed. "But you know we're going to track down every lead we can. Miller's going to find out where Mike is right now, and we're going to dig back into all the other people you and I talked about before we thought it was Russell."

I stared off at the trees. "Maybe it *was* Russell."

Greg cocked his head. "How do you figure?"

"We're fairly certain Russell was here, right? And that he was targeting Allison to get to me."

"Right. That's where the evidence pointed."

"One of Russell's favorite games was to manipulate people. I mean, you know what he went to prison for."

Greg nodded. "Yep. Convincing his friends to play Russian roulette. Guy died, it looked like a suicide, and Russell almost got away with it."

"Exactly. Sometimes Russell likes—liked—to get someone else to accomplish his end game." I thought it over more and more. "Mike's always been an ass, but Allison wouldn't have dated him if he treated her like this before. If Russell did his research and found Mike, he may have manipulated him into this kind of anger and possessiveness. Or...if it isn't Mike, Russell may have manipulated someone else."

Greg glanced at Miller. "You've still got Russell's cell phone, right? Double-check to see if there's a connection to Mike there. In fact, get me a list of everyone he was talking to in the weeks before his death."

Miller nodded. "On it." He walked off to make a call.

"You never told me what the update was on Russell," I said.

Greg cleared his throat. "The report's back from the crime lab. We've got an official cause of death. Looks like we were right about an accidental overdose. He died of fentanyl poisoning."

The news wasn't surprising. Fentanyl was dirt cheap and nearly one hundred times stronger than morphine. And since drug producers had started lacing their products with it, it was also the cause of nearly 70% of drug overdoses.

"Are you going after his supplier?"

"Yeah." Greg nodded. He stuck a hand on my shoulder. "But right now, Allison's my top priority."

"What can I do?" I asked, sticking my hands in my pockets. I felt completely helpless, being unable to do what I normally did.

"Stick with Allison like glue. Come stay with me and Janet, even though I know it sucks to leave your own place as a grown man—especially in the beginning of a new relationship." A hint of a smile crossed his face.

"I love her," I confessed. "I haven't told her that yet, but..."

"We're going to find out who's behind this, Jackson. We'll get him."

I nodded. "I'm trusting you."

Chapter Thirty-Five

I SHOVED CLOTHES INTO A BAG, NOT EVEN BOTHERING TO think through whether or not they would be appropriate for the next few days. I couldn't believe this was happening.

Mike had been in my home without me. Had taken my underwear and cut it up for his disgusting threat. Had watched as Jackson and I had kissed in the lake.

Had claimed me as his.

Had I just been too busy with residency to see what a creep he really was? Admittedly, I had never been entirely comfortable with him, and looking back now, I wasn't sure why I had even been with him in the first place. He had been convenient, he had understood my schedule, and he had even been a great study partner. But maybe the reason I had never really opened my heart to him was because part of me had sensed something was wrong, even if I had been unwilling to look at it closely.

Unless this wasn't Mike at all. But if not Mike, who else could it have been? It didn't make sense.

My cell phone buzzed. *Mama.* I groaned, not wanting to talk to her right now—especially after what I had learned from Beverly. But I knew she would keep calling, and I really didn't want to talk to her at the Morrisons'. Better to get it over with and keep all the negativity here, in a house I was starting to seriously dislike.

"Hey, Mama," I answered, knowing I couldn't keep the exhaustion out of my voice.

"Mike's mother and I had lunch today, and we're both wondering when you're going to put all this nonsense behind you and take him back. She told me he made a grand romantic gesture, but you sent him away without any hope. Tell me that's not true."

I closed my eyes, raising my fingers to my forehead as I sighed. "It's one hundred percent true."

"Allison," she began in the tone that let me know I was in for a lecture.

"Stop. This is not up for discussion."

At that moment, Jackson came in, asking if my suitcase was ready. I nodded, tensing as I braced myself for Mama's reaction to *that* one.

"Allison Bell, what man is there with you asking about your *suitcase?* You better be packing up to come back to Memphis."

"No, Mama, I'm not." I shook my head, steeling myself against her anger. Jackson raised his eyebrows before grabbing the suitcase and carrying it down the stairs. "'That man' is Jackson. I'm staying with him."

"Jackson Sharp. You have to be kidding me."

"It's Jackson *Ford,*" I reminded her, "and he's protecting me. Because I happen to have a stalker, and by the way, the number one suspect is Mike. So perhaps you should stop lecturing me on how I need to give him another chance."

The phone was dead silent for a moment. "What do you mean you have a stalker?" Her voice was strained and quiet.

"Mike hasn't been asking me for a second chance. He's practically been harassing me. And today, I got a bunch of cut-up roses and a letter saying I'm his, and—" I stopped suddenly, realizing if I went any further, I would have to reveal that Jackson and I were together romantically. And I wasn't sure I was ready for that conversation.

"And what?" she pressed.

I sank onto my bed, sighing. Things were bad enough. Might as well just get it over with. "That I'd regret it if I let Jackson put his hands on me again."

"You've let that boy touch you?"

"We're together, Mama."

"Over my dead body."

Anger bubbled up inside me. Considering her track record, she had no right to lecture me over my choices. Jackson was a good man, and I was done letting her speak about him like that. "What on earth do you have against him? You haven't even met him as an adult, and he never did anything you could hold against him as a kid. He was my best friend!"

"He's Russell Sharp's son!"

"So? If that doesn't bother me, why on earth would it bother you?"

"You don't understand," she began.

"Then explain it to me. Does this have anything to do with the fact that Dad used to make you pay off his gambling debts?" I didn't mean to ask it, but I couldn't stop it from coming out—especially as a terrible, horrible thought crossed my mind. Was there a chance—any chance at all—that Russell could have been... No. I couldn't even think it.

"Where did you hear that?" Her tone had changed again. This time, there was fear in it. A fear that confirmed the truth.

"My receptionist," I said. "Apparently everyone in Rosemary Mountain knew what was going on except me."

Silence.

"Mama, I have to know. Was my father not my actual..." I couldn't even finish the question.

"Your father is your father," she replied frostily. "We married as teenagers and I'd never been with anyone else until years after you were born, when he'd lost everything we owned and was given a chance to get off the hook by trading me instead. I never wanted you to know about that shame."

A tiny bit of relief passed through me. "So you're not against Jackson because we're...related in any way."

"Related? Of course not. No, I'm against him because he's a Sharp."

I had to roll my eyes, considering how people felt about Bells in this neck of the woods.

"He's a *Ford*," I said, emphasizing the difference. "He's nothing like Russell. I met his parents. His *real* parents. They're wonderful people."

Mama sighed in defeat. "I'm sure they are. And I'm glad he's made a change in life. But you have no business there. I've been saying that ever since you took that job. Now that you know the truth, do you not understand? Do you not realize what terrible people live there? They hide behind the veneer of their beautiful small town and their self-proclaimed family values. Allison, you're in danger. I risked everything to get you out of that place! How could you throw that away and walk back into the heart of the lion's den?"

"The lion's den?" I wanted to laugh out loud. "I'm not denying there are bad people here. There are bad people everywhere. But compared to Memphis this place is a paradise. And in case you've forgotten, it's my Memphis ex who is stalking me and making my life miserable."

"I don't—"

I interrupted her, softening my voice to reassure her. "Mama, I know you're worried. But I'm happy here. Really. And Jackson's taking great care of me. You'll see when you meet him. Maybe we'll drive down next month so you can get to know him. I promise, you'll love him."

Jackson reappeared at the doorway. Just seeing his face melted away the tension from Mama's phone call.

"Listen, I've got to go," I said, standing up and grabbing my purse. "I'll call you later, okay?"

"But, Allison—"

I hung up and turned my cell phone off completely.

SITTING AROUND GREG AND JANET'S DINING ROOM TABLE Monday morning, I found it hard to believe we were all here because of any kind of threat. It felt more like a weekend getaway with good friends. I didn't ask for updates on the case, even though I noticed Greg and Jackson occasionally slipping off for private discussions. They were handling it, and I was happy to let them.

I'd kept my cell phone off and basically disassociated from the entire situation, which I knew wasn't technically the healthiest response to what was happening. On the other hand, I was so blissfully happy to be with Jackson that I didn't want to let any of that chaos close to us. Here, we were safe. We were whole.

The mood was light and cheerful as Janet served up a delicious quiche and fruit salad, saying we all needed a decent meal to fortify us for the workday ahead. Greg kissed her and said he always appreciated her cooking, no matter what the day held.

I smiled over my cup of coffee, watching them together. Technically speaking, they were practically newlyweds, having found each other later in life. But I liked to think that Jackson and I would share that same chemistry years from now, even after having been married for a decade.

It startled me, realizing how easy it was to picture marriage with him. Three years with Mike and I'd never once imagined married life or what we'd be like when we were older. I'd never wanted to share a home with him, always preferring my townhouse with my girlfriends over renting something together. I'd assumed I was simply more career-minded than marriage-focused. But with Jackson, I was already dreaming about what life would be like five, ten, twenty years down the road.

And when I caught him smiling at me, I knew it would be beautiful no matter what, because we would be together.

"So you have a big day at the store?" Greg asked, directing the question to Janet as he sat down at the head of the table, digging into the plate she had placed in front of him.

"I do. Willa just finished up her fall designs and we're going to start changing our inventory over," she said as she gracefully tucked a napkin into her lap. Janet was elegant in all the ways Mama had always wanted to be. I knew that, when they finally met, Mama would hate her for it.

"Isn't it a little early for fall clothes?" Jackson asked, raising an eyebrow. "It's going to be over a hundred degrees today."

Janet just brushed him off with a wave of her hand. "Women like to start planning for the season ahead of time. You can't wait until the last minute."

"She knows what she's doing," Greg said, beaming with pride. "She's turned that place into the most successful boutique Rosemary Mountain's ever had." He turned toward me. "Don't worry. We'll show you how to set the alarm when we leave. You'll be safe here today. Help yourself to anything in the house. And Jackson, of course, if you need to take the day to stay with Allison, you're welcome to do so. Hopefully we'll have this wrapped up quickly and you guys can go back to your normal lives."

"Um, I can't stay here today," I said, dabbing my lips with my napkin.

Greg and Jackson both jerked their heads to look at me.

"Why not?" Jackson asked.

"Because I have patients to see." The idea of skipping work had never even crossed my mind.

"Surely you can cancel your day," Greg said, placing both of his palms on the table like he was ready to spring into action. "Everyone will understand."

"Will they?" I doubted it. "I'm just now actually getting a decent panel going. It took weeks for people to trust me enough to come see me. Besides, why would they understand when there's no way I'm going to tell them what's happening? This situation won't help my credibility."

"But—" Jackson started to speak, but I interrupted him.

"Mike's not going to do anything today," I said gently. "I know him. He may want to terrorize me, but I guarantee you he wants to succeed professionally more. His new job matters to him. He won't blow off work to be here."

Greg and Jackson exchanged glances. I saw Jackson give a tiny, almost imperceptible nod.

Then Greg cleared his throat. "Allison, we haven't been able to locate Mike. We know he wasn't home this weekend, and he hasn't shown up there yet. He might still be here."

I felt the first flutters of anxiety but refused to give them space. "He won't do anything at my job. That would destroy his career."

"Maybe you're right." Greg nodded. "But I don't think we can count on that. Assuming this is him, he's already crossed the lines into criminal behavior. That's enough to destroy his career too."

"Maybe," I admitted.

"I've got a BOLO out for his car. I got the make, model, and license number from his mom. Hopefully we'll locate him quickly and can wrap all this up."

I felt myself go pale. "You called his mom?"

"Yep. She hasn't been able to get in touch with him this weekend, either. And there's more you should know," he continued. "Mike's desperate. His parents were furious when they heard what happened between you two. Put the blame entirely on him. Told him to make things right or risk losing his trust fund. Could be why he's spiraled."

"I can't just blow off work," I said helplessly, although the truth was I was starting to reconsider. This was Mike though. He was a creep, but I'd never seen even a hint of violence in him.

"I don't like it," Jackson said. The look in his eyes made me want to agree to stay with him. But I couldn't.

"I'll be fine," I said, trying to reassure myself as much as him. "Beverly and Danny will be there. We'll keep the back door locked all day. You can drop me off and pick me up."

"Mike's our number-one suspect at this point, but that doesn't mean you should let your guard down. With anyone," Jackson warned.

"I know. But I can't just run away and hide because of personal drama. If I do, everyone will gossip about it for ages."

Jackson put his hand on mine. "I don't want to lose you again."

"You won't," I promised.

I only hoped I wasn't telling him a lie.

Chapter Thirty-Six

Jackson

"Can you stop that?" Greg asked mildly.

I looked up, startled, before realizing I was drumming my fingers on his desk. "Sorry."

"It's alright. I'm just trying to think here."

"Same." I got up and paced the room, trying to relax the knot of tension in my gut. I couldn't force Allison to miss work. Well, I *could*. But I knew she wouldn't like it, and I didn't want to be that guy.

"What are you thinking?" Greg leaned back in his chair and put his hands behind his head, spreading his elbows wide. It was a pose I'd seen many times before, the one he always took when he wanted to bounce ideas back and forth about a case. I was just glad he was letting me be in the loop on this one, even though technically speaking, I shouldn't be anywhere near it.

He understood though. He'd been there.

I shook my head. "I feel like we're missing something."

"Same."

I turned back and faced him. "I'm also thinking I should be at the clinic right now, making sure he can't get near her."

"She told you not to do that."

"I know." I went back to pacing before letting out a growl of frustration. "She's not ready for Danny and Beverly to know we're together, and she doesn't want anyone to know she's being stalked, either." I wasn't sure which one annoyed me worse.

"I've got Parker and Sanderson stationed outside the clinic," Greg reminded me—for the third time that morning. "If he shows up, he'll have to go through them. And God help him if he has to go through Parker."

I grinned, despite my worry. Parker was one of our female deputies. She was only five-two and couldn't have weighed more than a hundred pounds. But she was a third-degree black belt who could lay out a man twice her size without breaking a sweat. Training with Cole had made her even deadlier. If I couldn't be the one to take this guy down, Parker would be my first choice to do it. I just hoped I'd get a chance to watch.

Greg's phone rang. I immediately stopped pacing and took my seat across from him. He answered, then put it on speaker, his face dark. "Can you repeat that?" he asked. "I have Ford here and I'd like him to hear it too."

"Yep. Like I was saying, we got a hit on your BOLO. Found the vehicle at a vacation rental outside Chattanooga."

I frowned. *Chattanooga?* What the hell was he doing there?

"Have you made contact?" Greg asked.

"Not yet. I'll update you if and when we do."

"Thanks." He clicked off and looked at me, mirroring the expression on my face. "Thoughts?"

"Odd place for him to be," I said. "Too far from here, but not really on the way back to Memphis."

"It's a detour for sure," Greg agreed. "Could be on vacation. Could be visiting family. Who knows?"

I nodded. "More importantly though, it means he's probably not here."

"Probably not," Greg agreed. "The question is, what's your gut saying? Relief or… "

I crossed my arms. "Honestly?"

"Always."

I shook my head, flattening my lips. "My gut says this isn't over."

"Same." His phone rang again. He picked it up and listened, then closed his eyes and hung up.

"What is it?"

"I know this is the last thing you want to hear right now, but I need you on a case."

"Now?"

"Now. There's a missing kid."

Chapter Thirty-Seven

Allison

I had put on a brave face before heading to work, kissing Jackson and telling him that everything would be fine. And really, I believed it would be. Mike had proven to be a terrible person, but that didn't make him violent. Plus, I knew the sheriff had stationed two deputies outside the clinic—an honor that made me feel guilty, honestly, since he was understaffed as it was. But guilt or no guilt, I couldn't just hide out and leave my patients hanging.

My relationship with Jackson had made me fully invested in staying in Rosemary Mountain, and I knew if I couldn't get this clinic in the black, I wouldn't have a job here for long. Funding the clinic meant billing for appointments. Every day mattered.

"Good morning, Beverly!" I called out when I walked through the clinic doors.

"Good morning, Dr. Bell," she said, her tone guarded.

"How does our schedule look today?"

This time, she smiled. "You've got a full patient load. Eighteen on the schedule."

"Eighteen?" My eyes widened. "That's more than double my usual here."

"I called a few patients who were, um, overdue for appointments and got them on the schedule," she explained, her guilty expression betraying her. "We have a full docket all week."

I took a breath. "Excellent." I smiled, deciding to take it as a win instead of focusing on the past.

If Beverly actually started scheduling patients and Danny started logging accurate vitals, this clinic might have a shot.

"Where's Danny?" I asked, realizing I hadn't seen him yet.

Beverly frowned. "Must be running late. I'll try to call him."

"Thanks," I said, glancing up as the front door opened. My first patients were already arriving at 8:15—something unheard of since I'd started here. I ducked out, letting Beverly start checking people in, while I congratulated myself on our progress.

AFTER A LONG DAY, WHERE ALL EIGHTEEN PATIENTS SHOWED —but my nurse didn't, leaving me to do all the intakes myself—I felt exhausted but happy. It was the kind of day I had imagined when I first took the job. I felt like I had actually helped some people, and happily, I hadn't had a single patient demand narcotics.

On top of that, Mike hadn't pulled anything else, and I was starting to think maybe we had blown the whole thing out of proportion.

I was packing up my things for the day when Beverly knocked on my office door.

"Come in," I called out while tucking a medical book into my bag so I could review a protocol later.

"I'm about to leave, but I was wondering if you wanted me to stay for your meeting?" She let the words hang in the air.

"What meeting?" I frowned.

"With Dr. Johnson. Remember? You asked me to schedule a meeting with him about the medication-assisted drug treatment program. I put it on your calendar—and told you about it—last Friday. It's scheduled for six tonight."

"Oh my goodness." She *had* told me. I had just been too busy enjoying the flowers I'd assumed were from Jackson to actually pay attention to what she was saying. "I remember now." I glanced at my phone. "Oh man. It's too late to cancel, isn't it?"

"I could try," she offered.

I groaned. "No, that wouldn't make a very good impression, would it? After all, I'm the one who asked for his help applying for this grant. It's fine. I was just looking forward to getting home." More like looking forward to getting home to *Jackson.* I knew he had gotten called out to a case though and would likely be working late anyway.

"Okay," she said. She was hesitant, like there was something she wanted to say. "So do you want me to hang around for it, or..."

I realized she was worried I'd make her stay late for the meeting, which was above and beyond the call of duty. "No, no," I said, waving her off. "It's fine. Go on home and enjoy your evening."

"Are you sure?"

"Of course. I wouldn't put you out like that."

"Okay. Well, goodnight, then." She still looked hesitant.

"Goodnight, Beverly. See you tomorrow. And great work on the schedule this week!"

She gave me a faint smile, then closed the door and left.

With Beverly gone, I felt oddly unnerved about being alone at the clinic. I shot Jackson a quick text, letting him know I had a meeting I had forgotten about and would be working later than normal. Then I peeked outside the front window. The two deputies were still stationed out front.

"Everything's fine," I said, feeling jarred by the sound of my own voice in the empty building.

I had fifteen minutes before Dr. Johnson was scheduled to arrive. It only took five to pull the files I had prepped with my ideas for the program, so I killed time by playing on my cell phone.

My call log showed five missed calls from Mama from over the weekend, and I toyed with the idea of calling her back. But I just wasn't ready for another conversation with her. Not when she seemed intent on souring everything I was building for myself here. So I played solitaire instead, distracting myself from the anxiety building within me.

DR. JOHNSON ARRIVED WITH PRECISE PUNCTUALITY, knocking on the clinic doors at exactly 6:00. I unlocked them for him and waved to the deputies on the street, letting them know he was okay. Then I locked the door behind him and invited him into my office.

He walked in and looked around before taking the seat across from my desk.

"It's good to see you here," he said, a proud smile on his face. "I think you're exactly what this clinic needed. Fresh blood. New ideas. Everything worked out, didn't it?"

"It did," I said, smiling warmly. "Thanks to you. I really appreciate your vote of confidence. I know I wouldn't have gotten this job without you."

He bowed his head, accepting my thanks.

"Now," I said, pulling out the files I had prepared. "Here's what I'm thinking about for the program."

He took the file from me, thumbed through it briefly, then set it aside. "I assure you, you'll have the hospital's full support in setting it up however you wish," he said. "But that's not really why I'm here."

I knew immediately I had made a mistake. "Then why are you here?"

He stared at me a moment, then smiled. "You look so much like your mother. It's shocking, really. You didn't always. As a child, I thought you resembled your father more, but with every year that passed, you looked more like her. Then she took you away. And somehow, with her as your only influence, you seem to have transformed even more into her likeness."

A new question formed. "Dr. Johnson. How well did you know my mother?"

He smiled again. "Intimately."

I felt my face flush. "Are you... Are you my..." I couldn't even bring myself to ask the question.

He cocked his head, giving me a strange look. "Am I your what?"

I swallowed hard. "My biological father?"

Shock appeared in his eyes. Then he softened and laughed. "Goodness, no. Though I suppose I can understand why you'd jump to that conclusion."

I sank back in my chair, relieved. "Dr. Johnson, I wish you'd get to the point. You're not here to talk about my program, and you're not here to tell me you're my father. Please don't tell me you're here to rehash an affair with my mother."

He shook his head. "Of course not. We have much more to discuss than that."

"What do we need to discuss?" Fear began to rise. I had no logical reason to be afraid of Dr. Johnson, who had always been kind to me. But I also knew that a kind exterior could hide a predator's heart, and everything in my body was telling me to run.

He pulled a piece of paper out of his pocket. "This," he said, holding it up. But he didn't pass it to me. He cocked his head again. "Did you know that I'm not only responsible for getting you this job, but I got you into the residency program in Memphis as well?"

I was taken aback. "No. No, I didn't."

He nodded. "I've been watching you for a long time, Allison. It's been hard waiting for you. But I understand the need to pursue a vocation, and I admit, I was delighted you chose medicine. So I've waited patiently. And now, here you are."

"Yes..." I forced myself to act calm.

"I must say, you're more beautiful in person than I ever imagined. You were worth the wait. But..." he frowned. "I was very disappointed that you didn't wait for me, too. That's why I got a bit angry Saturday and left that mess at your house."

My hands began to shake. "That was you?"

"It was out of character," he admitted. "And I realized after that my reaction wasn't fair to you. After all, you didn't know about our agreement. I apologize for overreacting. I hope you'll forgive me the way I decided to forgive you."

"What agreement?" I asked, trying to keep my voice steady.

He smiled. "The one that made you mine." He tossed the paper he was holding onto my desk.

I picked it up with trembling fingers, not knowing what to expect.

But nothing would have prepared me for what I read.

It was a letter from my father. A signed letter promising me to Dr. Johnson in exchange for the release of his gambling debts.

Horror flooded my body as I read the words. When I was finished, I dropped it like a hot coal onto the desk.

"This doesn't mean anything," I said, shaking my head. "I'm not property, and this document is meaningless."

Dr. Johnson just smiled. "No. You're right of course. Legally speaking, it means nothing. But you owe me, Allison, just the same."

"I don't owe you anything." My voice trembled.

"Allison, your father owed me a great deal of money. An astonishing amount, actually." Dr. Johnson actually chuckled. "He was as bad at poker as he was at everything else in life. It was quite easy to force him into debts he could never pay."

"That has nothing to do with me."

"Oh, but it does," he said. "Because originally, I agreed to let your mother pay off those debts. It was an arrangement I was very pleased with, actually. She was a very beautiful woman, and the arrangement was quite pleasing. Until she got pregnant and lost the baby, then refused to continue on."

I flashed back to her miscarriage, the one where she hadn't gotten out of bed for three days—the shame on her face, Fiona's sadness. How after that, she'd stopped getting dressed up and working nights like she had before.

My heart sank, because I knew it was true.

"Again," I said, my voice shaking. "That has nothing to do with me. I was not my father's property, this is not even legal, and I owe you nothing."

"Did you forget how I got you this job? Or your residency? You do owe me." He shook his head in disappointment. "Oh, Allison. Your family wouldn't even have made it if not for me. Who do you think made sure your mother had money for groceries every week? Or that the light bill got paid when your father pissed away everything on gin?"

I couldn't speak.

"After your mother refused to keep up her end of the bargain, your father and I spoke. I offered to let you fulfill it instead. Not until you were eighteen, of course," he said, holding his hands up in defense. "Though I admit, I did wonder—even imagine—what it would be like to be with someone so...innocent." His eyes flickered with desire before he frowned again. "I think that's why I got so angry Saturday. I always imagined you'd stay innocent for me. I can't help but feel disappointed that you didn't."

My stomach shuddered as my body went cold.

"You should have always been mine," he continued, his voice hardening. "It was all arranged. Then, when your mother found out, she did the unthinkable. She disappeared with you."

There are monsters in Rosemary Mountain. Mama's words came back to me, and suddenly it all made sense. Why she had left, why she had been devastated by my taking this job, and why she wanted me back in Memphis—away from Dr. Johnson.

"I don't know what you thought you'd accomplish by telling me any of this," I said, fighting to keep my voice steady. "I have no intention of becoming your mistress in order to pay off my father's old debts."

"You don't understand. Debt or no debt, you're mine, Allison," he said softly. "You always have been. And one way or another, I intend on having you."

He pulled out a syringe and moved toward me.

Chapter Thirty-Eight

Jackson

I clenched my fist and counted to ten inside my head. All I wanted was to wipe the smirk off the man sitting across from me. I'd brought him in after I'd found his ten-year-old son hiding out in the woods, covered in cuts and bruises.

The kid wasn't talking. The dad's story was that the kid had run away earlier that morning because he was mad about being grounded for bad grades. The bruises and cuts must have happened while he was attempting to create a shelter in the woods.

Which, admittedly, was plausible based on what I'd seen.

But right now, all I could see was this guy's smirk. His arrogance. His complete lack of concern for his son.

In other words, all I could see was Russell.

I reached ten and took a deep breath. "Let's go over it one more time," I said before my phone vibrated. "Just a minute," I said, grateful for an excuse to step out and gather myself. "Hello?" I answered, as I closed the door of the room behind me.

"Detective Ford?"

"Yeah?"

"It's Beverly." Her voice was hesitant. "I feel stupid calling you about this, but…"

"What's going on?" I asked as I started moving toward the door. Somehow I knew, even before she said it—Allison was in trouble.

"Dr. Bell has a meeting tonight with Dr. Johnson."

"Right, I know," I said. "She texted me about it a few minutes ago."

Beverly sighed. "Listen, I don't know how to say this, but I know you two are involved. I think you should know there was a rumor going around that Dr. Bell slept with Dr. Johnson to get this job. I had changed my mind about her, but then she asked me to schedule this meeting with him for tonight. Right after I did, he sent her roses. She got all starry-eyed over them and wouldn't admit who they were from. Then tonight, I offered to stay for the meeting, but she sent me home, and, well, they're alone at the office together…"

I froze as puzzle pieces from the past started sliding together in a way I had never expected.

"Beverly, where did you hear that rumor?"

She didn't answer.

"Beverly," I said more forcefully. "I need to know where you heard that rumor."

"From Penny, Dr. Johnson's wife," she finally admitted. "Dr. Johnson had an arrangement with Dr. Bell's mom years ago. When the announcement was made about Dr. Bell coming to take over the clinic, Penny was furious. Said she shouldn't have been surprised—all Bells were the same, and for some unknown reason, Dr. Johnson couldn't get enough of them."

I closed my eyes as what Allison had told me about her mom lined up with everything else.

The poker games.

Russell's jokes about my mother not being as valuable as Allison's.

Jokes about how he wished Brent owed him as much money as he owed the doc.

His warning to me about how Allison was already spoken for.

The way Penny had treated her at the town dance.

The letter that said Allison had always been his.

My eyes opened again. Russell had been at the dance. I thought he had been there for Allison, but what if he had been meeting Dr. Johnson instead? What if the "doc" he had referred to so often in my childhood wasn't Doc Rogers, like I'd always assumed, but...

What if Dr. Johnson had used Russell to do his dirty work all along?

"Where are you?" I demanded, motioning to the front desk that I had an emergency and had to leave.

"I'm at home," she said. "I wasn't sure if I should tell you or not, but you're a nice man, and well, you just don't deserve a woman who cheats on you."

"Allison didn't sleep with him," I almost yelled. "She's in trouble. I've got to go."

I hung up the phone and jumped into my truck, praying I wasn't too late.

I RACED TO THE CLINIC, CURSING WHEN I SAW THERE WAS NO longer a patrol vehicle out front. Their shift would have just ended, but surely a replacement was coming.

Or not, since everyone would have expected Allison to be back at Greg's by this point.

I pulled my truck up onto the sidewalk, threw it into park, jumped out, and ran to the door.

Locked.

In an instant, I flashed back to the worst day of my life—the day I'd lost Allison.

I wasn't going to lose her again.

One solid kick and the old door gave way. I pushed through and ran toward Allison's office, feeling the same terror and loss I'd felt so many years before when I'd run toward her bedroom and discovered she was really gone.

No. Not again. I couldn't lose her.

When I threw her office door open, I almost vomited.

They were gone.

I heard the sound of a door opening in the back and took off, running past the exam rooms. I turned the corner and saw what had to be a nightmare. Allison's body was crumpled on the floor, her eyes closed and her face drained of all color, as Dr. Johnson dragged her by her wrists toward the exit that led to the alleyway. He dropped her immediately when he saw me and turned to run, but I was faster.

I flew toward him and grabbed his shirt, pulling him to the ground. Then I jumped on top of him and slammed my fist into his jaw, knocking him unconscious with a single punch.

I stared at him, seeing his face, but also more—I saw the doctor who'd screwed up Allison's life in Memphis. I saw her lousy ex, who'd thrown her away and then harassed her to take him back. I saw Willa's ex, who'd abused her in horrific ways. I saw the man who'd tried to kill Daphne and take her away from all of us. I saw the face of every single bad guy I'd ever taken down.

And I saw Russell.

And I knew I was going to kill him.

Every bit of rage I'd shoved down my entire life seemed to well up in a single moment with a single target. Russell had finally gotten what he'd always wanted. The Sharp blood had awakened in me, and for the first time in my life, I was so angry I felt like I could kill this man with my bare hands and not feel an ounce of remorse for it. I grabbed his collar with one hand and pulled my other back in a fist, ready to end this once and for all.

But then Allison groaned. Her hand fluttered toward me as she fought to open her eyes. "Jackson," she mumbled. "You came. I knew you'd come."

I dropped Dr. Johnson and went to her, pulling her weak body into my arms. She forced her heavy lids open and gave me the sweetest smile before her eyes shuttered again. But in that one look, I saw everything that really mattered. Her. Our future. The life we could build together. The children that would never have to be afraid to come home to us. The love and joy that would fill our home and our lives.

And in one astonishing moment, I realized Russell was wrong. That I wasn't the same as him at all. Because all that love, all that goodness—it was a thousand times stronger than the hate I had just felt. Our future meant a million times more than revenge. And I'd walk away from Dr. Johnson in a heartbeat if it meant having all that with Allison.

"I'm here," I said, tenderly stroking her face. "I've got you. You're going to be okay. Whatever he did to you, we'll fix it. I promise. You'll be okay. You have to."

She managed a nod. "Don't worry," she murmured, slurring her words slightly. "Just sleepy meds. Not dangerous."

Thank God. My eyes filled with tears. "I don't ever want to lose you again."

"You won't," she managed to whisper before squeezing my hand.

"I love you," I said. "More than anything. More than I ever thought it was possible to love anyone. I love you so much, Allison."

"I love you, too." She smiled as she said the words. Then she opened her eyes and met my gaze for just a moment before slipping back into her sleepy haze.

Dr. Johnson moaned as he began to regain consciousness. I gently laid Allison back down, then went to deal with him. No revenge this time, just procedure. I flipped him onto his stomach and cuffed him, rattling off his rights as I did. Then I called Greg and let him know what had happened, asking for backup and an ambulance.

With Dr. Johnson secured, I went back to the love of my life and held her as we waited, knowing I was never going to let go.

ONE WEEK LATER

It didn't take long for that night to seem like nothing more than a bad dream. Allison was safe and we were whole in ways I'd never expected to be. And when our chosen family gathered for a Fourth of July picnic, I knew there was only one thing that could make the night better.

"More tea, Jackson?" Janet asked, filling up my glass before I could even answer.

"Thanks," I said, smiling as I lifted the cold drink to my mouth. It had been a scorcher of a day, but this time of year usually was. We'd brave the stifling heat anyway, hoping it cooled off at least a little when the sun went down and the fireworks began.

"Will Allison be here soon?"

I checked my watch. "Any minute."

"Actually, I'm already here," said the sweetest voice in the entire world before she plopped down beside me on the quilt and passed Janet a bottle of champagne to add to the spread.

"Hey," I said, leaning over to kiss her—and marveling at how every kiss felt both normal and extraordinary at the same time.

Emerson elbowed Cole. "The fireworks haven't started yet. You owe me ten bucks."

"I didn't take that bet," Cole replied, rolling his eyes.

Daphne spoke up. "I know it's a party, but since this is the first time we've all been together since everything happened..." She trailed off, glancing between me, Greg, and Allison. She obviously hoped one of us would volunteer the scoop.

I had to laugh. Daphne couldn't help herself. She loved a good story about a bad guy getting what was coming to him.

I glanced at Allison, unsure how much she wanted to share. After all, it was mostly her family history. But she surprised me by launching into the story without a bit of embarrassment at all.

"Basically," she said, "what everyone in Rosemary Mountain seemed to know—except for me and Jackson, apparently—was that my father made my mother pay off his gambling debt to Dr. Johnson. Although some people thought it was an affair and didn't realize my mother wasn't exactly a willing participant."

"Oh." Daphne cringed. "I'm so sorry."

"It's okay," Allison said quietly. "Mama and I have had a lot of good talks about it, and I understand her more now. It's helped me have empathy for why she was the way she was and why she pulled me out of Rosemary Mountain in the middle of the night."

"I can certainly relate to that," Daphne said, exchanging glances with Janet.

"Anyway," Allison continued, "my dad had apparently signed something agreeing to give *me* to Dr. Johnson when Mama refused to continue. And when Mama found out, she left to protect me."

I squeezed Allison's hand. As much as it had hurt for her to disappear like that, now that I knew the truth, I was so grateful her mother had taken her away. And in a lot of ways, it had saved me, too. With her gone, Russell hadn't had the same leverage over me. It was something I'd never really thought about, but looking back, I could see how getting Allison away from his reach had changed the course of my life for the better. I needed to thank Allison's mom the next time I saw her.

"Dr. Johnson never gave up though," I added. "In fact, I think Allison leaving made it more of an obsession for him. He watched her career from a distance and kept tabs on her. It seemed innocent—a family friend who was rooting for a young girl to succeed. But in reality, he had these crazy fantasies about her still belonging to him, and when he saw an opportunity to get her here, he made it happen."

Willa shook her head. "That's awful," she murmured. "Are you okay, Allison?"

Allison nodded, then glanced up at me. "Yes, thanks to Jackson. Dr. Johnson started stalking me, but I didn't even realize it was him."

"He used Russell to do his dirty work," I explained. "Paid him to spy on Allison. Dr. Johnson wanted to know everything—if she was seeing someone, what her hobbies were, what movies she watched, everything. He wanted to know her daily routines. He was gathering information, trying to figure out how to play it. I think at first, he was hoping to seduce her. He delivered flowers to her when she first arrived in town, though she assumed they were from the rental agency."

Greg jumped in. "What he didn't realize was that Russell had an agenda of his own."

"What do you mean?" Daphne asked.

Greg looked at me and I nodded, letting him know I was fine with him sharing all the details.

"Russell was angry at Jackson. He realized the assignment wasn't just a paycheck. It was a way to get back at the person he blamed for destroying his livelihood. He knew he was at the end of his life and didn't care about keeping a good working relationship with Dr. Johnson. He just wanted revenge. When he saw how close Jackson and Allison had grown, he decided to kill her. Dr. Johnson realized it and killed him instead."

Emerson's eyebrows shot up. "Russell was murdered? I thought it was an overdose."

"It was," I confirmed. "Dr. Johnson switched out his meds to ones laced with a lethal dose of fentanyl. The pills looked exactly like legit pharmaceuticals. Dr. Johnson knew that, even if we sent the body to the crime lab and discovered the cause of death, we would go looking for Russell's heroin suppliers—not suspect legitimate prescriptions."

"So how did you know it was Dr. Johnson?" Daphne asked, those curious eyes of hers all lit up.

"After Jackson arrested him—ever so gently"—Greg coughed behind his hand—"Dr. Johnson wasn't talking. Lawyered up right away, even though he'd been caught literally red-handed. Jackson's gut told him to look for a connection with Russell's death, so he tested the pills. Confronted Dr. Johnson, who then decided to make a deal."

"Wow," Daphne said, shaking her head. "So what was the deal with Mike? Was he not stalking you at all?"

Allison glanced my way, knowing I still got annoyed at hearing Mike's name. "Not exactly, no. He *was* trying desperately to get me back —for all the wrong reasons." She rolled her eyes.

Willa shuddered. "Men like that are bad news. I have to tell you, I ran into Beverly at the grocery store yesterday. She was singing your praises. I guess you won her over."

Allison nodded, smiling. "Yeah, we're good now that she knows the whole story. We're developing a solid working relationship. *And* I have a new nurse, so things are going much better at the clinic."

"A new nurse?" Janet asked, popping the champagne and pouring glasses for everyone.

"Yeah. Danny quit when I tried to hold him responsible for his job performance." Allison shook her head. "He has some major growing up to do. Everyone always let him get away with whatever because of his connection to Doc Rogers. He wasn't interested in working for someone who expected him to actually do his job."

"Well, I'm glad everything is going better." Daphne leaned against Emerson, letting him wrap his arms around her.

"Me too," Allison said. "And I'm sorry to have brought so much drama with me to Rosemary Mountain."

Daphne and Willa looked at each other and started giggling.

"Welcome to the club," Daphne said.

. . .

AFTER THE SUN SET AND THE DARK SKY LIT UP WITH fireworks, Allison leaned against me, tucking her arm underneath mine.

"Freedom," she whispered. "I think we finally found it."

I kissed the top of her head. "I think you're right. But does any part of you still want to go find it in one of those places you always dreamed about? New York or San Diego?"

She looked up at me. "Are you serious?"

"Dead serious. I know you're under contract here, but after that, would you ever want to try somewhere new?"

Her eyes got dreamy and she smiled. "Maybe. But maybe not. I've visited a lot of those places, and I have to say—none of them are quite as pretty as Rosemary Mountain. What about you? Do you want to try somewhere new?"

I looked around at the people surrounding us—our chosen family—and knew I was exactly where I wanted to be. "I love it here," I said. "But I love you more. You're my home now. All that really matters is that we're together."

"That's exactly how I feel," she said.

I cleared my throat. "Hey, let's make a pact."

She looked up at me and smiled. "Another one?"

"Yeah." Nerves fluttered as I gathered up courage for what I needed to ask.

"Okay. What pact is that?"

I slipped a hand inside my pocket and pulled out the diamond ring I'd bought that morning. "A pact to love each other forever. Allison, will you marry me?"

Her face lit up, brighter than the brightest firework in the sky. "Yes."

"Yes?"

"Yes. I can't wait to be your wife. Forever." She kissed me.

"Forever."

Epilogue

Allison
The following spring

"Stop fussing, Mama," I said as she adjusted my veil for what felt like the millionth time that day.

"I just want everything to be perfect," she said, sniffling.

"It is," I said. "How could it not be? I'm marrying my best friend."

"Are you sure?" she asked. "I mean—" She cut off when I gave her a warning look.

"Why don't you go ahead and find your seat?" I suggested, trying hard to keep my tone pleasant.

She sighed but did as I'd asked.

"I'm sorry," Daphne said, giving me a conspiratorial look. "I guess things are still strained there?"

I shrugged. "Yes. But that's okay. Nothing could put a damper on today."

"Not even that?" Willa winced as raindrops began to fall.

Daphne and I looked at each other, grinning.

"Rain on your wedding day is good luck," Daphne said. "And thankfully, I brought umbrellas." She popped a clear umbrella open and held it above my head.

I smiled. "Our first kiss was in the rain. This feels fitting somehow."

"It's time," Janet said, grabbing one of the umbrellas for herself. "You look absolutely lovely, Allison." She quickly kissed my cheek, then headed down the pathway.

Daphne and Willa both gave me one last squeeze before following Janet, one by one. All three of them were serving as my bridesmaids, while Greg, Cole, and Emerson stood beside Jackson.

We'd turned the creek into the most beautiful wedding location I'd ever seen, with rented wooden chairs, Japanese lanterns, and a glorious arbor absolutely covered with blooms. And somehow, we'd managed to cram in enough seats for nearly the whole town. Everyone wanted to be here to support the town doctor and the hero detective.

But despite the crowd, all I could see was Jackson standing beside the preacher at the water's edge.

We had chosen the creek for our wedding because it was where we'd made our first vow—a pact we'd managed to keep despite years apart. We'd been best friends then, and today we'd vow to be best friends until death did us part.

So I walked barefoot toward Jackson, discarding the umbrella so I could feel the rain hitting my face. Freedom. It's all we'd longed for as children, and we'd found it, together, on the mountain he loved so dearly. He grinned at me and my heart melted.

"I love you," he whispered as I took my place next to him.

"I love you too," I whispered back. "Forever."

THANK YOU FOR READING *MOUNTAIN FREEDOM*! I HOPE YOU enjoyed this return to Rosemary Mountain as much as I did. Can I ask a huge favor of you? If you enjoyed this story, I would so appreciate you taking the time to leave a review at your preferred vendor. It truly means the world.

Ready for the next story? Check out *The Death Cabin,* a fast-paced, twisty murder mystery with a strong dash of romance!

Can't get enough of Rosemary Mountain? Sign up for my mailing list and receive Fiona's Hawthorn Tea recipe. You'll also be the first to know about upcoming releases, sneak peeks, and more! I would also love for you to come hang out with me on Facebook or Instagram. I love getting to know my readers!

Acknowledgments

Each book I've written has been a unique experience. But the one thing they all have in common is that I couldn't possibly have done it without my incredible support system. To each of you, I owe a debt of gratitude.

My husband: I'm certain I've said it before, but you are the most incredible life partner. Thank you for always being there to listen when I need to bounce ideas off of someone, thank you for being a source of information on so many subjects that seem to find their way into my books, and thank you for being my very best friend. While our love story is different than Jackson and Allison's, I love that ours, too, began by being childhood best friends.

To my sons: there are no words. You light up my life in a million ways. Thank you for pulling me off my computer to get sunshine and fresh air. Thank you for always being up for story-time on the couch with cups of chamomile tea. Thank you for being the resilient, amazing, brave-hearted boys you are. Most of all, thank you for letting me be your mom.

Dr. Catherine Kim: thank you for allowing me to run my crazy ideas past you, and for answering so many questions about the hiring process for physicians! You are truly one of the most authentic, beautiful souls I've ever met and I'm glad our paths crossed all those years ago.

Detective Jacob Higdon: thank you for once again allowing me to pick your brain as I explored different plotlines. Many of the scenes in this book were inspired by our conversations. As always, a note to my readers: any procedural mistakes made in this story are mine, not his. Detective Higdon often tells me "you can't do that." My characters usually decide to do it anyway.

To my beta team for this book: Courtney, Elsa, Camille, Jessica, and Deondra. Thank you all for taking the time to read Jackson's story and give your feedback! Your insight is so appreciated.

My editor, Mickey Reed: Thank you for catching all the things I miss and for being a truly exceptional human being. You are lovely, and I'm so glad to have you on my team!

My cover artist, Brooke Passmore: Once again, you've captured such a warm, cozy vibe for this book. Thank you for your thoughtfulness and commitment to making the Rosemary Mountain stories so beautiful!

Finally, thank you to all my readers. Many of you gave me a chance with "Secrets in the Cottage" and have stuck with me through six Rosemary Mountain stories. I am so grateful for you, and love that we get to share this world together.

Is this the end of Rosemary Mountain? Possibly. Jackson's story feels like closure to me. Then again, Fiona seems to be whispering that she has a story of her own...

About the Author

Nicole Gardner lives in NE Arkansas with her husband, their two sons, and their two crazy dogs. If she's not at her desk, you'll likely find her either in the garden, or creating teas and tinctures in the kitchen.

Nicole's background is in psychology. This fascination with human behavior and relationship dynamics plays a significant role in her writing and the way she shapes her characters.

www.nicolegardnerbooks.com